THE AMAZON PRINCESS

THE AMAZON PRINCESS

JJ DAVITT

Bankshott
BOOKS

First edition, softcover

ISBN: 978-1-63591-802-1

Dustjacket cover art by Tanner Henderson

Bankshott Books
An imprint of Pulp-Lit Productions
Corvallis, Oregon

http://bankshott.pulp-lit.com

For Nat

TABLE OF CONTENTS.

I.

THE DREAM.

The little girl sat bolt upright in bed with a little shriek. It had been ... *such* a dream.

She tried not to think about it, but she couldn't block it out. Her mind was still playing the dream back. It would keep playing it back, though she didn't know it yet, every night for years to come.

But tonight was the first time. And it was the first nightmare she had ever had ... if one could call it a nightmare.

It had started out, fading in from the murkiness of sleep, with her looking out on the great river that ran by her home. In her dream, she didn't recognize the place — or perhaps she did; it had a feel of deep familiarity to her. The night was very dark; only a tiny silver sliver of crescent moon dappled the river's dark waters. But by its light, a short distance away from the riverbank, she was able to make out the bulky outlines of some kind of big boat. And in her dream, she seemed to be peering out of the bushes at it, with a fierce expectancy, from the shore.

Then came a faint creak and splash from the distant boat, and a small white thing detached itself and started gliding toward the shore…a tiny boat, short and wide. Inside it she was able to see the shadowy outlines of two men in large, clunky hats. A thrill of savage exultation, a feeling completely alien to her, went through her when she saw that they were coming right to her. She realized that she hated these men. This was strange, because it was the first time in her young life that she had ever felt the emotion of hatred for anyone. Certainly she had no reason to hate these strange men in her dream. She didn't even know who they were.

But then she realized that no, she actually did know who they were. In her dream, she recognized them as men who had come to steal her family, her mother and father and sisters and brothers and friends and everyone except for Auntie, who had stayed behind with her when the others had gone away.

Wait, what *was* all that? She was an orphan. Her parents had died when she was just a baby; she had no memories of them at all. She had no sisters. She had no brothers. And her only friend was the little girl from her dreams, the girl she dreamed with every night, and talked to and played with. Her imaginary friend.

But her imaginary friend wasn't in this dream. And in this dream, she felt like a completely different person. Hard, resolved, fierce, she was waiting for those men to get to shore in their boat, and then she was going to — what?

Finally the small rowboat touched the riverbank. One

of the men stepped out onto a grassy tussock and started pulling the little boat up onto the shore. The other climbed out and helped. The two of them spoke to each other, and she couldn't quite make out what they were saying, but they seemed to be arguing. They pulled the boat a long way up onto the shore, as if worried that someone might come by and steal it. Then they turned back to face the river.

Her dream-body was moving now, moving far more athletically than she was capable of in waking life, stealthily creeping through the underbrush, coming closer and closer to the men in the boat. They were still arguing about something. One of them held a massive golden headdress in his left hand, a headdress shaped like a great serpent that wound around the wearer's head and finished with a fierce-looking crocodilian head just over where the wearer's brow would be. In her dream, she knew that headdress was the most important thing in the world; she could scarcely take her eyes off of it.

The man who was holding the headdress was holding it firmly yet diffidently, as one might hold a poisonous snake by the throat to keep its fangs at bay. "It's no good, Percy," he was telling his companion, speaking with a strange accent. "I'll not have the blasted thing on my boat. There are plenty of other valuable pieces we can take with us. This one's bad luck. It gives me a bad feeling. I'm putting it back."

"Just chuck it in the bushes here somewhere, or drop it in the river," the other urged. "Don't be so damned sensitive, Alfred."

"No. I am returning it. I believe — I verily believe doing so is our only hope of getting home alive, Percy."

Percy gave a short, scornful laugh.

"Scoff all you like," Alfred said in a level voice. "It's my boat, it's my expedition, and I make the rules."

The scant moonlight gleamed on the headdress in Alfred's hand as he turned his back on the other, apparently intending to continue walking up the riverbank; but as he did so, the man called Percy moved like a striking viper in the inky darkness. There was a flash of pale skin, a snicking sound of a knife coming out of its sheath and a thump like the sound of a ripe melon being dropped.

Alfred gasped. He ran a couple of steps and collapsed to the bank. Then he rolled over and looked up at the man called Percy.

"Wh — wh —" he gasped.

"Why?" said Percy coldly. "Because that's one less hand reaching out for a share of the treasure, and one less mouth to open in the wrong place and at the wrong time and ruin everything. Because now that you are dead, it's my boat and my treasure. All mine. I'll tell James back on the boat that you were shot with an arrow from ambush. And I suppose I shall find a way to rid myself of James later, on the trip back."

The dying man stared back at him. "It won't work, you know," he told him. "I was your last hope. You shall never leave this place now. We are going to die here, you and I. If you make it back to the boat, tell James I'm sorry I let him down."

And he closed his eyes. The little dreamer knew he was dead, and hot tears welled out of her sleeping eyes. All her mysterious hatred was focused now on the man who had killed him.

Percy reached down and took the headdress out of the limp hand of the other, and stood erect and looked out at the boat floating in the river. In her dream, the little girl looked out over the river too.

And then the moon's reflections in the glassy surface

of the water started to dance in a sinister way, the river's surface rippling as if a powerful current were starting just beneath the big boat.

"What the hell?" gasped Percy, sounding frightened for the first time.

Then something gray and shadowy broke the surface of the water, seemingly all around the boat. A fine mist erupted from the river like a great curtain, blocking the boat from view. There was a great splashing sound, followed by a heavy crunch that trailed off into a sound like bubbles rising to the surface.

Then the mist was dissipating and all that remained on the surface of the river were a few specks of debris floating on the still-rippling waters.

Then, in her dream, the little girl was moving in, gliding up behind Percy in deadly silence as he stood staring at the now-empty river as if frozen in horror, until she was just a few feet away from him.

Then he turned, and locked eyes with her.

It was his scream that had been ringing in her ears as she bolted up out of bed.

The little girl slipped out from under the covers and ran to Auntie's bed, the cold wooden floor feeling comfortingly real under her feet. She wanted Auntie. She wanted to curl up with Auntie and have her stroke her forehead and tell her it was all right, that it was only a bad dream. She was a good and kind-hearted little soul, who had never seen anyone so much as slapped, much less stabbed. She was horrified, traumatized, raw on the inside — terrified.

But Auntie's bed was empty.

She lay down in it and tried to sleep. But she was still

awake when, two hours later, as the gray light of the pre-dawn morning started to spread over the room, she heard Auntie and Uncle come inside.

Auntie took the little girl in her arms and stroked her forehead and told her everything was going to be all right, and assured her again and again that it had only been a dream, that the men and the ship were all imaginary, that she was safe.

The little girl quieted down. Auntie dressed for bed, even though it was already morning, and laid down with the little girl in her arms. Sleep had started to beckon once again, when suddenly the little girl's eyes snapped open. A thought had just flashed across her mind:

How had Auntie known what she'd been dreaming about?

II.

THE AMAZON PRINCESS.

Prudence McMarion perched on the hard teakwood bench and tried to be a good sport. It wasn't coming easily to her, though.

She knew she should be extremely pleased to be here, on the observation deck of this tiny run-down riverboat in the frontier town of Porto Escuro, deep in the heart of the Amazon Basin. Adventure of a lifetime, and all that, right?

But the fact was, she wasn't really here because she wanted to be here. She was here because she felt that she *should* want to be here. She was a modern young woman, a liberated woman, a woman of the 1920s. She voted, she visited speakeasies, she even occasionally smoked cigarettes. She hadn't worn a corset since 1919, when she'd felt the need to look as "respectable" as possible while marching in the street with her "VOTES FOR WOMEN" sign. She worked a job that many still thought only a man could do, and she rightly considered that she did it better than any man ever could.

So could she have turned down the opportunity to plunge deep into the darkest, most exotic place in the Western Hemisphere on the adventure of a lifetime — to stay safe and comfortable at home in Los Angeles, going to work, coming home, dusting furniture, and baking pies? — unthinkable!

But if she was honest with herself, that was really why she was here.

It hadn't been too bad, so far. The great ocean liner she'd boarded in Los Angeles had been very comfortable. She'd never been able to afford to travel first class before, but Eleanor had insisted. "Things will be much more primitive when we get there, dear," Eleanor had said with a benign smile. "We shall enjoy the luxurious life while we still can."

And that had been all right, because Eleanor was the one with the money.

When they'd arrived at Belem, they'd transferred to one of the big shallow-draft riverboats that ply the lower Amazon. There things had been considerably less posh. Still, it had been far more comfortable than the boat she'd just boarded promised to be.

She looked around for Eleanor, who had stepped away to powder her nose or something. Eleanor wasn't in sight, but there weren't many places she could hide on this little passenger-freight boat. It was a modest-looking thing, long and narrow, with a sleek but badly weather-beaten hull on which the name, *Amazon Princess*, could barely be made out. It boasted a single covered deck, open at the stern and with cabins forward. *That must be where the staterooms are*, she thought.

The observation deck was narrow, no more than seven feet wide, with a hard bench lining each side, topped with a few flat cushions. Seated on the benches with Prudence were several other passengers: a worried-looking Brazilian woman in a white cotton house dress, with a girl of twelve or so, obviously her daughter; and a well-dressed man who looked crisp and cool in a pale-yellow linen suit and white bow tie.

The man, she allowed herself to notice at length, was a bit of a sheik. He had black hair, stylishly molded, over a delicate brow and intense blue eyes; a muscular, clean-shaven chin; and a pencil-thin mustache over lips that looked just a little too full and shapely for his otherwise-rugged-looking face. It might have been the cut of his suit jacket, but the outline of his upper body formed a sort of V-shape that suggested power, and something in the way he held his head made her think he might be just a little bit dangerous.

Then he caught her eying him and his stylishly slender mustache curled smoothly up into an ingratiating smile. She turned her eyes away, abashed.

As she did so, she caught a glimpse of the woman's face. It was really worried now, startlingly so. The man noticed too, and turned toward her.

"What is the matter, *Senhora* Ribeiro?" he inquired solicitously, in Portuguese.

"Oh, Dr. LeCourt, it is Alberto," she replied. "He should be back by now. I told him to be back before eleven or he might be left behind. He is always such a good boy, I just know he wouldn't disobey. Something has happened to him and I don't know what to do."

"Please allow me to be of service," Dr. LeCourt replied smoothly, rising to his feet. Prudence stood up as well. She didn't know the missing lad, but surely she could do something to help. And just where on Earth was Eleanor, anyway?

Just then came a shout from far up the wharf, and then a gunshot rang out. It was followed by a bellowing howl — it sounded like a cry of rage, not of pain — and more shouting.

Dr. LeCourt leaped for the gangway, landed on the dock outside, and then stopped short. Prudence, who was following behind almost by instinct, just barely managed to avoid crashing into him from behind.

Running toward them at a dead sprint was a small Brazilian boy, perhaps ten years old.

"Alberto!" cried *Senhora* Ribeiro, who had left the boat just behind Prudence. "What has happened to you?"

Indeed, Alberto looked as if something had happened to him — something bad. His face was a mask of fear, he was running at top speed, and as he drew near Prudence could see that his left eye was swollen almost closed.

Alberto never slackened his pace. He dodged around the little party on the wharf and, with a flying leap accompanied by what sounded like a sob of relief, soared over the gangway and onto the deck of the *Amazon Princess*. Then, safely on board his personal sanctuary, he turned to his mother.

"Don't let them get me, Mama," he cried.

"Alberto, calm down," said his sister, who was still sitting where she had been before. "You are so embarrassing sometimes."

Prudence wanted to go see what the gunshot had been. She could still hear angry shouting from the other end of the wharf, and peering down the walkway she could see a small crowd beginning to gather near the gangplank of a big sailing ship. But both Dr. LeCourt and *Senhora* Ribeiro now seemed completely uninterested in whatever was happening down there. Both of them unhurriedly re-boarded the *Amazon Princess* and gathered around young Alberto. So, with one more quizzical look down the wharf, Prudence stepped back aboard the boat.

"I was looking at that ship down there at the end of the wharf," Alberto was explaining earnestly. His voice trembled a bit, but he was obviously making a real effort to sound calm and collected. "A man came down the ramp and asked me if I'd like to have a tour of the ship. So he was showing me around the ship and he asked me what my name was. And I told him, and then I asked him what his name was, and instead of answering he asked me if I'd like a piece of cake from the ship's galley."

LeCourt looked very grave. "And then what, Alberto?" he prodded.

"I — I said I would," said Alberto. "So he went into a door, but it wasn't the galley. We had been to the galley on my tour and I didn't see any cake there. But another man poked his head out the door after he went in. I think it was the captain. He stared at me for a minute. I didn't like him staring at me like that. Then he nodded and disappeared and a little later the first man came out again. Only this time he wasn't smiling like he had been before. He started yelling at me in English."

"How do you know it was English?" his sister cut in.

"*Senhor* Bancroft has been teaching me," Alberto replied proudly. "You should let him teach you too, Imelda. It is good to know English."

Imelda let out an exasperated sigh and rolled her eyes. Her brother was already continuing his story.

"He was yelling too fast for me to understand," he said. "And pointing at a door in the deck."

"A hatch. That's called a hatch, dummy," said Imelda.

"Imelda," said *Senhora* Ribeiro, "be quiet and let him talk."

Imelda rolled her eyes again as Alberto continued. "I said, 'What did you say?' but that seemed to make him angrier. He came right up to me and punched me in the eye so hard I thought my head would break. Then he yelled at me again, and that's when Mr. Bancroft rescued me."

"How did he rescue you, Alberto?" asked Imelda, her curiosity about the adventure finally overcoming her exasperation with her brother's drama.

"Well, I didn't see him arrive," Alberto said. "Just suddenly he was there. He said something in English to the man. He was talking too fast for me to understand but he sounded funny, cold-like. The man yelled something back at him and grabbed one of those wooden club things and went to hit Mr. Bancroft with it."

"A belaying pin, no doubt," murmured Dr. LeCourt.

"I don't know," said Alberto, "but anyway he didn't get to use it. I couldn't even see what he did, it was so fast, but he must have punched him or something. He fell down. Then Mr. Bancroft said, 'Show me the ship's particles.'"

Alberto delivered this last quotation in heavily accented English, with no small amount of pride. Prudence heard a short, hard chuckle just behind her, and turned to see a medium-sized man standing there, hands on hips. He was wearing a battered and filthy captain's hat; his face, craggy and browned, had obviously not been shaved in a week; and his short-sleeve khaki shirt was stained with sweat and what looked like engine grease.

"That's 'articles,' not 'particles,'" he said, switching easily from a fluent-but-barbarously-accented Portuguese to pronounce the English words. "It's the list of sailors who've signed up to sail on a ship. You must have given the captain your name, Alberto, because he forged it on the ship's articles. You were about to be shanghaied. Good thing I got there when I did. And you oughtta thank that mate for being so loud about it, because if he hadn't started bellowing at you to get below, I wouldn't ever have known what was happening."

"What was that shot?" asked Prudence, unable to restrain herself any longer.

Bancroft — for this could be none but he — glanced over at her briefly, then looked again with greater interest, apparently surprised by her Old World Portuguese accent. "What?" he said. "Oh. The captain of the *Swathmore* tried to get his ship's articles back by pointing a revolver at me. Expensive mistake. That was a very nice revolver. Colt, as a matter of fact."

"The *Swathmore?*" Dr. LeCourt said, switching to English and speaking with a thick French accent — and Prudence could clearly hear the malice in his voice. "That could be trouble for you, my friend. You know, do you not, who it is that owns that ship?"

"Yep," said Bancroft shortly, not bothering to look at him. "I'll straighten it out with him next time I'm in port. Right now, I've got a schedule to keep."

He then turned to the others. "Everybody ready to go?" he said.

"My companion is still missing," said Prudence in English, looking around again for Eleanor.

"You mean the tall dishy doll with the long black hair?" Bancroft replied breezily. "She'll be here before we're ready to blow. Don't worry, I won't leave *her* behind."

Something in the way he said this bothered Prudence. It must have shown in her eyes, because Bancroft followed up immediately: "Hey, take it easy, sister, I don't mean anything by it."

He didn't wait for a reply, but started toward the front of the boat, calling back over his shoulder, "Gotta step out before the Vigilance Committee gets the tar warmed up and the feathers out of the ducks."

Prudence gazed after him, almost but not quite entirely sure that he was joking. Did they have Vigilance Committees in jumping-off port towns deep in the Amazon, like Porto Escuro? She wouldn't be surprised.

But beside her, she heard LeCourt snort derisively.

"Prudence darling," said a voice behind them. "Who is your friend?"

"Eleanor!" Prudence cried, turning quickly. "I was beginning to worry. This is — Dr. LeCourt, right? We haven't been introduced either. I'm Prudence McMarion, and this is Eleanor Martins."

"*Enchanté*," purred LeCourt smoothly. "I am Raoul LeCourt, at your service."

Prudence thought his eyes rested longer on Eleanor than was quite polite — or was she imagining it? In any case, she was already well accustomed to men staring at Eleanor. Eleanor was a truly striking beauty, tall and slender and with an elegance of bearing that could only be described as "regal." Her face, naturally the exact color of the suntan Prudence always hoped to achieve by the end of each summer, was the perfect shape, with strong but feminine chin and noble cheekbones beneath a luxuriant cascade of straight black hair that seemed to glow with dark golds and deep reds when the sun shone on it. She always dressed just right, never a wrinkle or button out of place, but with a simple elegance that Prudence herself could only vainly aspire to. At that moment, she was dressed for travel in a sort of iridescent bronze rayon afternoon dress with a particularly glamourous but simple garden hat tinted to match it. White gloves and two-tone color-matched strap shoes with sensibly low heels completed the ensemble.

Prudence herself, although no ugly duckling, was quite plain by contrast with her glamorous friend. Her wavy hair, cut fashionably short, was a dull dark-brown and her face round and cherubic, and she was a good five inches shorter than Eleanor. She was also about twenty pounds heavier than she wanted to be, and carried most of it in her upper body, which made her look quite unfashionably busty by modern late-1920s standards. And although she'd tried to do better since meeting Eleanor, her style of dress was dated and frumpy in comparison. On this particular day, she was wearing a French-blue day dress with a straw cloche hat and plain brown Oxfords.

Bancroft now returned to the deck. "Everyone ready to cast off?" he said curtly. "Last call."

"Oh!" said Eleanor. "Our equipment hasn't been loaded yet." And she pointed to a stack of boxes and crates, still sitting on the wharf.

Bancroft glanced at it. "Oh, that's your loot, is it?" he grunted. "I was wondering. Nobody told me anything about you having freight. There's gonna be a surcharge for that, you know."

"What?" Prudence said, feeling herself reddening. "I've never heard of such a thing."

"Sure," said Bancroft. "I run a freight operation here, sister. If people could load all the goods they wanted on my boat, just for the cost of a passenger ticket, I'd never make a nickel on this river."

"And *Monsieur* Bancroft is always very interested in making a nickel," sneered Dr. LeCourt.

Bancroft ignored him. "Speaking of which, it's time for everyone to pay up. It's fifty *reais* per, plus an extra five for the stack of junk."

"Excuse me?" Prudence said tartly. "That's twice the price you quoted."

"That's right," said Bancroft, sounding a little irritated now. "Round trip. Carraçao is the only stop on this river and I'm the only boat. I'm not taking a chance on somebody ending up stranded there begging me for a charity passage. I'm trying to make money, not friends."

"Oh, good Lord," said Prudence. "You are a mercenary creature, aren't you?"

"Oh, it's all right, Prudence," said Eleanor serenely, laying an exquisite, immaculately gloved hand on the other's forearm and smiling sweetly. "We pay it now or we pay it later; what does it matter? And five *reais* sounds quite reasonable to me."

She withdrew a roll of banknotes from her purse and paid.

"Thank you, miss," Bancroft intoned, never taking his eyes off the roll of banknotes until it was safely stashed away once again in Eleanor's purse. "Also, don't flash those around like that. This is a dangerous place. Just stack the crates on the deck here, between the seats, and I'll take care of stowing them. And get a wiggle on, would you? We need to cast off before that tar from the *Swathmore* starts making trouble."

Bancroft obviously didn't intend to help load the crates, and for some reason that struck Prudence as inappropriate. She opened her mouth to protest, then suddenly realized how silly it would sound and closed her mouth again. Eleanor, who'd caught her look, smiled serenely at her.

"It's all right, Prudence," she said smoothly. "We can

load it all. We're not helpless waifs."

"And I will be glad to be of service," interjected Dr. LeCourt. "In fact, I insist. Perhaps also, Alberto —?"

Dr. LeCourt directed a paternal smile at the boy, who was still visibly shaken from his recent ordeal; Alberto leaped to his feet with commendable eagerness. Bancroft looked uncomfortable for just a moment, then shrugged and without a word started forward toward the steering station.

Standing over the stack of crates, LeCourt introduced Prudence and Eleanor to young Alberto; then, seizing the largest costume crate, he hurried off toward the *Amazon Princess* with it.

"What is all this stuff, *Senhorita* McMarion?" the youngster asked, picking up one of the smaller boxes.

"Well," said Prudence, "this long box is tripods; and this crate is full of movie film cartridges for the cameras. And the box you're holding there, see how it says "Kinamo" on the side, like these other two? Those are the movie cameras. Most of these crates are full of costumes."

"Movie cameras? You're making movies?"

"Yes," said Prudence.

"Here?"

"Well," Prudence said, "not here in Porto Escuro, but in your town, in … er …"

"Carraçao? In Carraçao? You're making a movie in Carraçao?"

"Maybe you would like to be in our movie, Alberto," said Eleanor, leaning toward him with a graceful smile.

"You bet I would!" Alberto chirped.

"Well," said Prudence, charmed by the youngster's enthusiasm, "why don't you carry the cameras, and we'll get the rest?"

With the four of them working, it was a matter of a minute or two before the equipment was safely stowed on board the *Amazon Princess*. And a few minutes later, with a rumble and a hiss of escaping steam, the slender steamboat was sliding away from the wharf.

Prudence looked back at the dock as they glided away, wanting a better look at the *Swathmore*. It was a large, generally nondescript sailing ship, three-masted, its hull painted white, with rust stains running down from its gunwales. It was the biggest sailing ship at the wharf. Prudence wondered idly who the owner was, of whom Dr. LeCourt had spoken so ominously.

Then she saw a group of seven policemen, moving along the dock toward where the *Amazon Princess* had been docked. They stopped when they saw that the *Amazon Princess* was no longer moored there, then looked out at the departing riverboat. They stood there staring at it for a moment, then turned and walked back to shore. It could not have been more obvious that they had been sent to intercept it.

The *Swathmore's* owner must be a real big cheese, Prudence thought.

III.

THE JOURNEY BEGINS.

As the *Amazon Princess* glided smoothly on up the placid green river, Prudence remained by the rail on the observation deck and watched the little port town dwindling slowly away into the distance behind them. It got smaller and smaller, and the forestland around got larger and larger, until a bend in the river cut them off and the wild scene looked as it had looked for a hundred thousand years before humans ever walked the Earth.

The river here was narrower than she had seen it before. She couldn't remember its name — it wasn't the main-stem Amazon, she knew, but one of its tributaries, and if she remembered correctly from Eleanor's description, they'd be turning off onto a tributary of the tributary sometime the next day.

Prudence was still a little taken aback by the scenic

beauty surrounding her, even after three days' journey from Belem. It was nothing like what she'd expected. She'd thought they'd find a jungle of the classic Congo River type as seen in the Tarzan pictures, dense and humid and deadly and full of thick vines with monkeys swinging on them and maybe "Numa, the Lion" stalking through the brush. What the Amazon really was, she'd quickly realized, was a wild woodland, dense and deep green and full of life. And she could see why Eleanor loved it so — although she couldn't understand how Eleanor could show so little fear of the great snakes that seemed to be everywhere.

She heard a soft step behind her and turned to see Eleanor, stepping up to the rail beside her. She smiled sweetly, and Prudence smiled back. Anyone watching the two of them would have assumed they were sisters, or lifelong friends at the very least — perhaps even parties to a "Boston marriage." But in truth, they'd only just met a few months before.

But there was something between the two of them that felt far older. Prudence felt as if she'd known Eleanor all her life, and she knew Eleanor felt the same way about her. Without saying anything, both of them had known they were destined to be best friends from the moment they'd met.

They had met in the lodge at Crater Lake while both were on vacation, in early autumn of the previous year. Prudence had been sitting there reading in a rustic Morris chair by the fire when Eleanor had come into the hall and stopped short when she'd seen Prudence. Prudence had met Eleanor's eyes and smiled. "I'm so sorry," Eleanor had said then, in her creamy musical voice with its faint hint of an exotic accent. "I've forgotten your name. I'm so awful that way."

"It's Prudence," Prudence had replied. "But I've forgotten yours too. Or is it possible — we've met, haven't we?"

"I think we have," said Eleanor. "In Los Angeles, right?"

"Yes…" Prudence had replied. "I think so. But I can't think where."

"I'm Eleanor," the other had continued. "Eleanor Martins."

And for the rest of their time at the lake, the two of them had been inseparable.

Prudence had learned that Eleanor had been born in Brazil, in a small village deep in the Amazon rainforest, and moved to the U.S. when she was just eight years old.

"But Eleanor isn't a Brazilian name, is it?" Prudence had said, puzzled. "And you haven't got an accent. I mean, you have the faintest trace of one, but not — "

"People have told me I do sound Brazilian, sometimes," Eleanor had replied with a smile. "And," she'd added with a rich and musical sort of Portuguese accent that had sounded impossibly exotic to Prudence, "I can make my accent come back when I wish to. And Eleanor is very Brazilian, or at least very Portuguese. It was the name of several queens and a Holy Roman Emperor. Although they usually spell it differently."

B y the end of that day, Prudence and Eleanor had concluded that they hadn't ever met before, because both knew they would have remembered if they had; rather, as Prudence jokingly suggested, they must have been twin sisters in a past life.

Not that Prudence had ever had any patience for metaphysical nonsense of that sort. Still, the coincidences had been a little uncanny. Both of them turned out to speak Portuguese — Prudence having been learned it from her mother, who had been born and raised in Lisbon, and Eleanor having grown up speaking it in her home village. More oddly, the two of them also shared some linguistic idiosyncracies of the type that develop among family members and close friends — pet names for things, obscure metaphors, and the like. For Prudence, it felt exactly as if she'd known Eleanor all her life, as if they'd sat around the same dinner table every night like sisters. And the strangeness had been crowned by a coincidence that really did make Prudence wonder just a little bit, even now, if there might be some supernatural explanation. It had come to light late in the afternoon of that first day.

"Eleanor is such a lovely name," Prudence had remarked, while standing on the rim of the lake and looking out over its blue expanse. "When I was just a little girl, you know, I had an imaginary friend named Eleanor. I drove my parents crazy talking about her, for years."

Eleanor had smiled then, the sort of dreamy, misty smile that appears when one is thinking back on an lovely and distant memory. "I had an imaginary friend, too, when I was a child," she murmured. "Her name was Trudie."

That had been a pleasant surprise. Trudie, as Eleanor had not yet known, was Prudence's nickname, which she had adopted at a very young age to stop people from calling her "Prudie." She laughingly told Eleanor about the coincidence.

"You know, Trudie," she'd said, "it's a funny thing. You are exactly the sort of person I'd always imagined my Trudie as."

Prudence had replied with a light, nervous laugh, a little embarrassed by the personal turn the conversation had taken. Perhaps because of her embarrassment, she hadn't told Eleanor the feeling was mutual. Eleanor would have been a perfect fit for a movie role as Prudence's Childhood Imaginary Friend. Except, of course, for the silly back-story she had made up for her imaginary Eleanor as a little girl: that she was a lonely princess from a hidden kingdom in a faraway land, who lived in an empty castle with loving but distant parents and nobody to play with or be friends with but Prudence.

Still, in all, it had been quite a coincidence.

The two of them had stayed up talking and drinking coffee on into the night, and then arranged to meet for breakfast the next morning. Both had been at Crater Lake for extended stays — Eleanor for a week, and Prudence for three days; but on the third day, Prudence had sent a telegram to her boss, Walter, requesting permission to stay an extra few days so she could travel home with Eleanor. (It had been promptly granted. Walter was one of those highly driven men who see time off as an investment in future productivity.)

The two of them had spent the next five days enjoying each other's company. Prudence's travel funds had started running low on the fourth day, and when she'd ordered nothing but toast for breakfast that morning, Eleanor had deduced the problem, and gracefully insisted on paying for everything for the rest of the trip.

"You may reimburse me later if you like," she'd said with soft firmness. "But, Prudence darling, I have just inherited a great deal of money from — from my family in Brazil. It means much less to me just now than it does to you."

And, although Prudence would never have considered accepting such an offer from any other friend, somehow with Eleanor it was different.

Over the rest of their breakfast, Eleanor had told Prudence she was hoping to use the inheritance to make a movie in her home town, the village of Carraçao, nestled on the shore of a small tributary to the Amazon River deep in the rainforest. But she knew nothing about movies, and the directors and movie people she'd approached about it — all men, of course — had not been good fits for the project. One had told her he'd need full creative control; another had said he'd do it, but insisted that she stay behind in Los Angeles while he traveled to Carraçao and shot the film unsupervised ("The savage jungle can be a dangerous and frightful place for a lovely and delicate maiden such as yourself," he'd informed her paternally, apparently forgetting that she'd grown up there); and the last one had actually asked her to sign a power of attorney so that he could draw funds from her personal bank accounts. All three had tried shamelessly to take her to bed, not even bothering to remove or conceal their wedding rings. It had been very discouraging, and she'd been on the verge of giving up.

"Why, Eleanor, that's my business," Prudence had said, when she heard this story. "I've been working in movie and animation production for years. I've never been The Director, but I've done everything a director does. You should hire me!"

"Oh, I couldn't!" Eleanor had said. "We're friends, Trudie, we can't be employer-employee."

"Partners, then?"

"Partners!"

Today, standing beside Eleanor on the observation deck of the little riverboat and gazing out over the primordial Amazon river scene, Prudence felt as if she really were with a childhood friend rather than someone she'd only just met earlier that year.

Footsteps behind them on the boat brought both women around. Dr. LeCourt was walking up to them.

"Is not ze afternoon lovely?" he murmured, speaking English with his heavy French accent. "You are traveling to Carraçao, no? I also am traveling there. I am one of the village physicians."

"Carraçao has more than one doctor?" said Prudence, turning to Eleanor. "You always described it as such a tiny place, Eleanor, I thought —"

"*Mais oui*, if you can believe it, we actually have three!" LeCourt said. "There is Dr. Jones, Dr. Rodriques and myself. But you are right, it is a very small village for so many doctors, and the people there are healthy. Fortunately we all have other things we do to occupy ourselves."

"Such a lovely little town," LeCourt went on, and Prudence thought he sounded as if he were hurrying to say something, as if he'd just suddenly realized that she might ask him to elaborate on the "other things we do to occupy ourselves" and wanted to forestall her. "The perfect place to retire from a career of hurrying about the field hospitals in the war, and attending silly parties during peacetime. Here, life is simple and beautiful. I will not make my fortune here, but I will be happy here, for it is my home. And the people are my friends."

A curt, mirthless laugh rang out behind them after that, and all three turned and saw that it was Bancroft. The scruffy captain was coiling up a white rope by the rail, having left the steering station for a moment. He made no further comment and did not meet the ladies' eyes, quickly finishing up his task and moving forward again. LeCourt turned back to the ladies and smiled ruefully.

"Perhaps not all the people are my friends," he

murmured, sounding a little abashed but still very smooth and extraordinarily French. "There may be … an exception, or perhaps two."

"What's he got against you, anyway?" Prudence said, her words sounding a little sharper than she'd intended. Bancroft's rudeness bothered her. She felt strongly that if a person really wanted to be grouchy, that was fine; but pressing one's bad humor upon other people was unacceptably piggish behavior.

"I do not know," said LeCourt ruefully. "Unless it is that I hired another boat to bring some of my laboratory *equipage* up the river to the town. *Monsieur* Bancroft likes to charge as much money as he can for his services, he is, how you say — very mercenary, greedy even. He quoted me a price to bring my *equipage* that was so high, I was able to save money by hiring another boatman who does not usually come to Carraçao. So, *Monsieur* Bancroft got nothing, and it is since that day that he has been like this."

"Oh," said Prudence.

Eleanor glanced at him for a moment, looking slightly puzzled. Then she smiled as if dismissing a troublesome thought from her mind and turned her eyes out upon the river. The *Amazon Princess* had reached a part of the river that was broad and shallow, like a great green lake. She gazed dreamily out over its surface, her strong yet delicate features relaxing naturally into a soft smile.

"It is like a dream," she murmured, the Brazilian accent stirring in her words more strongly than Prudence had ever before heard it. "A dream of coming home."

Prudence shifted uncomfortably. She herself did not feel very homey here. She watched a foot-thick snake moving slowly through the mud along the near shore of the river. It was at least twenty feet long. She shuddered a little.

"Please excuse me," LeCourt murmured, and as he turned to go, Prudence caught his eye. There was something in his expression that caused her pulse to quicken for a moment.

Eleanor watched him walk away, then turned to Prudence. "He's sweet on you, Trudie," she said laughingly. "You be careful with him, darling. He seems a little dangerous."

"Yes," Prudence said. "Yes, he does."

That night, the passengers took their evening meal seated on the observation deck. Captain Bancroft brought out a great basket of stale bread and a platter of rubbery cheese, which the passengers all augmented with fruits and snack foods that they had brought along with them.

Prudence learned that she had been right about the location of the "staterooms" — but on this boat there were only two of them: the captain's cabin, and another identical cabin on the opposite side. Between the two cabins were the boat's steam engine, toward the front; and behind that, a tiny, cramped bathroom that Bancroft referred to as "the head." When it was time for sleep, the men of the party — Bancroft, LeCourt and young Alberto — repaired to the captain's cabin, and the ladies — Prudence, Eleanor, *Senhora* Ribeiro (who introduced herself as Izabel) and young Imelda — took the other.

"Don't be such a Gibson Girl, Prudence," Eleanor had whispered to her when she'd complained about the arrangement. "Most of these riverboats haven't even got cabins. Everyone just climbs into hammocks on the observation deck."

The cabin held three bunks, plus a hammock that had

been strung across the corner. Young Imelda claimed this, and the other ladies started preparing themselves to sleep on the bunks.

"I do hope poor Alberto isn't having to put up with too much over there," remarked Izabel in Portuguese, speaking to Eleanor. "Those two men — I had so hoped Alberto and I wouldn't have to sail back to the village with Dr. LeCourt on board."

"Why, Dr. LeCourt seems like such a nice man," said Prudence, a little alarmed. "Is there something we should know about him?"

"Oh, no," said Izabel, smiling. "It is just that he and *Senhor* Bancroft detest each other so. It is hard to be around two people who are so full of hate for each other, and we will be on this river for three full days together."

"It will not be so bad," said Eleanor, giving one of her creamy smiles. "They can make themselves miserable if they like, but Captain Bancroft can seldom leave the steering station, which makes him easy to avoid. And at night, I am quite sure Alberto will be well able to sleep. The two gentlemen's style of fighting appears to me to be more along the lines of haughty silence rather than angry shouting."

Izabel looked startled. "Excuse me, *Senhorita*," she said. "I thought you were a North American, but I see from your accent that you are not. Your accent almost sounds like —"

"Yes," Eleanor said, smiling mistily. "Yes, I was a North American. But now I am coming home."

Prudence stirred uneasily, sitting on the edge of her bunk, and glanced at Eleanor out of the corners of her eyes. Eleanor might have wanted to stay here in this rainforest forever, but she, Prudence, very much did not. Nor did she relish the thought of leaving behind the woman whom she had already come to view as her best friend, when she returned home to Los Angeles.

"Home?" Izabel was saying, sounding delighted. "Where is home?"

"Carraçao," said Eleanor. "I am from Carraçao. My family left when I was just a little girl."

"Really?" Imelda chimed in. She'd sat up in her hammock and was looking down at them. "Who are they?"

"My parents both died when I was a baby," Eleanor replied. "I was raised by my aunt Marcita and uncle Carlo. Our last name is Martins."

At the sound of the name, Prudence saw an odd look cross Izabel's face for a fleeting instant. It looked like shock, maybe even alarm — with possibly even a hint of fear. Then it faded rapidly into a look that was even more disturbing — a look of sad, gentle sympathy. Then even that was gone, and Izabel looked awkwardly at the floor.

Eleanor seemed not to notice. But a moment later, when Izabel had turned her attention back to preparing herself for bed, Eleanor met Prudence's eye, and they exchanged puzzled frowns.

Prudence found it easier to sleep on the boat than she'd thought she would, owing no doubt to the gentle rocking motion of the boat in the river. The following morning, the first pre-dawn glow outside the windows awakened her. She pulled her little travel alarm clock out of her purse and checked the time. It was just before five in the morning.

She rolled out of her narrow berth and hurriedly got dressed. Prudence's favorite time of day was the sunrise, and she very much wanted to be up on deck to see and hear it in this new and exotic place.

She slipped out the cabin door, leaving her companions

undisturbed, and made her way on to the observation deck, padding along in stocking feet.

As she reached the corner of the cabin and stepped out onto the observation deck, she heard a quick, stealthy scuffling sound behind her, and she whirled, alarmed, groping for some kind of weapon and finding only her travel alarm clock. Then the door of the captain's cabin flew open and Bancroft leaped out, a big black revolver in his right hand.

"Oh, it's you," he growled, sounding vaguely disgusted.

Prudence dropped the clock back into her purse. "And a very pleasant good morning to you, too, Captain," she said icily.

"Sorry," Bancroft mumbled, looking sheepish. He stowed the revolver in his pajama pocket, where its weight distorted the fabric noticeably. "When I feel somebody walking on deck without making any noise, I get worried."

"Oh!" Prudence said in surprise. "Is there any danger here, then? From hostile natives or something like that?"

"Hostile natives? Maybe, but I don't think so, not on this river, and certainly not to my boat. No, not from the natives."

"From something else, then?"

Bancroft now seemed slightly impatient. "No. Everything's fine, everything's jake. Just, somebody pussyfooting around on the deck of my boat in the middle of the night, trying not to make noise, that's something I want to know about, that's all."

He glanced back into his cabin, then looked out at the lightening sky. "It's about time for me to start building the boiler fire anyway," he said. "Excuse me."

And he made his way forward, toward the pilothouse.

Shivering just a little in the early-morning chill — or what passed for a chill, anyway, on a late-summer day in the Amazon Basin — Prudence settled herself down on one of the settees under the canopy, pulled her shawl around herself, and watched and listened as the rainforest around her slowly came to life under the rays of the rising sun.

The day passed in pastoral quiet, with the scenery gliding relentlessly by as the little vessel wended its way up the river. The river they were on was broad and placid, and its waters were an opaque, murky brown. It was also a busy river — much busier than Prudence had thought it would be. They passed dozens of vessels ranging in size from small scows to very large side-wheel riverboats.

Midway through that afternoon, Prudence noticed that there were two different colors of water in the river, flowing side by side and seeming reluctant to mix: opaque and murky brown on the right, and clear but dark on the left. The riverboat seemed to be following directly over the boundary between the two waters. Then it slid over into the clear, dark waters on the left, and Prudence realized the river in front of them was splitting in two. There was a sunny, broad, open channel flowing with muddy brown water; and a dark, shadowy channel, covered completely over with the canopies of great trees like a tunnel, looking improbably narrow by contrast, branching off to the left.

They soon plunged into the comparative darkness of the smaller river, and Prudence noticed it had a much brisker current than the big muddy river did. It also had an indefinable character, wholly missing from the bigger river, of mystery — with the faintest touch of the sinister.

"Is this the river Carraçao is on?" she asked Eleanor,

who was also watching, with shining eyes.

"Yes," said Eleanor. "This is the Arapaima River. You can see its water is not muddy like that of the big river. It is not so large, either. But it is unusually deep."

Eleanor paused for a moment, and seemed to want to say more. But she remained silent. Prudence wondered what was on her mind, but didn't press her.

They stopped for the night at a dilapidated dock jutting out into a broad lagoon of sorts, in the middle of the river. And once again, at five the next morning, Prudence slipped out of her cabin, this time keeping a watchful eye on the captain's cabin door. She'd brought her journal with her this time, because although there wasn't enough light to really write in it, she wanted to be able to jot down any thoughts that came to her.

Then she turned toward the settee on the observation deck, and stopped short, giving a startled gasp that was almost a muffled shriek. Seated expansively on the settee was Captain Bancroft.

"Good morning, ma'am," he said.

Prudence did not try to conceal her annoyance. She didn't get up at such an early hour every morning because she wanted company, and she felt vaguely cheated by his presence.

"Off to a great start," she said tartly.

Oddly enough, he seemed to understand. He nodded. "I'm a morning person too," he told her. "I won't bother you for long, and anyway I've got the boiler fire to get started. I just wanted to — to warn you."

Her eyebrows shot up. "Warn me?"

"Yes," said Bancroft, now looking distinctly uncomfortable for the first time. "It's about — look, Miss, um —"

"It's McMarion," she said. "Prudence McMarion."

"Miss McMarion. Like I said, it's none of my business, and I feel a bit of a chump butting in, but. . ."

His voice trailed off awkwardly.

"Well?" Prudence said, growing exasperated.

"I just — it's LeCourt. Don't trust him. He's not a trustworthy man. That's all."

Prudence looked at him, her surprise starting to harden into a sort of frosty indignation.

"I see," she said icily. "Captain Bancroft, much as I appreciate your concern for my womanly virtue, I must ask you please in the future to mind your own business."

"I've said my bit," Bancroft shot back crisply. "You're now free to ignore it, or misinterpret it however you like, but I've said my bit and now I can get back to, as you say, minding my own damn business, with a clear conscience. So you can save your little lecture about etiquette, it won't be needed."

He surged to his feet and stormed off the deck, heading toward the wheelhouse. Prudence sat down where he had been, fidgeting with her travel journal, still simmering with resentment at Bancroft's apparent assumption that she would be putty in the hands of the smooth-talking Frenchman.

Finally she managed to calm herself down. A glance at her travel clock showed it was still only five fifteen; there was plenty of time to enjoy the sunrise. She opened her travel journal, uncapped her pen, and wrote the date in the top corner of the page.

Then the captain's cabin door opened again, and Dr. Raoul LeCourt emerged.

"*Mademoiselle* McMarion," he said smoothly in greeting. "But what brings you out upon the day so early?"

Prudence cringed inwardly, trying to hide her embarrassment. Ordinarily she would have welcomed a chance to get to know Raoul better — but then again, ordinarily she would not be just out of bed, in a rumpled cotton house dress, bare-legged, hatless, and without having had the chance to so much as run a brush through her hair. Always before she had found that waking up before the chickens started to crow was the best way to find uninterrupted quiet time. Apparently, though, the Amazon Basin was special in that regard.

She composed herself, and looked up at him with a smile. "The sunrise. Isn't it beautiful?"

"Yes. Yes, it certainly is," he murmured distractedly, glancing briefly in the direction of the softly glowing sky. "But it is a little early for me, *ma foi*. You are, how you say, morning person?"

"*Bien sûr*," she replied. "*Le matin, c'est bien l'heure que j'aime le mieux.*"

"Ah, very good," LeCourt replied. "Your *Français*, she is excellent, *Mademoiselle*. But it reminds me of things I try to forget, of the heartbreak that I left behind me in gay *Paris*. I much prefer to speak ze English."

"As you wish," murmured Prudence, trying not to show her puzzlement.

"And did I hear the voice of our captain out here this morning?" LeCourt continued.

"Yes," she replied. "He was out here a moment ago. He's gone forward, I think, to start the boiler fire."

"What brought him out upon the deck so early, do you suppose, eh?"

Prudence frowned. "Does he not get up this early most mornings, to start the boiler fire?" she said.

"*Ah oui*. And did he say something to you?"

"No," said Prudence crisply. "Nothing of any interest whatsoever."

LeCourt looked at her searchingly for a split second, and she met his eyes with a firm mind-your-own-business look — not a glare, but something close to it. He responded by murmuring some sort of French-accented pleasantry and moving back to the cabin, leaving Prudence alone at last. She stared after him, glanced up at the pilothouse beyond, and then looked down at her travel journal.

"These people are very strange," Prudence told Eleanor an hour later, after Eleanor had emerged sleepily from the ladies' cabin. "This morning, our surly captain got up even before me, and was waiting for me when I got on deck. Apparently he wanted to tell me not to trust Raoul."

"Raoul?" Eleanor said, surprised. "Surely not."

"Well, that's what I thought," said Prudence. "I rather assumed he meant that I would need to guard my womanly virtue particularly diligently because Raoul was such a smooth-talking ladies' man, or something like that. I have to admit that I was thinking the same thing myself. But then Raoul himself came out and we had the most remarkable conversation. He seemed to want to know, in the worst way, what Captain Bancroft had said. He interrogated me almost to the point of being rude. Do you know, Eleanor, I don't believe that man is really French. He talks like no real Frenchman I've ever met. He sounds like a Vaudeville Frenchman. And when I actually addressed him in French, he continued speaking English to me. And he made the most remarkable gender error."

"Perhaps he prefers to practice his English?" Eleanor said.

Prudence smiled at her. "You don't know many Frenchmen, do you, Eleanor?"

The little riverboat steamed onward, ever deeper into the woodland. The river had become noticeably narrower now, and in a few spots Prudence was sure she could have thrown a stone all the way across it. It almost seemed to tunnel through the foliage in places—like a secret river, close and green and intimate.

"I hope we don't meet a big riverboat here," she remarked to Eleanor, while they were traversing one such stretch of river. "There wouldn't be room."

"Oh, there aren't any other riverboats on this river," Eleanor assured her. "Captain Bancroft is the only one, other than the government mail boat once every two weeks. The Arapaima has a… strange reputation. Most of the other operators avoid it."

"Really? Is it dangerous?"

"No, not dangerous," Eleanor laughed. But she didn't elaborate, and seemed not to want to talk about it, so Prudence changed the subject.

"Eleanor," she said, "you saw the look on Izabel's face when she found out who you were, didn't you? What did you make of it?"

A soft shadow seemed to drift across Eleanor's beautiful smile. She looked away over the river, her eyes focused on infinity, obviously lost for a moment in thought.

"Yes," she said. "I wondered about that. I waited for her to tell me something about it but she hasn't, and I keep catching her looking at me with that wistful, sympathetic look. I hope Aunt Marcita and Uncle Carlo are not sick or hurt."

She was silent for a moment, then continued: "But

Trudie, did you notice — did you think — there was something odd about — "

"I think I know what you mean," said Prudence.
"Something is different, something changed after Izabel
learned who we are. Something in her eyes. Something
almost like fear. Does your family have a strange reputation
in the village or something?"

"Not that I know of," said Eleanor. "But I was very
young when I left."

She looked sad and worried for a moment, then shook
her head and seemed to put the matter out of her mind.
But Prudence could tell it was still bothering her, deep
down inside.

T he next morning, Prudence was journaling on the
observation deck when Bancroft emerged from
his cabin to light the boiler fire.

"Good morning, Captain," Prudence said with what
she hoped was a gracious smile.

"Morning," he grunted cautiously, as if suspecting that
her politeness was a setup for some kind of trap.

She smiled reassuringly at him and turned back to the
journal. He lingered there for a moment, seemingly debating
whether to say something more or go forward and start the
fires; then he turned.

"Listen, Miss McMarion, I apologize for making you
uncomfortable yesterday," he said rapidly. "It's just that
you're not from here, and you — need to know something
about the expatriate community here in the Amazon. Guys
like me and Raoul LeCourt and Hy Jones, the — well, you'll
probably meet him later. See, tourists like you come to
places like this and they end up palling around with the
expats because they're from north America, or Europe, or

Australia; and they're familiar types, speak English, and all that. But here's the thing. None of us is here because we want to be. Not one of us expats living here in the middle of nowhere is here because we looked at a map and said, 'I dream of living here.' All of us are on the lam, sister. All of us."

"Including you?" Prudence said, engaging in spite of herself.

"Including me. Some of us are running from the law; some are running from lovers, some are on the lam from whole families they've abandoned; some are hiding out from gangsters they've ratted out. Lenny DeKock, down in Porto Escuro, rumor has it he's actually running from a murder rap. We're all fugitives. So when I tell you not to trust Raoul LeCourt, I'm not implying—what you think I'm implying. I'm just saying, he's an expat, he's running from something, don't trust him, don't trust any of us."

"What are you running from?"

Bancroft's only reply was a wry, jaded little smirk that said, plain as speech, "You know better than to ask me that."

Prudence smirked back; then her face became serious again. "Captain," she said, "if it's all right to ask, why do you hate him so?"

Bancroft looked at his feet. For a moment he looked slightly shamefaced. Then his face hardened again and he turned away from her and started for the bows.

"I don't want to talk about it," he grunted as he went.

Prudence scowled after his retreating back. "What a cake-eater," she muttered.

They arrived at Carraçao late the next morning. Captain Bancroft announced their arrival—as, Prudence would soon learn, he always did—with a long blast on the steamboat's whistle, a low-pitched, almost ghostly flute-like wailing sound, very distinctive and like no steam whistle she had ever heard. As they got closer and closer to the final bend in the river around which her hometown would appear, Eleanor got progressively more and more excited. Finally the little steamboat rounded that bend, and there before them lay the village — a collection of rustic huts made of rough-sawn planks with roofs made of grass and a small pier extending along the river in front. Toward the rear of the town, a tall and improbable-looking steeple rose from the top of the village church, an all-wood structure that did not quite fit in with the surrounding architecture. The village looked pleasantly alive, with smoke rising from a chimney or two here and there and figures bustling around in its streets.

Standing at the rail in the seating area, Eleanor gave a small joyful cry.

"It is Carraçao! Just as I remember it!" she cried.

Glancing up at her friend, Prudence caught sight of Izabel Ribeiro, standing nearby with Imelda and Alberto and looking at Eleanor with a strange, sad expression on her face. She looked as if she wanted to tell Eleanor something, but was afraid to.

Then they were pulling up to the pier, and Bancroft was bustling about tying the boat off.

As she watched him doing this, Prudence saw Dr. LeCourt approaching with Izabel in tow. Izabel now looked distinctly distressed, and LeCourt bore a look that Prudence found even more disturbing — a look of professional sympathy, the sort of look a doctor wears when giving a terminal patient the bad news. She wheeled round to face them, then realized they were looking not at her, but at Eleanor.

"*Mademoiselle* Martins?" Dr. LeCourt intoned, speaking Portuguese so that Izabel could understand him. "*Madame* Ribeiro has asked me for my assistance. She feels you should know a thing, but is too, how you say, overcome to tell you directly. I regret terribly to give you this news. It is about your aunt and uncle."

Prudence felt as if a heavy lump was forming in the pit of her stomach at this alarming preface to what was clearly a piece of very bad news. But Eleanor maintained her usual uncanny calm. "Oh!" said she, looking mildly surprised and curious. "Is there a problem?"

"Well, you see, just a few weeks ago, your aunt and uncle, Carlo and Marcita Martins, left in their canoe to go up the river for something," LeCourt said. "They may have been hunting the caiman, I do not know. But they never returned. Their canoe was found floating in the river, and it looked as if the caimans had bitten upon it."

Eleanor's smile froze momentarily and an indefinable look flashed across her face — something like dread. Then she composed herself with a visible effort and flashed a sad, misty little smile. "I'm so sad to hear this. I haven't seen my aunt and uncle since I was eight years old. And I have no other relatives in town."

"No, *Senhorita*," said Izabel, "but I hope that you will consider my family to be yours as well."

"Thank you, Izabel," Eleanor said. "You are so sweet, and I am honored."

"The Martins house is empty," Alberto said then. "I guess it's yours now, *Senhorita* Martins. Would you like to go see it? Imelda and I will show you. Come on, Imelda."

Imelda rolled her eyes, then looked at Eleanor and smiled shyly.

Prudence looked at Eleanor closely. *She doesn't believe*

it, she thought to herself. *She doesn't really believe they're dead.*

The Martins home was very similar to the other houses in the village, although it clearly had gone unoccupied for some time. It was a large cabin atop posts or stilts, five feet high, with a single interior partition across the center separating the sleeping area from the living room. Across its front was a full-width sitting porch. A steep-sloping grass-thatched roof covered everything. The four of them stepped inside and waited a moment or two for their eyes to get used to the darkness.

From the distant wharf came faintly the sound of a well-muffled automobile engine, an incongruous sound amid the sylvan stillness.

"That's Dr. LeCourt's automobile," Alberto said proudly. "He doesn't get it out very often. One time he let me ride in it with him. I wonder if he's driving somewhere?"

They continued their exploration. Inside the sleeping room, there was a single double-size bed topped with a mattress stuffed with straw, and a single smaller bed made the same way. Eleanor smiled when she saw it.

"That was my bed, when I was a little girl," she said. "It looks just as it did when I last slept in it. Only it seems as if it is much smaller now that I am grown!"

In the living room stood a modest table with chairs and what looked like a hand-built couch or settee. The furnishings were very modest, but looked comfortable.

The automobile engine, which had been growing steadily louder as if drawing near, now settled down to a sedate two-cylinder murmur just outside the front door. Something creaked and clanged.

"Well," said Eleanor, "I had expected that we would

stay with Aunt Marcita and Uncle Carlo. I had not anticipated staying in their home without them. It feels odd,
but I suppose this is where we should stay."

"Hello ladies, and master Alberto," called a voice from
the front porch. "Where may I place these things for you?"

Stepping to the door, Prudence and Eleanor saw that
it was Raoul LeCourt, holding one of the big crates in
which they'd packed their camera gear. Behind him they
saw the automobile, a tiny coal-black two-seater that looked
to be at least 15 years old, with a sloping bonnet and large
wood-spoked wheels.

"Oh, Dr. LeCourt, thank you," Prudence called out.
"You can just put it down on the porch there."

"Oh, do please to call me Raoul," he replied.

LeCourt insisted on using the little motorcar to help
the two women haul the rest of their gear back from the
wharf to the Martins cabin. It took four trips. When they
were finished, the two ladies walked back to the wharf with
LeCourt puttering alongside in the car, the two children
perched happily in the passenger seat. There the youngsters
jumped down and LeCourt retrieved his own luggage.

"Raoul," Eleanor said then, "there is a restaurant in the
village, no? Or are there now more than one?"

"There are two, *mademoiselle*," replied LeCourt. "Me,
I prefer to dine at Marcello's. It is just there, you see? Where
the chimney smokes? It is more, how you say, *élégant*. But
it is not *élégant*. Both our restaurants are crude and of the
frontier, not like what you would find in Paris."

He paused. Prudence, who had looked away toward
the restaurant with the smoking chimney, turned back just
in time to catch Raoul letting his eyes linger on her. He
didn't seem embarrassed at being caught; he merely smiled,
and she returned the smile with what she hoped was not

too high a degree of flirtatiousness. Prudence really wasn't used to this sort of attention when in Eleanor's company; most men seemed to find the tall Brazilian so attractive that they barely noticed Prudence. Most of the time, it was kind of nice.

"Would you ladies care to join me for the luncheon?" Raoul said then. "I would be, how you say, *enchanté* to have such lovely company on such a beautiful day."

"Why, thank you, Raoul," purred Eleanor, and Prudence wondered if she also had noticed LeCourt eying her. "Prudence?"

Prudence really wanted to say something flirty to Raoul, but she knew it was too soon. So instead, she simply said, "I think we would both love to join you for lunch."

As the three of them strolled away from the dock, Prudence caught the eye of Captain Bancroft, who was moving about the boat cleaning things and shutting everything down after the run on the river. His look was cold and disapproving; then she saw his eyes slide away from hers and onto LeCourt, and they hardened in a flash into little slits of hate. She saw LeCourt stiffen slightly, and knew they'd made eye contact.

Not my business, she reminded herself firmly, and went with her two companions to the luncheon table.

IV.

THE FILMING STARTS.

Prudence and Eleanor spent the rest of their first day in Carraçao exploring the village, meeting people and reconnecting Eleanor with people who had last seen her when she was a little girl. They were invited in for innumerable cups of thick black Brazilian coffee sipped on porches and in living rooms. Prudence had been eager to get started with filming, but Eleanor had insisted that she make the rounds, assuring her not doing so would be seen as a slight.

So the two women set out to reconnect Eleanor with her past.

By the end of the day, Prudence was frankly envious. Her own upbringing as the daughter of Vaudeville performers had been very nomadic, and there really wasn't a place that she could think of as a childhood home. The experience Eleanor was having, as she trooped dutifully from one house to the next, was one Prudence would never have. Tears were being shed, and great joyful hugs were being exchanged, and Eleanor was glowing with pleasure at the welcome from her old friends and neighbors. Standing there watching this, Prudence felt oddly left out, like an unseen ghost. By the end of the day, a soft melancholy had settled over her.

But when she turned to Eleanor, at the end of the day, she saw her own melancholy reflected in the taller woman's eyes as well.

"Why, whatever is the matter, Eleanor?" she said.

Eleanor flashed a soft smile. "I couldn't say," she said quietly. "It's just that there is — something. With every person we met today, when I first started talking and they could tell from my accent that I was from here, their eyes lit up and they looked so happy to see me. But then, when they learned who I was, when they heard the surname Martins —"

She broke off, but Prudence understood. She'd seen it too, although she hadn't realized what it was. And, come to think of it, she'd seen it in the eyes of Izabel Ribeiro on the boat ride to town. Not fear, not even nervousness — just a subtle sort of awareness of other-ness. The shouts of joy, the hugs, and the "my-how-you've-growns" had not been able to conceal it. Something — something had been there.

"At first I thought that it was just that they felt bad for me because Aunt Marcita and Uncle Carlo have disappeared," Eleanor said. "But I think it's something else. I think my family has some sort of — reputation here. Something I know nothing about, something everybody knows but nobody talks about."

She was silent for a moment, gazing out over the village

toward the river as Prudence silently groped for something to say.

"All my life I've dreamed of this day," Eleanor continued. "Dreamed of meeting the people I loved so long ago, and who loved me; of being home, in my village, the place where no matter where I've been and what I've done, I will always have a place, a community. But now I am starting to feel that perhaps I — I don't."

Prudence laid a hand on her forearm and looked into her eyes. "Eleanor, darling, I understand you perfectly," she said. "When I was growing up we never stayed in one place. I never got to know a place as home. I was like a little gypsy girl. I understand that feeling, that longing. I've known it all my life. And — just know that I'm here for you."

Eleanor smiled by way of reply. Then, a moment later, she spoke. "Thank you, Trudie," she said, "for being such a good friend."

By now it was time for dinner, and although Eleanor had collected several invitations to dine, she hadn't accepted any of them. The two of them made their way to the other restaurant in Carraçao, a tavern improbably named "Smithy's" even though no one by that name was connected to it.

They found the food there to be coarse, but cheap and served in large quantities, so they fell to with gusto. Prudence ordered a double Scotch to start things off, but found she was unable to drink the stuff; it tasted like cheap speakeasy "dehorn" with moss soaked in it. There were, however, nine different kinds of rum and *cachaça* — a popular Brazilian liquor made with fresh sugar cane juice. So, figuring that when in Rome one must do as a Roman does, she asked for a double shot of the darkest rum they had. Neat, no chaser: Prudence was not a drinker of girly drinks.

Eleanor ordered a glass of white wine.

After dinner, the two of them walked through the gathering darkness to the empty Martins home, ready to settle in for the night.

"How do you feel about this?" Prudence asked. "Going to spend the night in your aunt and uncle's home, when their loss is still so fresh?"

"I don't much like it," Eleanor said slowly. "I did not think it would be a problem earlier today. But now, it's dark, and — well, it's what we must do, isn't it?"

They arrived at the bottom of the porch steps just as the last light was fading, and entered the house, which was now in total darkness.

"Do you know where Carlo and Marcita kept the candles?" Prudence asked then.

"They were in this little bureau by the door," said Eleanor. "I still remember the stern lecture from Uncle Carlo the day I found them and tried to eat them, when I was just three or four."

There was a sound of wood scraping on wood, and Prudence knew that Eleanor had opened the drawer; but then, there was a moment of silence, followed by a little squeak of surprise.

"They are not here!" Eleanor said. "They must have moved them. Will you help me look?"

"I don't know how I can," said Prudence. "I can't see anything and I don't know where anything is in the house."

Nonetheless, the two women fumbled about in the house, locating furniture by touch, going through drawers and boxes as best they could.

Finally, Eleanor said, "It's no use. We should just go to bed and in the morning, be sure and find the candles. Or we can buy some from Old Man Paulo at the general store."

Prudence fumbled about until she found her suitcase. Then she paused.

"I think I'll just sleep in my clothes," she said.

"I — I can't," Eleanor said, and her voice quavered just a little for the first time since Prudence had met her. "I can't lie down on this bed without checking it for snakes. I'm going to wait up until dawn comes."

Prudence hadn't considered the possibility of snakes. Or spiders — did the Amazon have deadly spiders too? She wasn't sure, but she thought it probably did.

"I'm going to do the same thing," she said firmly. "We'll sit together here and stay up all night together talking."

"Oh! Yes! Like two girls at a slumber party!" Eleanor said, all the fear and worry suddenly gone from her voice. "What a stellar idea, Prudence. And what a lovely friend you are."

Then, out of the darkness beyond the porch of the house, a voice called out in heavily French-accented English: "Prudence? Eleanor? Is it that you are at home?"

"It's Raoul!" cried Prudence. "Yes, Raoul, we are here. Sitting in the dark, because we cannot find the candles."

"It is just as I thought when I walked by and saw that no light burned in your home," the Frenchman replied. "I will not ask to come in, for I expect that you are not dressed to receive company. But I hope that you will allow me to place these candles and matches just inside the front door. I also wish to tell you that I took the liberty of entering the house while you were out, for purposes of sweeping away the cobwebs and making sure no serpents lurked within."

"Oh, thank you, Raoul!" Eleanor called out musically, with gratitude sounding strong in her voice.

"I will not keep you, nor will I strike a light knowing

you are in your nighttime dress," LeCourt continued. "*A demain, mesdemoiselles.* Perhaps we may again enjoy breakfast together tomorrow?"

"We would love that," Eleanor answered. "Wouldn't we, Prudence?"

"*Mais oui,*" Prudence replied. "*A demain, Raoul, et encore nous vous remercions! Vous nous avez sauvé!*"

"But of course!" said LeCourt. "It is my very great pleasure to be of service."

And they heard his footsteps descend the front steps and disappear into the night.

Prudence found the candles and matches, and struck a light; and neither of the ladies thought they had ever been so grateful for such a tiny point of light as they were for the one they now sat before, in the warm inky blackness of a rainforest night.

"Still, though, it would have been such fun to stay up all night with you," Eleanor murmured, suddenly sounding very sleepy.

Prudence nodded and stifled a yawn.

The next morning, Prudence once again awakened at five. But once again, she was frustrated in her desire to savor that golden hour of solitude, because in climbing out of bed and trying to sneak out the door onto the porch, she tripped over the crate that held their camera tripods, and pitched headlong to the floor with a crash that brought Eleanor bolt upright in bed with a little shriek.

"I'm so sorry," Prudence stammered, picking herself up as Eleanor struck a match and lit the candle by her bed. "I couldn't see."

"It's OK, Trudie," Eleanor whispered. "Such a dream I

had — such a strange dream. I am grateful to have been awakened from it."

"Want to tell me about it?" Prudence asked, seating herself on the crate and rubbing her bruised shin.

"Not — not by candlelight in a strange room, no," said Eleanor. "Let us get ready for today. An early start, no?"

Over an early breakfast at Marcello's, Prudence laid out her plans for the movie.

"We'll get started right away filming the scenes that don't involve Charles," she said. "There are quite a few of them. If we plan right, we can have almost half the movie shot in a week, and then when he arrives, we'll be able to make maximal use of his very expensive time."

"Good," said Eleanor. "It's just as well he was delayed, isn't it?"

"I guess so," said Prudence. "If we shoot every scene without him in it before he arrives, and then finish up with him here, we don't have to worry about realizing at the last minute that we forgot to shoot some scene that can't be shot without him."

She was referring to Charles Conners, the star actor they had hired to play the lead role in the film opposite Eleanor. Conners was expected to arrive via passenger steamer a few days after Prudence and Eleanor, and they had him for just one week before he'd have to return for his next job. Really, they were lucky to have him. Prudence didn't like to speculate on how much Eleanor must have had to pay to get him.

"I was told his ship was due in Belem today, and then he'll be another three days on the riverboat to Porto Escuro," Prudence said. "There, he'll meet up with Leonard, and the two of them will come up the river in the little steam launch.

So we have about a week before he'll be here.

"Wait until you see the launch, Eleanor," she added. "It's designed to be sunk and re-floated on command."

"That sounds clever," said Eleanor. "So we should be hearing from them perhaps in three days?"

"No, probably later today — tomorrow at the latest," Prudence replied. "I asked Leonard to send me a telegram when he arrives in Belem. Leonard tells me the general store here is a telegraph office."

"Yes," said Eleanor. "Yes, it is. I remember how excited everyone got when a telegram used to arrive there, when I was a little girl."

"Good," said Prudence.

"Are you quite sure those odd little movie cameras will be good enough?" Eleanor asked, looking a little worried. "They look so — different from the ones I saw in the studios. And they are so tiny. Like toys."

"Yes," said Prudence. "They're German. A company called Ica makes them, in Dresden. Walter, you know, my boss, he's the one who told me about them. They use standard movie film, and it comes in those metal cartridges so that we can change films without a darkroom, and they wind up like a clock, so they don't have to be cranked."

"Oh," said Eleanor. "If Walter says they're good, that's good enough for me.

"I do so love the story you wrote for our movie, the — is it called a photoplay?" he added.

"Photoplay, yes," said Prudence.

"And are you sure I'll be good enough as a film actress? I've never done anything like this before."

"Yes," said Prudence. "Just act naturally, the way you always do, and you'll be fine."

"Well, good morning, *mesdemoiselles*," purred a smooth

voice at Prudence's elbow, and she turned with Eleanor to bid good morning to the seemingly ubiquitous Raoul LeCourt.

"Hello, Raoul," said Eleanor, sounding distracted.

"I see that you were unable to wait for me to come for breakfast," he said then. "But that is all right. May I join you now?"

"Oh yes, please do!" said Prudence.

LeCourt seated himself a little closer to Prudence than she was quite comfortable with, and sipped gingerly at his coffee. "And what are your plans on this fine morning?" he said then. "Would you care to join me on a tour of the village and surrounding countryside? As you are new to the town, you might like to meet some of our local residents, eh?"

Prudence wondered if Raoul somehow didn't know that everybody in town already knew Eleanor from her childhood. If so, he would learn of his mistake soon enough, she thought; there was no need to rub his nose in it by publicly correcting him now.

"We'd love to, but we have work to do today," she told him. "But perhaps — do you know a good place to get good, scary shots of alligators swimming in the river?"

LeCourt smiled, and Eleanor's tinkling laugh pealed out for a second before she caught it back, snatching a delicate tan hand to her mouth. Prudence looked back and forth between them. "What is it?" she asked, trying not to sound irritated.

"It is just that we have no alligators here," said Eleanor. "They are caimans. Alligators are from the north, and they are much larger."

"*Oui*, but *ma foi*, the caimans, they are large enough!" exclaimed LeCourt.

"Well, we're going to want them to be pretty large," said Prudence. "Big enough to be credible as a threat to three men swimming in the water."

"There is no difficulty there," said LeCourt. "They are just as deadly as their larger cousins, and just as hungry. I can take you to where the beasts sun themselves in the river. It is just a mile or two upstream, where the river opens into a broad, sun-soaked shallow flat. They love to float just under the water and be warm. But why do you want to see caimans?"

"For the picture we're making, of course," said Eleanor.

"Picture? You mean a moving picture? You're making a moving picture?"

Prudence looked at him in some astonishment.

"You didn't know?" she said. "But you helped us carry all our supplies yesterday. Did you not wonder what was in all those cases?"

"I did. But I did not consider it gentlemanly to pry. So, tell me about this picture. What is she called?"

"It's called 'The Golden Curse of Death," said Eleanor proudly. "Prudence wrote the— the photoplay. So I'll let her explain."

"OK," said Prudence. "I'll just give you the overview. Here it goes: The story follows a dashing adventurer named Steve Cordite, who has found a map in a tomb—a map that seems to show the way to a rich treasure of Spanish conquistadors. He comes up the river in his little steam launch, following this map, and arrives at a charming little village… this village.

"There he meets a local maiden named Maya, who finds out what he's doing and tells him the treasure is real, but it is cursed. She refuses to help him to retrieve it. He, thinking to be clever, asks her if she will show it to him so that he can look upon it, and she reluctantly agrees to take him. His plan is, after she shows him where it is, he'll come back later on and get it and slip out of town in the middle of the night.

"Well, up they go to an ancient hidden ruined city deep in the forest, and she shows him a room full of more gold than he even knew existed. But a gang of treasure hunters is already there, and they catch Steve and Maya and tie them both up and then carry all the gold out and down and load it onto Steve's boat. While they're gone Steve wriggles out of his ropes and cuts Maya loose, and the two of them get down to the boat just in time to see the bad guys pushing off. But the boat is dangerously overloaded. Steve shouts to them that they need to throw some gold overboard because they're overloaded; the main bad guy rushes out on deck with a rifle and takes a shot at Steve; Maya, seeing what's about to happen, leaps in front of the rifle and takes the bullet; the recoil of the shot pushes the overloaded boat over. Then we see a bunch of allig — er, cai — caimen —"

"Caimans," said Eleanor quietly.

"Caimans," said Prudence. "We see a bunch of caimans sliding into the water and swimming toward the men splashing around in the water as the boat sinks. Then we see Steve holding Maya in his arms as she tragically dies. Then he sits there weeping for a minute, and gets up, and we see a piece of gold jewelry that the thieves dropped on their way to the boat. He's looking down on it, and it's in the mud by the bank of the river. And then he turns and walks away into the woods, stepping on the piece of gold as he does so and treading it into the mud. And we fade out on him walking away into the rainforest."

There was a half-second of silence after she finished

this synopsis — or as close to silence as one could find in a restaurant at breakfast time — and Prudence glanced up at LeCourt. She was surprised to see him standing there with a distinctly stricken look on his face.

"Pardon me, Raoul, I'm very sorry," she said hastily. "But you pay me the best compliment a writer can ever aspire to! If by just hearing a short overview of my story, you are affected —"

"*Mais oui, mais oui*! And it is I who should apologize," cried the Frenchman in tones that almost sounded more like relief than discomfiture. "But I got caught up in the story. I do not like it that *Mademoiselle* Maya dies in the end. But I can see that is the only way, and it is very brave of you to write it that way."

Prudence beamed.

"I must go, *mesdemoiselles*," he said quickly then. "It is necessary for me to catch the mail boat before she leaves today."

There it was again, Prudence thought. "Boat" in French was not a feminine word — it was masculine, *le bateau*. But LeCourt was calling the mail boat "she."

On a mischievous whim, she answered him again in French: "*Ah oui, bien sûr*," she said. "*Quand il y a beaucoup des moutons, faut qu'on en parle bientot.*"

"*Mais oui*, it is just so," said LeCourt, and decamped, leaving Prudence gazing after him with a mischievous look on her face.

"What did you say to him, Trudie?" Eleanor asked, a curious smile on her sunny face.

"I said, 'When there are lots of sheep about, it's necessary to talk about them right away,' " Prudence replied. "I really don't think he's French, Eleanor, and I just thought I'd have a little fun testing my theory."

"I suppose it isn't really necessary to call it a theory any more, darling," said Eleanor, with a conspiratorial little smile.

"Precisely. No Frenchman would reply to such a ridiculous lot of nonsense without at least giving me a funny look. Raoul does not speak French."

"Well, perhaps he is from a part of France where they speak a dialect?"

"Hah," Prudence snorted. "If that guy's from anyplace, I bet he's from the Bronx or New Jersey. He's faking it."

"Well," said Eleanor thoughtfully, "if so, he's a pretty good actor, isn't he? Should we offer him a part in our movie?"

Prudence thought about this for a moment. "He's certainly handsome enough," she mused, "and he manages to be pretty well dressed. I'd be more comfortable, though, if we knew why he's pretending to be French."

"That bothers me as well," said Eleanor, shooting one of her vanishingly rare serious looks at Prudence. "But I think it would be well for us to offer him something, to encourage him to work closely with us. Eventually he will slip up, and we will know more, and then we will know if we should trust him or no."

Prudence laughed. "So what you're saying is that we should keep our friends close, our enemies closer, and those we can't classify closest of all?"

Eleanor smiled indulgently. "Surely Raoul is no enemy," she said, slightly reprovingly. "I would merely like to know his secret; that is all. Did Captain Bancroft ever tell you why he dislikes him so?"

"I asked him, and he wouldn't say," said Prudence. "But he had a look on his face that made me think it was his fault, not Raoul's. But he told me not to trust any of the expatriated Americans and Europeans here. They're all on the run from something, he said. From the law, from an angry spouse, or from the mob, or whatever."

"What is Captain Bancroft running from? Did he say?"

"No. But I bet it's some crime. Smuggling or bank robbery or something like that. Or bootlegging. He seems like the bootlegger type."

"And Raoul?"

"I don't know," said Prudence. "He doesn't seem like the criminal type. I suppose he could be running from an ex-lover."

"Ah," said Eleanor. "But I am sure that whatever he wants to get away from is not French. So, he tries to be French. It is best to play along and not ask questions … and to be as observant as one possibly can."

"You're right, of course," said Prudence. "I'm just so curious. I would love to know what those reasons are. Raoul is — a mystery. And rather a dishy one at that."

"Just be careful, Trudie," Eleanor said.

"I will," said Prudence.

Eleanor smiled at her, but said nothing, and the silence fit close and comfortable around the two of them as they finished their breakfast.

"My dream last night," Eleanor said at last. "It was a little frightening. So vivid."

"Mm?" said Prudence, her mouth full of tapioca pancakes.

"Yes. It was as if I were flying, slowly, just a few feet above the ground," Eleanor continued. "I flew slowly up the river and then drifted through a dense forest along a path, so close that the branches brushed by me on both sides. And then I came out into a clearing and saw a city before me, an ancient city made of stone and with vines covering the walls, looking abandoned but somehow—*alive*. And I could feel that city calling to me. Something inside me wanted to go inside and rest. I can still remember how I felt looking at it, happy and worried at the same time. But I went to it. And just as I reached the door, it was then that I woke up, from you tripping over the camera."

"That's interesting," Prudence murmured vaguely, gazing out the window at the waterfront, where she could see Raoul apparently having an engrossing conversation with a short, powerfully built man with bushy black hair.

Eleanor looked at her and sighed.

Two hours later, one of the cameras was securely stowed in a big wooden canoe along with a half dozen 25-meter film cartridges, and the two of them were paddling off on the river's glassy green surface with LeCourt and the bushy-haired man, who introduced himself with none too friendly a demeanor as Marco Morais.

The shooting went very smoothly indeed, except for one moment when Prudence nearly dropped the movie camera in the river. Eleanor was not in any of the river shots, so she was able to wear plus-fours rather than one of the filmy Rayon dresses she'd brought as movie costumes; this turned out to be a good thing, as canoeing turned out not to be the sort of activity that lent itself easily to feminine modesty. Morais, who seemed to be the resident caiman expert, led the way to a sunny lagoon where dozens of the big water lizards lounged and swam. At first the caimans seemed nervous about the visitors, but after a couple hours the big reptiles seemed to forget they were there. Prudence shot all day, and by the time they were paddling home for dinner she had undeveloped footage of caimans swimming, sliding into the water, sliding out of the water, fighting over a particularly comfortable basking beach and once even ambushing a small deer that came to the river to drink.

Once back on the dock, Morais trooped off without a glance backward and without a single word to either of the ladies. LeCourt gazed ruefully after him, then glanced back at Eleanor.

"He is very shy," he said. "He is also a little grouchy. I asked him to come as a special favor, and he owed me a favor, so I do not think he felt he could say no. Perhaps I should have made it more clear."

"We all have bad days," said Eleanor serenely.

Prudence was glad no one asked her for her opinion of Morais, because it would have been considerably less charitable than Eleanor's.

Once again, LeCourt invited them to join him for dinner, and once again they cheerfully did so. This time, he flirted a little more overtly with Prudence, who bit her tongue and limited her French speaking to the occasional "m'sieur" or "qu'est-ce que c'est."

And that night found the ladies much better prepared. Prudence had bought a box of candles from Old Man Paulo, the garrulous old fellow who ran the town's general store and post office, and she started setting them out well before nightfall. In contrast to the frightening and chaotic scene of the previous day, their cabin was actually cozy as the daylight faded, and they were able to settle in comfortably, getting ready for bed.

"You know, Trudie," Eleanor said, gazing contemplatively at the bare top of the little table and vanity nearby, "I wonder what happened to Uncle Carlo and Aunt Marcita. I mean, what really happened."

Prudence stirred uncomfortably. She knew Eleanor

didn't really believe her aunt and uncle were dead, but she didn't see how they could still be alive. Sooner or later, she was convinced, their bodies would be found, and she knew this would devastate her friend.

"You... you don't think —"

"No," said Eleanor dreamily. "No, I don't. The two of them went up the river, in the middle of the night, in a canoe. And only their boat returned, swamped and with the marks of caiman teeth upon it. But caimans don't eat canoes. If they did, we would never have survived our shoot today. Why would a caiman chew on an overturned canoe?"

Prudence was silent for a time, turning this over in her mind, and noticing the sinister implications. If caimans didn't chew on canoes, then either a caiman had made a special exception for this one canoe, or some unknown person had —

"We are in no danger," intoned Eleanor, apparently reading Prudence's thoughts.

"But how do you know that?" said Prudence, with mounting alarm. "Regardless of what happened to them, somebody marked up their canoe to look like a caiman ate them. Why would somebody do that, other than to cover up a murder?"

Eleanor's laugh, as it tinkled out, seemed to chase all the ghouls from the room. "Why indeed? Perhaps to cover up their own plan to leave the village. Who knows? But I would like to learn. And Prudence... I do not believe they are dead. I believe I would have — would have felt their loss if they had died."

Prudence gave Eleanor a long, silent look in the dim candlelight. Sometimes her placid good cheer seemed almost inhuman, and this was one of those times.

"You don't believe me," Eleanor said mildly. "That's all

right. You don't have to. But I would have felt it, I promise you. I believe they are alive."

Prudence smiled. "You know me so well," she said. "I just can't make myself believe in things like that."

"You will before too much longer," Eleanor said softly. "But don't ask me how I know."

Prudence only chuckled indulgently. Eleanor blew out the candle by her bed, climbed in and arranged herself for sleep; Prudence poured herself a small glass of *cachaça* and sat sipping it quietly, contemplating the tiny flame of her candle, until she reached the bottom of her glass. Then she blew out the candle and went to bed herself.

V.

THE STAR IS DEPORTED.

The next morning, for the first time since they'd stepped off the big riverboat in Porto Escuro, Prudence got her quiet morning time. She rose before dawn, around five o'clock, and padded carefully out of the little house without tripping over anything. On the porch, she settled into one of the surprisingly comfortable rustic chairs there and opened her journal, then gazed out into the darkness and silence. Somewhere in the distance, a chicken crowed.

She looked down at the river, which she could just see in the dim moonlight at the end of the village street. It was like the edge of civilization, dark and silent and wild. She felt an impulse to go to it, to commandeer a canoe and paddle out on its black waters and experience the coming-to-life of the rainforest from the middle of the river. She wondered if she'd actually have the courage to try such a thing. Were there night-beasts, she wondered, like the caimans and snakes, that might be bolder in the darkness than during the day? She'd have to ask Raoul; he would know. She'd have to be careful, though, for she knew the Frenchman was enough of a traditional daddy type to try to prevent her from doing such a thing if he knew she was contemplating it.

By the time Eleanor had stumbled, bleary-eyed, out onto the porch to greet her, the sun had come up, and Prudence had enjoyed the full wild orchestral performance of the rainforest greeting the day. She smiled up at her friend.

"I can see why you love this place so much," she said.

After dressing for breakfast, the two of them strolled down to the restaurant to get the day started. LeCourt, to Prudence's surprise, was already there, and seemed to be waiting for them.

"*Bonjour!*" he cried, affably and with a slightly overdone Gallic charm. "And how are you ladies on this fine morning, eh?"

"Well, thank you," said Prudence, with a charmed smile.

"Oh," said Eleanor, "thank you for asking, Raoul, but I did not sleep so well last night."

"Have some coffee," Prudence suggested.

"Thank you," Eleanor said, "I think I'll need it."

"Was it another bad dream?" Prudence asked her.

"Ah, the dreams," murmured Raoul distractedly. "They can be so hard on the ladies."

Prudence bristled a little at this, but Eleanor seemed not to notice — or perhaps she was simply ignoring him. "Yes," she continued, still speaking directly to Prudence. "It was like the one the night before, but — different. I was approaching the same stone city, floating just like before, but this time it was covered with weeds and vines and instead of opening invitingly, the doors and windows gaped like the mouths of some menacing beast. And I went inside the great door, and —"

There was a dramatic crash and tinkle of broken crockery, and Eleanor stopped, eyebrows raised in surprise. Raoul's coffee cup had slipped from his fingers and crashed to the restaurant's rough-sawn hardwood floor.

"*Mon Dieu*, I am so sorry, *mesdemoiselles*!" he cried, producing a tiny and inadequate handkerchief and sopping up a half-ounce of the spilled coffee with it.

Marcello, the proprietor, hurried over with a small towel and, while LeCourt gingerly picked up the big pieces of broken crockery, cleaned up the smaller shards and the puddle of coffee. Then he disappeared into the kitchen and returned with a fresh steaming cup, which he handed to LeCourt, waving aside the Frenchman's red-faced apologies.

"It is of nothing," he said, in halting English. "Accidents are happen."

"Marcello, it's so kind of you to think of us," Eleanor said in Portuguese, "but both of us speak Portuguese, so you needn't worry about being rude."

"Thank you, but I like practice," Marcello said, still in English.

Raoul was gripping his new cup of coffee tightly, but Prudence thought she could see a slight tremor in his hand. She wondered if Raoul suffered from a medical condition like palsy. He seemed young for that.

"I am so sorry," he said to Eleanor. "You were saying?"

"Oh, I was just telling you of my dream. Nobody really

likes to hear other people's dreams, do they?"

"I should very much like to hear of yours," Raoul said.

"There's not much to tell," she said. "My beautiful city had been overgrown with weeds, and when I went inside I found it full of — full of evil. Evil had come into it while I was away."

"Full of evil?" said Prudence with the beginnings of a teasing smile dying on her lips as her eyes met Eleanor's. "Oh, I'm sorry, Eleanor. I can't remember any of my dreams these past two nights."

Then she glanced at the two men. Both seemed to her to be acting strangely. Marcello's broad smile had faded to an expression of vague uneasiness, and LeCourt looked positively grim. Both were looking at the floor and would not meet her eye.

But before she could ask them what was wrong, LeCourt gave a slight start and looked at Eleanor.

"I beg you to excuse me," he mumbled, setting his still-full coffee cup down on their table. "I have a project that I must start this morning."

And he disappeared from the restaurant with surprising speed as Prudence watched his retreating form; when she turned back she found Marcello had moved back into the kitchen. She wondered if she or Eleanor had somehow offended him.

But Marcello was back to his affable, broken-English-speaking self when he returned with their breakfast plates — *pão francês*, the ubiquitous buttery Brazilian "French" bread, with cubes of melon and other fruits and cheese. The two ladies tucked into it with gusto.

"What are we doing today?" Eleanor asked.

"Auditions, I think," said Prudence. "Charles and Leonard should be here with the boat in a few days. It would be good to have the cast assembled, and maybe some early shooting done."

After breakfast, Eleanor set out to recruit actors, wandering through the village and talking to everyone she saw about the movie, leveraging her local ties. Meanwhile, Prudence went to the general store by the wharf to ask Old Man Paulo if there were any telegrams for her. There were not.

"What could be keeping them?" she asked Eleanor when next she saw her, walking back from a villager's house. "I really want to start shooting today, but what if I get a bunch of it done and Charles has been delayed or missed his boat and doesn't come for another month? I can't ask these actors to stand around for weeks doing nothing while we wait because we can't shoot any of the scenes they're in with Charles. And what if he's changed his mind? You know how fickle these movie stars can be. Should we delay the whole thing, do you think, until we know?"

"Yes," said Eleanor. "But if he has changed his mind, or we haven't heard from him tonight — what can we do?"

"Well," said Prudence slowly, "we can telegraph Los Angeles, to inquire about hiring another leading man. But that will take time, and we'll have to take whatever we can get. I can ask my boss to vet them; Walt has great instincts and he knows our script, he won't let us down; but so much of these things come down to personal chemistry. I think it would be better to try to find an understudy here, locally."

"So in other words, we'd have no professional actors at all in our movie?"

There was a moment of silence. Then Eleanor looked at Prudence with slight exasperation on her face.

"Prudence," she said, "you are such a worrier. One day

with no contact and you're already imagining the worst, and I'm getting caught up in it too! Relax. It will all turn out all right."

Prudence sighed. Eleanor was right.

They spent the rest of the morning talking to villagers and casting them in various roles. By lunchtime, Prudence had filled all the roles and was ready to start the shooting.

"Now, let's see," said Prudence, after they'd eaten. "There's something I hadn't thought of. We have a lot of shooting to do on the river, and I want to do it at a spot near where the caimans were yesterday; but I don't want to be paddling two hours each way, for the next four days."

"Shall we ask Captain Bancroft?" said Eleanor. "I'm sure he will help us, for the right price."

Prudence snorted. "For the right price. I'm sure of that. Let's ask him."

As the two ladies walked down to the docks to do this, Old Man Paulo hurried out of the general store and called after them.

"*Senhorita* Martins!" he called. "I have a telegram for you. It sounds not so good."

"Oh?" replied Eleanor. "Thank you, Paulo."

She took the telegram from him with a gracious nod, read it, and then handed it to Prudence with a sober look.

Prudence read:

STILL IN BELEM STOP CHARLES ARRESTED IN JAIL STOP TO BE DEPORTED TOMORROW STOP CHARGES UNCLEAR STOP PLEASE ADVISE STOP LEONARD.

Prudence looked up and met Eleanor's eyes gravely. Their leading man — deported?

"Well," she said. "Now what?"

"It's good that you were thinking ahead," said Eleanor. "You must have had a feeling something like this was going to happen. If we have to, of course, we can go back to Los Angeles and audition a replacement. Or we can complain to the U.S. embassy and wait and see if they can fix this. How long do you think that would take?"

"I have no idea," said Prudence. "I could telegraph down there and ask. But either way, we'll have to stop what we're doing, and that's half a day wasted, plus the actors likely won't be very happy."

"Oh, I think they'll be fine," said Eleanor. "I'm prepared to pay them for their time even though we're not starting our shooting. Relax, Trudie. This isn't a big thing. Well, it is a big thing, but not a big-big thing, if you follow me."

Prudence wondered if the real secret of Eleanor's placid demeanor was that she never had to worry about money. If she'd been financing this movie with investors, something like this certainly would have been both a big thing and a "big-big" thing.

The two ladies hurried back to Old Man Paulo's store and composed a reply to the telegram:

NOTIFY EMBASSY STOP ANY CHANCE WE CAN FIGHT THIS STOP PRUDENCE.

"I wonder if he's still in the telegraph office," Prudence mused as Old Man Paulo sent the message.

"Let's wait and have a cup of coffee and see," said Eleanor.

So the two of them settled down on the porch in front of the store and waited. Sure enough, a few minutes later, the ancient teletype machine clattered to life.

EMBASSY WILLING TO HELP BUT CHARLES ANGRY REFUSES TO STAY STOP REQUEST INSTRUCTIONS STOP LEONARD.

Prudence and Eleanor exchanged meaningful glances. Then the door rattled and Raoul LeCourt strolled into the store.

"Ah! Mesdemoiselles Eleanor and Prudence. I had hoped that I might find you here," he purred. "I understand that you are casting actors for your movie. May I offer my candidacy as well?"

"Your timing is perfect, Raoul," said Prudence. "Frankly, I think you'd make an excellent Steve Cordite. Eleanor, what do you think?"

"Certainly," said Eleanor. "This surely helps us out of our bind. But we still need our boat, don't we?"

"Yes, that's OK," said Prudence. "I'll have Leonard bring it up the river to us immediately, now that the Charles situation is apparently beyond retrieval."

"So, we wait six days for Leonard to bring the boat here from Belem?" said Eleanor.

"Well, not necessarily," said Prudence. "Let's walk down and see if Mr. Bancroft is available to help us."

LeCourt looked pained. "Surely that isn't necessary?" he said. "Couldn't we just — er — use a canoe?"

Eleanor looked at Prudence, and Prudence shook her head.

"Canoes handle wrong for all the boat-on-the-water shots," she said, "and we'd be spending the whole day paddling around. Also, we've got an extra camera just in case, but all the same I'd rather not risk dropping one into the river. I almost did that while we were shooting the caimans, you know. And, well, I'd rather delay our start by a few days rather than wear myself out paddling all over the river in a canoe."

LeCourt sighed.

"Come on," said Prudence. "Let's talk to him."

She led the way down to the dock to the *Amazon Princess*, where they found Bancroft arranged in a leisurely way in a hammock, strung between the poles of the canopy over the observation deck at the stern.

"Ladies," he said, reaching up to tip his hat and finding that he wasn't wearing one. "Sorry to be rude and not stand up. Took me half an hour to get balanced right. How can I help?"

"We were wondering, Mr. Bancroft, if you'd be willing to take us out with our actors for some movie shots over the next few days," said Prudence.

"Sure," said Bancroft. "Hell, for the right price I'd even take that cake-eater out for some shots." And he jerked his head toward LeCourt, who stood several feet away, as if being careful not to get too close.

"Sharpen your pencil," said Prudence. "He's our leading man now."

Bancroft sat bolt upright in the hammock, causing one of the canopy poles to flex a little bit; rebounding, it flipped the hammock sideways just enough to put Bancroft off balance, and the hammock, quick as a flash, inverted itself, dumping Bancroft out into a heap on the deck like an overfilled wheelbarrow full of rocks tipping over sideways.

Several seconds of highly creative cursing later, Bancroft pulled himself to his feet.

"Are you all right, captain?" Prudence asked tentatively.

Bancroft ground his teeth, a look of exasperated fury

on his face. "Yes," he said. "Yes, thanks, I am. Now, as I was saying, I charge two hundred *reais* per day, plus expenses, and am free at present."

"Two — two hundred *reais*!" gasped Prudence.

"Yep," said Bancroft.

"But that's a ridiculous price!"

"Is it?" Bancroft shot back, a little sharply. "I have nothing scheduled this week — nothing. I'd planned on spending the whole thing doing absolutely nothing, loafing on my boat, drinking my Scotch, smoking my cigars, going on short excursions on the river and generally enjoying a little vacation. If I'm going to cancel my vacation and put on my work clothes and a work smile and have a man I don't like on my boat requiring constant surveillance, well, begging your pardon, ma'am, it's going to cost somebody some money."

"You are lucky there's no competition here, or you'd be out of business," Prudence snapped.

"Nothing would make me happier," Bancroft shot back. "Then you and your leading man could be somebody else's problem."

"You — you —"

Eleanor laid a hand on Prudence's arm. "It's OK, Trudie," she said quietly. "It's worth the price. And it's only for a few days."

She turned to Bancroft. "We'd like to book your services for the next four days," she said. "I can give you half the fee up front and the other half delivered at the end — will that work for you?"

Bancroft looked at her and shook his head. "I work one day at a time, and I need it all up front," he said. "Today's half over, so I'll take a hundred today, and then another two hundred tomorrow, and another two hundred the day after that. I don't like being obligated for more than one day at a time."

"Very well," said Eleanor, and pulled out her roll of bills again.

Then the two ladies returned to Smithy's Tavern to meet up with their newly assembled cast members. In addition to LeCourt, there were six men and women and two children.

"We'll be shooting this afternoon from the deck of the *Amazon Princess*," Prudence told them, and was somewhat surprised when the villagers murmured approvingly. Clearly her own opinion of Bancroft was not widely shared among Carraçao's residents.

Eleanor paid for a hearty lunch for everyone. After eating, the group trooped down to the waterfront, where Bancroft had the boilers heated up and ready.

That night, Prudence and Eleanor accepted a dinner invitation from Izabel Ribeiro and her family. They met Izabel's husband, Carlo, and visited again with Alberto and Imelda. Alberto's retelling of his close call at the hands of the shanghaiing first mate of the *Swathmore*, Prudence noticed, had acquired a few new details; now he was claiming that he'd actually punched the first mate, and Bancroft's fight with the belaying-pin-swinging mariner had become much more dramatic and less one-sided. At one point, Prudence caught Imelda's eye and almost burst out laughing at her exasperated look.

When it was time for the ladies to retire for the evening, Prudence was almost glowing with the warmth of their hospitality. And yet, on the inside, she felt that old familiar gypsy melancholy, the sense — so familiar to the children of migrant workers, Army officers and Vaudeville performers — that she wasn't really a part of the boisterous and happy community she moved in, that she could never truly be home, that the most she could aspire to was to be a tolerated outsider.

But she shook it off, as she always did, and walked on by Eleanor's side, strolling toward the river and Eleanor's aunt's house.

Eleanor, as they left the party, had been glowing a little with quiet happiness, but she'd grown quiet as they started strolling through the dirt street toward their house. Prudence wondered if she'd gotten over that sense of alienation she'd talked about on their first day in town.

Then she heard a tiny sniff from the statuesque beauty by her side, and she knew Eleanor had not — that it was still troubling her. She reached out in the darkness and took her hand and smiled at her, a beaming smile of warmth and acceptance and love; Eleanor's face brightened noticeably; and they walked on in happy companionable silence.

"A very good day," Prudence remarked as they entered the little house. "And Captain Bancroft and Dr. LeCourt barely even snarled at one another."

"Yes," said Eleanor. "But there is something... disquieting about the river, where we journeyed today. It seems familiar somehow. As if I've seen it before. No, more than that — as if I know it already."

"Well, don't you?" said Prudence. "This is your hometown, after all."

"Oh, no," said Eleanor. "We don't let eight-year-old girls play on the river. It's far too dangerous. There are many things in this river that are dangerous to eight-year-old girls. Caimans and snakes, piranhas, and there are... legends of other things as well. No, I was not allowed out on the river. And yet somehow I feel I know it, like the street leading to my home in Los Angeles."

Prudence thought for a moment. "That log," she said. "Did you —?"

There had been a moment, out on the river, when she had noticed Eleanor staring intently at the riverbank as the *Amazon Princess* chugged along the shore at its regular cruising speed, making for the sunny spot with the caimans again. Then, as Prudence had started to approach her to ask what was so interesting on the riverbank, Eleanor had abruptly left the rail and hurried to the wheelhouse. Almost immediately after she'd gone in with Bancroft, the boat had turned sharply and steamed out away from the shore — and as it had done so, Prudence had seen a shadow in the water alongside. The shadow, as they'd drawn near, had resolved itself into a massive, straight mahogany log just below the surface, not more than ten feet away. Had they hit it directly, the boat would certainly have been damaged, and might even have been sunk. It had seemed strange to Prudence at the time that Eleanor would have seen this nearly-invisible obstacle. Now she wondered if perhaps she hadn't.

Eleanor was nodding, deftly reading Prudence's thoughts. "Yes," she said. "I knew there was a tree that had stood there, long and straight and dead. I don't know how I knew that, but I did, and when we steamed toward it I saw only a jagged stump where it had been, and I knew it had to have fallen in the river. So I told Captain Bancroft."

"And saved our lives, maybe."

"Maybe."

Prudence shivered. "This is all so strange."

"Strange, yes," said Eleanor quietly. "And yet I feel,

somehow…"

Her voice trailed off, and the silence hung for a moment
or two. Then Eleanor spoke again, in an almost preternaturally tranquil yet strong voice.

"Do not fear for yourself, Prudence," she said. "You are
well protected here in my country. Nor is it the strangeness
that is to be feared."

"Pardon me?"

Prudence stared at Eleanor in the candlelight as she
in turn gazed with that odd tranquility at the flame of the
candle burning by her bed, like an eastern mystic in meditation. Then she started abruptly and looked up. "I'm sorry,"
she said then. "Did you say something?"

"Not really, but you did," said Prudence. "Something
about fear? I didn't understand."

"Me? No, I know nothing about anything that we
should fear, other than swimming with the caimans and
dancing with the jaguars."

"But you said —"

A sudden throb of headache inspired Prudence to stop
talking. It had been such a long, exhausting day. Perhaps
in the morning things would make more sense.

"Let's go to sleep," she murmured, pulling back the
blanket on her bed. "It's been such a day."

And both of them blew out their candles and settled
in for the night.

Many hours later, Prudence stirred awake to the
sound of movement in the hut. The candles
were out, of course, but they had left the
window open, and a thin, cool shaft of moonlight shone
on the floor. By its light, Prudence could see that Eleanor
had gotten up and changed into an afternoon dress, and

was moving toward the door of the little house.

Prudence started to say something, but then realized what was most likely happening. Eleanor was going to the outhouse. Because she slept in a wispy nightgown that was altogether too revealing for her to risk being seen in, she had gotten dressed, just in case someone else was out prowling about. That was all.

Still half asleep, Prudence watched her friend move with slow, regular steps to the door of the hut, slip out, and close it gently behind her. She heard Eleanor's soft, regular tread as she made her way down the steps. Then she fell back into a heavy, dreamless sleep.

But something must have bothered her about the incident, at least a little bit. Because when she awoke, several hours later, at her customary time of five o'clock, the first thing she did was peer over at Eleanor's bed, a dim and barely visible shape in the pre-dawn darkness.

Then, with fingers that were suddenly shaking, she groped for the box of matches on the bureau by her bed, struck one and held it over her head.

The other bed was empty. Eleanor was gone.

VI.

THE PRODUCER VANISHES.

Prudence bolted up out of her bed and raced to the door. "Eleanor!" she shouted.

There was no reply. Somewhere in the distance, a rooster crowed. When its call stopped, the silence seemed to gather around her like a thickening fog — a silence that was unusual in the rainforest, even just before dawn. She shivered a little.

Her mind raced, seeking the safe harbor of a plausible theory that did not involve something awful. Perhaps Eleanor had just gone for a walk? Yes, of course, that had to be it. She'd returned after her midnight trip to the outhouse, been unable to sleep, given up and gone for an early-morning stroll around the village. Or something else; Eleanor was a grown woman, she didn't have to file a report with Prudence every time she went out. And there was no reason to think she would not be back in a matter of minutes, her preternaturally sunny smile lighting up the world as it always did.

This made perfect sense. There was no reason to be alarmed.

So, why was she having so much trouble convincing herself that something had not gone horribly wrong?

Prudence lit the candle on the little table and forced herself to sit down. She scanned the table for a note; Eleanor surely would have left a note? But there was nothing. She felt the panicky feeling starting to rise inside her again, and she closed her eyes and tried once again to bludgeon her emotions back into line with the cool blue cudgel of reason. It had been dark, too dark to write, and Eleanor would not have lit a candle to write by, knowing that would disturb Prudence.

She would be back at any moment. She would.

Prudence's eyes snapped open. It was no use. She would just have to try to keep herself busy, too busy to worry, until Eleanor returned. With much businesslike bustle, she set about getting dressed.

Half an hour later, sunrise was well under way, and Prudence was sitting on the porch of the house watching the sun slowly lighten the forest canopy through the smoke of a long dark-brown cigarette. This was unusual for her — although she had been a regular if secretive smoker during and just after the war, she had forced herself to quit after noticing the habit's impact on her health, and now lit up only very rarely and at times of great stress. Her travel journal lay open in her lap; she'd opened it before there was even light enough to write in it, but she had written nothing other than the date and the words, "Eleanor gone when I awoke. Waiting for her now."

She sat, and she smoked, and still she got more and more restless. Finally she got to her feet, stubbed out the butt and started down the steps that led off the porch.

She made her way briskly toward the docks. Around her, the village still drowsed; the sun was barely up, and the morning chill was still on the air. But she saw a figure moving on the deck of the *Amazon Princess*, and knew that Captain Bancroft was up and about. She had little interest in a conversation with that unpleasant, mercenary man; but nobody else seemed to be stirring yet.

By the time she reached his boat, he'd disappeared into his cabin. She stepped gingerly onto the boat, walked to the cabin door, and knocked.

A moment later, it opened, and Bancroft was looking up the short stairway at her.

"What can I help you with, Miss McMarion?" he asked.

"Captain Bancroft, I — I'm very sorry to bother you so early in the morning, but — but I wonder if you've seen my companion, Eleanor."

Bancroft's eyes narrowed and for a moment he looked thoughtfully into the distance behind her, his lips pursed. He almost looked suspicious, although of what she could not guess. "Miss Martins is missing? That's very strange," he muttered.

Then he shook himself briefly, looked up at her again, met her eyes and shook his head. "No," he said. "I haven't seen her. But I think I might have heard her last night. Someone came down to the dock in the dark of the night, probably three, maybe four hours ago. I heard footsteps on the dock, a slow, very regular tread, of someone wearing shoes. Then I heard the sounds of someone getting into a canoe and paddling out into the river."

"And you didn't do anything?" Prudence said, her voice

rising as the panic she'd been quelling all morning suddenly burst free from its bonds. "How could you —"

"Hey, hey, take it easy," Bancroft interjected. "It's none of my business if somebody in the village wants to take a little moonlight paddle. Why would I have done anything other than sit here and mind my own business?"

Prudence bit her lip. She knew her angry words were as much directed at herself as they were at Bancroft — more so, in fact. If only she had said something to Eleanor when she got up, as she was dressing to go out — to go out for what Prudence was increasingly convinced was something far more sinister than a trip to the outhouse or to stretch her legs.

"You're right, of course," she said, feeling ashamed of herself. "I'm sorry. It's just — just that I have a bad feeling."

"Sure, sister," Bancroft said, a little distractedly. "But just relax. I'm sure she'll be around shortly."

"Well, thank you, Captain Bancroft. I'm sorry to have disturbed you."

"No trouble," said Bancroft, and closed the door before she'd turned away from it. Ordinarily such a rude gesture would have left her simmering, though she knew it was made in ignorance rather than malice; but today, she barely noticed it.

She stepped off the boat and went back up the main street of the village. Old Man Paulo was just opening his store; he knew nothing of Eleanor's whereabouts, he said, but would send his young assistant to find Prudence if he heard anything. She wandered on.

The village was now starting to awaken. Prudence stopped everyone she could, asking in her still-somewhat-rusty Portuguese if he or she had seen Eleanor. No one had.

No one, that is, until she knocked on the door of an

old woman who lived at the edge of town closest to the shallow end of the docks, whom she had seen sweeping dust from her porch a moment before. To her surprise, the old woman told her she *had* seen Eleanor — last night, she said, well after midnight.

After inviting Prudence inside, giving her a cup of coffee, introducing herself as Kylla Azvedo, and subjecting her frustrated guest to what seemed like a catechism of small talk — inquiries about her health and whether she was enjoying her stay in Carraçao, that sort of thing — the elderly woman got down to her story.

"Something awakened me, some noise," she said. "When you get to be eighty-three years old, you sleep very lightly. I heard footsteps, very even footsteps, on the wooden planking of the dock. So I pulled myself up and peered out the little window by my bed. The moon gave enough light to see your tall friend walking down across the docks. I easily recognized her; no other woman in this village is so tall and beautiful. The shadows were deep, and the docks are treacherous with uneven planks and gaps; but she walked as if she could see perfectly."

"So that was her," Prudence murmured. "Hmm. What could she have been doing at the docks?"

"She walked to the shallow end of the dock, by where the vines and bushes crowd thickly around the end of the boards, right over there next to the wall of my house," Kylla continued. "And then she stepped off the end of the dock into the river."

"What?" gasped Prudence in English, her hand snatched to her mouth in horror.

"That is what I thought," said Kylla. "I thought, 'She is sleepwalking! I must get down and help her out of the river! You know, it is not very deep there, no more than half a meter, but there are caimans and serpents and it is best not to be in the water."

"And then what?" said Prudence.

"As I emerged from my home, I saw that she was standing in a canoe. Or, not a canoe, really, but a sort of long, thin boat, and she was standing up in it, which we all learned very early in our lives that we must never do. You fall over, you know, when the boat scoots out from under your feet. But she seemed perfectly balanced. As I watched, she sat gracefully down, picked up a paddle and started away from the dock. She did not look like she was working very hard, paddling her boat, but it seemed to me that it sped away unusually fast. She went upriver, and was soon lost to my sight in the thin moonlight."

By now it was getting close to breakfast time. So Prudence started back toward Marcello's restaurant. As she walked, she worked hard to convince herself that in spite of the strange behavior the old woman had described, Eleanor had merely gone for a moonlight paddle to scout for locations, or to clear her mind, or maybe for reasons of nostalgia.

By the time she got there, she had nearly succeeded, having reduced her feelings of misgiving to a faint, vague shadow in her mind. Eleanor would be back soon, she told herself, and when she arrived Prudence would have some sharp words for her, for the first time since they had met.

She found LeCourt already at Marcello's, sipping coffee.

"Good morning, *Mademoiselle!*" he cried out, with slightly overwrought gladness. "But where is *Mademoiselle* Eleanor this morning?"

"I don't know," said Prudence crisply. "She went out for some kind of moonlight paddle before I got up this morning.

She's still not back yet."

An expression of alarm flashed across LeCourt's face, then quickly modulated into an expression of gravely sympathetic concern. "She is not yet returned? But what could be keeping her?"

"Damned if I know," said Prudence.

LeCourt did not flinch at Prudence's unladylike language. "Well," he said soothingly, "if I had to make a guess, I would say she has gone to some place she remembers from when she was a little *gamine*. She will be back shortly. Would you like me to ask among the villagers?"

All at once the bluster left Prudence, and she felt her face falling into lines of vulnerability and worry. And then suddenly she was more than worried. For the first time she felt the full awareness of her position. She was all alone in a strange country where she knew no one and barely spoke the language, and it was a country in which practically every living animal could and would kill her. If Eleanor didn't come back....

"I would like that very much," she said, in a very small voice.

"Very well," said LeCourt, his smooth equanimity sounding comforting in the cool morning air. "Meanwhile, such inquiries are hungry work, *non?* Let us enjoy our breakfast."

Eleanor was a significant character in the movie, so there weren't very many shots they could film without her. Prudence and her cast worked diligently until lunchtime, when Prudence found she had filmed all the land-based sequences that she could without her. After lunch, there would be about a half-day's worth of shooting that could be done from the boat; after that, they'd be stuck until Eleanor returned.

So Prudence finished her lunch and then strode briskly down the street to the docks, where she found Bancroft scraping at a patch of peeling paint on the cabin wall.

"Will you be ready to leave around one o'clock?" she asked him.

"Sure, if the money's ready before then," he replied.

"Eleanor didn't pay you?" Prudence said.

"Oh, she paid me for yesterday," said Bancroft. "I work one day at a time, remember? It's strictly pay-as-you-go with me, no prepayment and no credit. So here it is Day Two, and I need to be paid for it."

"But Eleanor is missing."

"Exactly why I'm concerned," said Bancroft. "For all I know she might have skipped on this whole operation, run off down the river and left you in the lurch. But I know she's the moneybags of the operation, and without her around to peel banknotes off that mammoth wad of shekels, I don't see myself getting paid for anything I do. Unless you've got another source you can draw on, that is."

"I — you — but — oh, you hateful mercenary pig!"

"Hey, don't take it personally," Bancroft said. "But I'm not here to lose money, sister. Nobody's going to look out for me if I don't do it."

She said nothing, merely glared. He let the silence hang for half a second; then a flicker of irritation crossed his face and he reached for his scraper again.

"I hope you find your friend," he said as he turned back to his work.

"Drop dead," Prudence advised him frostily, and spun on her heel and stalked away.

She returned directly to Marcello's to deliver the bad news to the crew members.

"So, does that — does that mean that if *Senhorita* Martins does not come back, we don't get paid?" asked one local actor.

"Oh!" Prudence stammered. "I — well — that is — well, I will have to do whatever I must to get you your pay. But perhaps we should not do any more work until Eleanor is back."

Prudence spent the entire afternoon looking for Eleanor. She borrowed a canoe from Old Man Paulo, and a broad-brimmed sun hat from Eleanor — the only hats she'd brought with her were cloches, berets and one dressy turban, nothing that would give her any protection from the sun — and paddled out upon the river looking for signs of her friend. She returned just as Bancroft, in the *Amazon Princess*, was casting off for some kind of errand down the river. She caught his eye briefly, and he nodded a greeting, to which she responded with an icy smile; then the sleek but battered riverboat was forging away downstream.

Then she wandered around the outskirts of town peering into the forest beyond.

By the end of the day she was exhausted. Her shoulders ached from paddling, her legs were scratched from the bushes and plants she'd waded through, and her navy-blue house dress was all but ruined.

Suppertime found Prudence back at Marcello's, where she gratefully accepted LeCourt's invitation to join him for dinner. Over their meal, knowing she could count on his sympathy, she gave full vent to her fury at Bancroft's rude refusal to continue working with them until Eleanor's return.

"But I guess it's just as well," she added. "Had he not been so rude, we would have run up more bills for the other actors as well. And if Eleanor gets — if she doesn't — if she —"

"Quite so, quite so," murmured LeCourt soothingly. "But the villagers to whom I have had the talk, they are not so worried about your friend. They say it is common, this thing. A newcomer will be so enchanted with the scenery that he will go paddling out upon the river in the night and stay away for several days. You will see, she will be there in the morning. Do not forget, she knows this place."

"I suppose you're right," said Prudence. "Eleanor can take care of herself. But I do wish she had told me where she was going."

She basked for a moment in a sense of relief as LeCourt's suave words swept the majority of doubts and worries from her mind. She was, she thought, so lucky to have found a good friend to lean on here in the middle of the wilderness. She looked at him with deep gratitude; he returned her gaze with a warm smile, a smile in which she thought she caught — not for the first time — the faintest traces of a well-concealed desire. She turned her eyes away, feeling a little abashed.

After dinner, as sunset neared, Raoul walked Prudence to the Martins house, and as they walked past the square by the town's wharf she idly noticed that the *Amazon Princess* was still gone from the dock.

And on her porch as she bade Raoul goodnight, before she could object or even react, he took her in his arms with natural smoothness and kissed her, long and tenderly and with a growing passion.

When their lips parted, her shields lay scattered around her feet, but she knew she must say no to the question that would come next.

But it didn't come.

"Goodnight, Prudence darling," LeCourt murmured. "I do hope we will see much more of each other. And please do not worry about your friend."

Inside, Prudence lit both candles — her own and Eleanor's — before getting dressed for bed. A vague anger was stirring inside herself. She knew a little bit of it was at Raoul, for stealing the kiss on the porch as brazenly as he had; but most of it was at herself for yielding to it so limpidly. She had played the part of a silly old-fashioned corseted maiden, not a modern — no! even worse! An old-fashioned corseted maiden would have finished the kiss with a slap across Raoul's face for such temerity!

But most of all she was angry with herself for being, deep down inside, secretly just a little disappointed that Raoul had not made an attempt to move beyond the kiss, to seduce her. She would have rejected him, of course, and forcefully at that; but —

She shook her head, exasperated with herself. Of course he hadn't made a move. What kind of a man takes advantage of a woman's temporary vulnerability for some cheap sex? She was all alone in a strange country with only himself for a friend, and sick with worry that her best friend might be — gone. Only the most horrid of men would try to turn a situation like that to his own carnal advantage.

She smiled then, and reached for her pajamas. It was time for bed. Eleanor, she thought, would surely be back by the next day.

With the drama of her evening with Raoul, and the lingering worries about Eleanor, Prudence anticipated terrible trouble getting to sleep. She poured herself an extra stiff jolt of *cachaça*, but found its taste somehow disagreed with her, so she set the glass on the table and started getting dressed for bed.

Then, just as she was buttoning up her pajama top, she heard footsteps outside. Could this be Eleanor coming back, she wondered? She hurried to the front window and peered out.

It wasn't Eleanor. It was two men, carrying a large canoe. They were hurrying past her house and headed down toward the docks.

Could this be Raoul, going out to search for Eleanor? But no, wouldn't he wait for daylight to do that?

Then she realized that it was probably a hunting party, going out to hunt caimans. She'd heard or read somewhere that the big water-lizards were easiest to hunt at night, when their eyes could be dazzled by bright lights thrown by carbide search lamps.

She climbed onto her large, hard bed. Eleanor, when they'd moved in, had insisted on taking her old bed, on which she'd slept as a little girl; that left the big double bed of Eleanor's aunt and uncle for her to sleep on.

Now it felt bigger and emptier than ever. She arranged her head upon the pillow and closed her eyes. The last thing she remembered was wondering how she would ever get to sleep.

When Prudence next opened her eyes, the room was bathed in the golden light of morning. She had slept late — very late; it was at least seven o'clock. She pulled herself upright and looked over at Eleanor's little bed. It was still empty.

She swung her feet out onto the floor and sat there on the edge of the bed for a moment, contemplating the dream she'd had the night before. It had felt strange, this dream — somehow threatening and comforting at the same time. Eleanor had been in it, that much she knew, but she couldn't remember how. All she remembered was floating in the air just above the river, flying through the air until she reached a certain point on the bank of the river beneath an enormous mahogany tree eerily shaped like a human skull and beside a mysterious looking river channel or deep creek leading off at right angles to the riverbank. She'd floated up a narrow winding path that had suddenly appeared beside that deep creek, which had led off up the side of a small hill and then wound and twisted through the forest for what seemed like miles and miles.

At last the path had opened up into a small clearing in the forest — at the edge of which was a giant wall, obviously the wall of a huge, ancient hidden city.

More than that she could not remember, although she knew there had been more. It reminded her, uncannily, of the dream Eleanor had tried to tell her about, the day before she'd vanished. At the time she hadn't been paying close attention, her mind drifting off onto matters relating to filming their movie; she'd been only half listening. Prudence now wished that she'd paid closer attention.

But now it was late. Raoul would have already been at Marcello's for breakfast, probably for some time; she was a little surprised the suave French doctor hadn't come looking for her.

She hurriedly dressed herself—plus-fours this time, rather than a skirt, just in case she got a chance to go out in a canoe — and left the house.

Marcello's was up the bank from her house, but as she started for it, she suddenly remembered the two men carrying the canoe in the night. She decided that, before going to get breakfast, she would follow their trail down to the river. She wasn't sure what she hoped to see there, but Eleanor had now been gone for well over twenty-four hours, and no amount of smooth assurance from LeCourt was going to soothe her anxiety about her now.

Down at the waterfront, she found a few people stirring about, although it was still plenty early for most people. Bancroft was out on the observation deck of the *Amazon Princess*, sipping what appeared to be a Bloody Mary. He peeled two fingers off the side of his glass to give her a perfunctory wave, to which she replied with a cold nod. She hurried to the edge of the dock and looked down, to see if the big canoe was still tied to it.

A flash of delight and relief surged through her as she saw, at the bottom of one of the pilings at the shallow end of the dock, a long slender skiff — a skiff that she somehow knew to be the boat Eleanor had paddled upstream in.

The feeling lasted less than half a second before it was replaced with a whiplash of shock, horror and alarm. She heard herself scream. Her vision seemed to tunnel in on the strange skiff — on the river water that filled it nearly to the gunwales, on the leaves and twigs that floated in it... and on the deep gouges left by hard, sharp things that had cut deep into its sides.

Tooth marks.

VII.

THE SEARCH.

Within a few seconds, Prudence was surrounded by villagers, rushing to see what she'd screamed about. The first on the scene was Kylla Azvedo, the matron who'd told her of Eleanor's midnight departure. She gazed down at the swamped boat and murmured, "Poor thing. Poor thing."

She gazed at it for a moment or two, then turned back to Prudence. "It is the very place where Carlo and Marcita Martins' boat was found," she added sadly, "also chewed, just like this. I am so sorry, dear, so very sorry."

As she was speaking, Captain Bancroft appeared. He'd left his breakfast cocktail on the boat and run the length of the wharf. Now as he stood gazing down at the swamped boat, his eyes narrowed and his mouth hardened noticeably; he looked almost suspicious. Then he turned to Prudence and opened his mouth, but just as he did so, Raoul raced up to her and seized control of the scene in an almost proprietary manner.

"What is it, *Mademoiselle*?" he panted. "I heard you scream!"

Prudence was no longer trying to hold back the tears, but was trying not to sob. She mutely pointed to the edge of the dock, and Raoul peered over the edge.

"But whose boat is that?" he exclaimed.

"Eleanor's," said Prudence, almost inaudibly. "I'm sure. Eleanor's."

"I very much doubt that, *Mademoiselle*," Raoul returned. "Miss Martins would not have —"

He broke off suddenly, gazing at the boat. Bancroft was watching him intently, although he seemed not to notice, lost in thought. Then Bancroft glanced at Prudence, flashed a disdainful look back at LeCourt, and turned and started back toward his boat.

Then the old woman, Kylla, spoke up. "That was the boat that I saw *Senhorita* Martins paddle away in," she said firmly. "That is her boat."

More villagers arrived. Then one of them, after looking long and fearfully at the boat, said something to another in a language that was not Portuguese, and the other crossed himself in response.

The old woman then said something very crisply in the same language, and both villagers looked a little ashamed. But Prudence noticed a particular sort of troubled look on the faces of several of the other villagers. It was the same look she'd noticed creeping into Izabel Ribeiro's eyes at unguarded moments, and the look she'd seen a hint of crossing the faces of villagers on the first day when Eleanor had been introducing herself to everyone.

"They worry about the tooth marks," said Kylla. "It is very uncommon for a caiman to attack a boat, and for two boats belonging to Martins family members to be attacked — that is most strange."

"It is," said Prudence. "Are they worried about some kind of curse, then?"

"In a way," said Kylla. "They are modern, twentieth-century Brazilians. They do not believe in such silliness as curses, or great legendary monsters of the river. But an event like this, it makes it hard not to wonder. I do not blame them for their fears, even as I chastise them for expressing them."

"Fears — of river monsters?" Prudence said.

Kylla was silent for a moment. Then she spoke: "There is a legend among the native tribes in this area," she said. "A legend of a monster that lurks in the Arapaima River's darkest depths, and is called the Yacumama."

"A monster?"

"Yes. A very large, cruel monster formed like a great snake with the jaws of a caiman, hundreds of feet long, with a head two meters wide. It does not, of course, exist. But you know how legends are. And our village was once a native tribe, encamped here on the river. We are modern Christian citizens of Brazil, but we are still part of the Cahuacaso tribe, and the tales and legends of our forefathers have a pull upon us."

Under ordinary circumstances, Prudence would have wanted to know more about the Cahuacaso Tribe and the origins of the village of Carraçao. Now, though, she was very distracted. She shivered. Then she gave a panicky start.

"Well, we've got to do something!" she cried. "Eleanor could be stranded on an island full of poisonous snakes and hungry tigers — I mean jaguars. We must go and look for her!"

One of the villagers now spoke up, in a firm voice full of authority: "We cannot," he said. "Someth — some caiman out there is attacking canoes. We do not believe in the Yacumama. But we do believe in very large, rogue caimans, and if one of them has learned to attack canoes to get the people inside them to fall into the river, who will take a chance on the river?"

The other villagers were nodding approval. LeCourt spoke up: "I think that is wise, Mayor Sunil. But no caiman is ever going to attack a steamboat. I will pay to have *Monsieur* Bancroft take us to search for *Mademoiselle* Martins. Although" — he turned to Prudence and his tone grew more tender — "I am afraid, my dear, you will have to prepare yourself for disappointment. I do not think we will see her again. I am … so sorry."

Prudence choked back a sob, turning away from him. "Thank you," she said thickly. "Excuse me. I need a moment."

She walked, as normally as she could, back to the Martins house, climbed the steps, walked inside, curled up on the bed in a fetal position — and, at long last, let the tears come freely.

W hen Prudence re-emerged from the house fifteen minutes later, the village was bustling with its usual morning activity, but she noticed that no one would meet her eye. Briefly she wondered if she'd done something wrong, or if it were fear of the curse that seemed to linger on the Martins family. The subtle alienation made her uncomfortable. She knew she should go down and eat breakfast, but she wouldn't be able to touch food now.

She walked down to the wharf — but this made things worse. She was unable to stop her eyes from drifting over to the end of the wharf where Eleanor's boat had been found. The tears threatened to well up in her eyes once again.

Then someone called her name and she turned and saw LeCourt, just stepping off the afterdeck of the *Amazon Princess*. He was gazing at her with a big, comforting smile.

"Ah, *Mademoiselle* McMarion," he said. "I have just made the arrangements to go out upon the river in search of our lost friend. We leave in thirty minutes. Have you had yet your breakfast?"

Prudence didn't trust her voice not to crack into a sob. So she just shook her head.

"Come with me, then," LeCourt told her, in a gentle and patronizing voice that ordinarily would have brought her hackles up. Today, though, it felt comforting rather than insulting.

Prudence was still not hungry, but she forced herself to eat some fruit and *pão francês*.

As the two of them walked back to the wharf after paying for breakfast, Prudence looked up at Raoul gratefully.

"I do feel better," she said. "Thank you, Raoul."

He merely smiled at her, and gestured graciously toward the docked steamboat.

On board the *Amazon Princess*, two villagers were already in the bows holding binoculars. Prudence noticed, with slight unease, that one of them was LeCourt's burly, taciturn friend Marco Morais.

LeCourt gallantly made rather a show of paying Captain Bancroft for the charter. Bancroft accepted the money with noticeable annoyance, greeted Prudence with a sincere if businesslike smile, and set about casting off the lines.

The *Amazon Princess* glided smoothly up the placid green river, hugging the near shoreline closely as Morais and the other villager scanned the bushes with their binoculars. Prudence, having borrowed a pair of binoculars from Bancroft, did likewise.

Under less stressful circumstances, Prudence would have loved that trip. She saw, through her binoculars, an astonishing panoply of tropical animals — monkeys and tapirs coming down to drink, snakes of every size, brilliantly colored birds of all sorts.

Once she watched as a jaguar stole up behind a medium-sized caiman that was sunning itself on a sandbar and pounced upon it. The caiman thrashed helplessly as the big cat bit deep into the base of its skull, then went limp, and the jaguar carried it away into the bushes for a private feast.

This drama would ordinarily have fascinated Prudence; now it almost made her hysterical. Although she knew the jaguars didn't eat people, she couldn't help picturing Prudence being mauled like that caiman. How people could stand to live in such a deadly place, so full of creatures that could kill one in an instant, was beyond her.

By about one o'clock, they had traveled several miles up the river, and Prudence had realized that it made little sense to continue. However preternatural Eleanor's speed might have seemed to old Kylla watching from the shore, she couldn't possibly have paddled herself this far up the river. So she went to the wheelhouse to ask Bancroft if he would turn the boat around.

She found LeCourt there with Bancroft, which surprised her a little; she had been under the impression that the enmity between the two of them was deep and lasting and mutual, not the sort of thing that fades in a day.

LeCourt was leaning close to Bancroft murmuring

something to him, and he was nodding curtly in response. Bancroft was puffing powerfully on the largest, ugliest black cigar she had ever seen, and the cabin air was thick and awful with foul-smelling smoke.

"Should we turn around now?" said Prudence, standing by the door so as to catch as much fresh air as possible. "I can't imagine she paddled up this far."

"I was just making a similar suggestion," LeCourt replied, smiling at her kindly.

"Suggestion, hell," grunted Bancroft.

"But first, we must stop for our lunch," LeCourt continued, ignoring Bancroft's interjection. "This searching, it cannot be done when the stomach is growling, no?"

So Bancroft steered the boat into the middle of the channel and let it drift slowly downstream while everyone assembled on the observation deck and ate sandwiches and drank white wine — all generously provided by LeCourt.

It was nearly two when they finally turned back toward the village.

At first, the return trip was a mirror of the trip out, only conducted along the far side of the river rather than the near. But after about three o'clock, when they were perhaps halfway back to the village, Prudence saw that they were moving away from the shore and the boat was picking up speed. Soon they were racing back down the river at what felt close to top speed, well away from the shore.

Puzzled, Prudence put down her binoculars and made her way to the pilothouse.

"LeCourt wants to get back to the village by four," Bancroft said shortly, in response to her inquiry.

"And he didn't know about this at lunch, when everybody was dawdling around like we had all the time in the world?" she said.

Bancroft turned to look at her. "It's not how I'd run a search operation," he said. "But I'm not in charge here. This is LeCourt's show. And I guess he suddenly remembered a pressing engagement at four, so he ordered me to step on it."

"But what does he need to do?" she said, trying not to let the question come out as a wail.

"No idea," Bancroft replied.

"Can we at least get a little closer to the shore?"

"Maybe a little closer," he said. "But not much. It's not safe. You saw that dead tree we almost hit the other day?"

"But this is terrible," Prudence said, wailing now in spite of herself. "This is the most likely place for her to have landed. And now we're going to race past with barely a chance to look."

"Yep," said Bancroft, his voice hard and unfriendly. "That's what LeCourt wants, and he's the man paying for this. You want me to take my time, talk to him about it."

Prudence sighed and stepped to the wheelhouse door.

"Keep an eye out, though," Bancroft said then, in a voice that sounded intentionally gruff. "If you see anything, we'll stop. The *Princess* is a fast boat, we can make up time if we have to."

"Thank you, Captain," she replied, as neutrally as she could, and stepped through the door to find LeCourt.

The Frenchman wasn't on the port side of the boat, so she rounded the corner of the cabin to look for him on the starboard side — the side facing the shore. As she did so, she stopped short with a little gasp. Groping for the binoculars dangling from their lanyard around her neck, she brought them to her eyes and stared.

She was looking at the same patch of shoreline that she remembered from her dream. There was the same great mahogany tree, eerily shaped like a human skull; the same dark little inlet leading away from the river at right angles; the same tiny, weed-choked game trail leading up into the forest.

She turned and ran back to the door of the wheelhouse.

"Captain Bancroft!" she panted. "We have to stop!"

Then she paused. What was she going to say? She couldn't tell Bancroft about her dream; he'd just laugh at her.

"I am so very sorry, *Mademoiselle*," purred a smooth voice just behind her and to the right. "It is my fault entirely. I had forgotten my confidential appointment with a very important patient. Perhaps we can reprise our search tomorrow."

She turned and saw that LeCourt was standing just to the right of the door, holding a slender gold-tipped cigarette. Bancroft, standing at the wheel, was puffing furiously at his cigar, its ember blazing like a beacon amid tremendous clouds of smoke.

"B— but — I just — I just saw a caiman. A very large caiman," she said, as a sudden and mysterious bit of inspiration flashed across her mind. "And I thought perhaps it was the one that chewed the boats."

LeCourt laughed. It was the kind of laugh that always infuriated Prudence — the laugh of a self-assured male chauvinist enjoying the silliness of "the Fair Sex," a laugh of a man who wondered how the little ladies could get such silly little ideas into their pretty little heads. Prudence, who had found LeCourt's patronizing attitude comforting earlier, now greeted it with her customary fierce resentment. She opened her mouth to say something sharp to him, but Bancroft spoke first.

"Too bad you didn't see it sooner," he remarked. "We could at least have shot it as we steamed by."

"*Mais oui*, what a shame," said LeCourt sadly. "And more of a shame that we have no time now to turn back to shoot it. If only we had broken away from our lunch a few minutes sooner."

Prudence happened to be looking at Bancroft as LeCourt said this. He turned his head now, and she saw a flash of something in his eye — a sort of malicious triumph.

"Naw, we got time," he said brusquely, and his hand shot out to the steam valve as he spun the wheel shoreward.

"No!" cried LeCourt, and it was almost a scream. He looked, and sounded, genuinely alarmed. "I cannot be late! We must continue! Sail on, I order you!"

"You're not gonna be late," said Bancroft. "I personally guarantee we will be back on time, by four o'clock, as I promised."

Prudence glanced at LeCourt; the Frenchman's mouth was opening and closing almost spasmodically, as if he were desperate to say something but couldn't. What had gotten into him? And was it just the smoke in the room, or was his face looking a little gray all of a sudden?

"Where did you see this caiman?" asked Bancroft, and she looked up to see that he had now maneuvered the boat up close to the shoreline and was heading back up the river.

Again, Prudence didn't want to say why she wanted to backtrack and look more closely at this spot in the river. She thought it must be because they would laugh at the thought that they were taking time to explore something she claimed to have seen in a dream; that they would disbelieve her, dismiss her as a vapid flapper making up silly stories and fooling herself into thinking they were true;

but it seemed, somehow, that there was more at stake than just that.

"It was up there, just past that outcropping," she said. "There, just below that far tree that looks like a — like a — monkey's head."

"Behind where that little creek comes in?" said Bancroft. "Funny, I'd more expect to see them waiting by the mouth of that creek."

LeCourt was now most definitely looking gray, or at least very pale.

"Just over there," said Prudence as the *Amazon Princess* motored slowly past the tree and creek. She surreptitiously looked at it out of the sides of her eyes while pretending to continue staring past it. Prudence could plainly see the little footpath that ascended the bank right next to it. And it was unquestionably the scene from her dream.

Which meant — what, exactly?

"I don't see anything," Bancroft was saying. "Are you sure you saw a caiman?"

"Yes," she said then. "But I don't see it now. It's gone."

"Well, we need to be going now," said Bancroft. "I'm going to have to flog her full tilt to get LeCourt back in time. Hold on, I'm going to open up the steam."

As the riverboat surged ahead, Prudence saw LeCourt gazing icily at Bancroft. She was puzzled. These two men clearly hated each other; why were they insisting on being in the same room together now?

She shrugged. Not my business, she thought again. Then she stepped over to the cabin door.

"Thank you, Captain," she said, and withdrew, grateful to be away from the cigar smoke.

The boat was just passing, once again, the shoreline scene from her dream. She stared at it openly now, scrutinizing it through her binoculars. And suddenly she thought she glimpsed something in the muddy shore—something she'd overlooked before. It almost looked like the mark of a boat's keel, where it has been dragged out of the river. Just the keel, though—no footprints—if Eleanor had disembarked there, surely she would have left footprints?

She turned toward the pilothouse, intending to ask Bancroft to turn back. But she never entered it, never made the request. As she turned, her gaze fell upon Raoul LeCourt, who was looking at her through the window. For the briefest fraction of a second, she caught his eyes, and there was something in them that froze her blood: a look of fear and determination and fierceness and coldness tempered with sadness and regret.

But the look was gone almost the instant she saw it. LeCourt smiled gallantly at her through the glass, touched the brim of his hat and strolled leisurely away to the other side of the wheelhouse.

VIII.

THE MIDNIGHT VISIT.

The rest of the journey, conducted as fast as Bancroft's boat could safely go, took less than half an hour. The spot certainly was within easy paddling distance of the village. Prudence continued to scan the riverbank for signs of the presence of Eleanor, but now she was also making a mental note of all the landmarks and waypoints along the way. She already knew that she must return to this place, by stealth if necessary.

It occurred to her that, now that Eleanor was gone, she should try to find a really good friend her age among the villagers. She had made some friends, notably with Izabel's family; but the only one she felt a real connection with was Kylla, the old woman who lived at the docks. Kylla would understand, she thought. She would talk to Kylla.

But even so, she knew her return trip to look for Eleanor

would have to be made alone. And she would have to make it in a canoe — caimans or no caimans.

Finally the riverboat arrived at the village wharf. As Bancroft had promised, it arrived at three-fifty — in plenty of time for LeCourt's appointment. LeCourt, who had been standing by the gunwale waiting for it to touch the quay, sprang over the rail and hurried off toward his offices, at the far downstream end of the village. Marco Morais, without a word or glance at anyone, hustled after.

Prudence watched him go. Then she turned to Bancroft, who was busy tying the boat of to the quay, to thank him.

"Don't thank me," Bancroft grunted curtly. "It was just a job for me. Thank LeCourt for hiring me to do it. But, Miss McMarion —" and he turned and looked at her — "don't forget what I said about LeCourt."

She nodded, her memory flashing back to that look she'd caught through the cabin window. What a difference a glance could make! "I remember," she said, and her voice was not as cold as it once had been. "Good day, Captain."

"Miss McMarion, wait a moment," Bancroft said. "We still have steam up. Can I take you back upriver to look for your friend? I'll have to charge you for it, of course, but we'll put it on credit. Something tells me you're good for it."

Prudence, of course, accepted gratefully and stepped back aboard. And for an hour and a half, the *Amazon Princess* chugged upriver, carefully covering the part of the river that they'd missed.

But when they got to the spot with the skull-shaped mahogany tree, Prudence stiffened. Something was different.

Stepping out of the pilothouse, she pressed her binoculars to her eyes.

"See something?" Bancroft called out over the hissing of the steam plant. "We can pull in again if you want. Is the caiman back?"

"Yes... yes, can we get a little closer?" she replied.

Prudence still didn't quite trust Bancroft. Her highly unfavorable first impressions of him had been tempered by occasional glimpses of humanity, which he seemed to try very hard to conceal; but she still was not comfortable telling him why she really was interested in this spot. She hoped he would not ask, as another line about a caiman would probably be a hard sell.

He didn't ask; he just steered the boat toward the mahogany tree as she intently scanned the bank with the binoculars.

It wasn't anything she saw there that disturbed her; it was what she didn't see. There was suddenly no sign of the trail leading up from the river. A thick wall of foliage seemed to have materialized in the spot where she thought she'd seen it, both in her dream and, two hours previously, from this very boat. And the mark of the boat's keel, there where she thought she'd seen it — there was nothing there but a large piece of driftwood.

And yet this was unquestionably the scene from her dream.

"What is going on?" she murmured, rubbing her forehead. "Is something wrong with me?"

"See anything?" Bancroft called out.

"No..." she replied. "I guess we can head back now."

B ack in the village at last, Prudence stepped off the deck of the boat with a final word of thanks to Captain Bancroft and walked up the quay toward the Martins house. As she did, she passed a small group of village women who had gathered to watch the *Amazon Princess* dock.

"*Senhorita* McMarion," said one, "we all feel terrible for you, losing your friend like this. We are gathering at Ana's house tomorrow after lunch to play bridge; would you like to join us? We would love to have you. And perhaps, after our game, we can go out with you to look for her, just in case —"

She stopped suddenly, looking awkward. Prudence, surprised, looked at her with a tentative smile. "You play bridge here?" she said.

The villager looked a little hurt. "Of course," she said. "We may live deep in the Amazon on the edge of the wilderness, but we aren't uncivilized."

"I'm so sorry," Prudence said. "I wasn't thinking. And I'm so new here. And everything is so different."

"Of course," said the other. "I am Camila, and this is Gabriela, Ana and Amanda."

Prudence was soon properly introduced, and the five of them chatted happily for a few minutes, the local women steering the topic scrupulously away from the subject of strange disappearances. When she left the little company, Prudence was almost glowing, despite her lingering worries about Eleanor. Camila and her friends, by reaching out to her as they had, had made her instantly feel welcome. She no longer felt like a frightened little girl alone in a strange place. She had friends now. And her friends were expecting her at Ana's house the next day.

Prudence smiled a little as she hurried on toward the Martins house. She was brought forcibly back to Earth, however, the moment she stepped inside and saw Eleanor's little childhood bed with the candle beside it. With an anguished sigh she sat down heavily on her bed, glanced at the bottle of *cachaça*, and then reached for it.

There was nothing for her to do now. All she could do was wait and hope Eleanor was OK and would soon return.

Prudence was not a patient woman. All her life she had been a person who, when something bad happened, took immediate action to attack the problem. Sitting around weepily waiting and hoping for things to get better was very much out of character for her, and she was having a great deal of difficulty doing that now.

She took another pull of the fiery *cachaça* and felt her inner anguish immediately grow more muted. Then she set the bottle down on the floor by the bed again and tried to think. If only there were something she could do — anything.

The movie, of course, was dead in the water until Eleanor came back. If she'd brought darkroom supplies, she might have been at least able to "soup" the film she'd shot over the previous few days, but, knowing it would be far easier and less chancy to wait and develop it at home after the shoot, she had planned to do all that after returning to Los Angeles. She could spend some time actively looking for Eleanor — that was surely what she would do when morning came, before it was time to go to Ana's — but she had no leads other than the odd spot in the river that she'd seen from the boat that afternoon, and she felt sure she'd have difficulty getting back to that spot for at least a day or two. Raoul, she knew, would do everything he could to prevent her, out of fear that she would become a fourth victim of whatever was out there chewing on canoes.

She sighed, taking another short pull on the bottle. A plan of action was starting to develop in her mind; that, in combination with the soothing effect of the alcohol, was starting to quiet her mind a little. She would set out on the river in a canoe, returning to the place on the river she'd dreamed about, and she would get out on the shore and see what was there — snakes or no snakes. But she would have to do it the very first thing in the morning, before Raoul LeCourt could catch her and try to prevent her. Especially if he knew she planned to get out and beat the bushes on shore, she felt sure he would do everything he could to "save" her.

But where would she find a canoe? She thought for a moment, then remembered the boat that Eleanor had left in. It had, of course, tooth marks all over it, and was still half full of water; but she could empty it out in a few minutes and be on her way. All she would need was a paddle, and she was pretty sure she could find one in another boat and borrow it for the day. She hoped its owner wouldn't be too angry.

Well, it was time. With another healthy pull from the *cachaça* bottle, Prudence drained it and stood up, noticing that the room wasn't quite as steady under her feet as it had been when she'd first sat down. She realized that she'd leaned a bit more heavily on the bottle of *cachaça* than she usually did, and was feeling more than a little tipsy.

She'd start at the general store, since she needed more candles and maybe a fresh bottle of *cachaça*, and she could check and see if any new telegrams had come in from Leonard. Then she'd head to Marcello's for a bite to eat, turn in early, and leave early the next morning in the canoe to find Eleanor.

The instant she walked into the general store, Old Man Paulo stepped forward to greet her. "*Senhorita* McMarion," he said earnestly, "I wish to offer my heartfelt condolences on the death of poor *Senhorita* Martins."

"Thank you," she said, "but how do you know she's dead?"

Paulo gave her a pitying look that put her hackles up and sent a wave of resentful adrenaline tingling in her fingertips.

In awkward silence she collected her candles and other things and started for home.

"*Senhorita* McMarion," said a man just outside the door. "I want to offer my heartfelt condolences on the loss of poor *Senhorita* Martins."

"Thank you," she said through gritted teeth. "But I'm not convinced yet that she's actually dead yet."

The man gave her the same look of condescending pity, but she was braced for it this time. Somewhat nettled nonetheless, she moved on without saying anything further.

Dropping her supplies off at the house, Prudence now made her way toward Marcello's for a solitary dinner. She hoped Raoul wouldn't stop in; she really was not in the mood to be sociable just now.

On the way, another villager stopped to offer her his most heartfelt condolences on the death of poor *Senhorita* Martins.

"Thank you," she replied. "But I refuse to believe she's dead until a little more time passes."

The man looked sadly and pityingly at her and moved on. This time, Prudence very nearly lost her temper and snapped at him. What was going on? Had the entire village rehearsed the same line, waiting to use it on her at the first opportunity?

With a muttered curse, she turned to the door of Marcello's, pulled it open and walked inside.

There were one or two dozen people in the restaurant having dinner. The ones nearest the door looked at her as she walked in, and gave her looks of pitying sympathy. "There goes poor *Senhorita* McMarion," the looks seemed to say. "Whatever will the poor little waif do now that her friend is gone?"

She didn't like it, but it was better than another round of heartfelt condolences on the death of poor *Senhorita* Martins. She moved to an empty table and seated herself.

Soon Marcello himself appeared before her.

"*Senhorita* McMarion," he said. "I wish to offer my most heartfelt condolences on the death of poor *Senhorita* Martins."

Prudence, half drunk to begin with and goaded beyond endurance by the constant repetition of those same hateful words, couldn't take it any more.

"She's NOT DEAD!" she screeched, as loud as she could and in English to boot. The murmur of conversation ended in shocked silence.

Then Marcello gave her The Look, and something snapped. Springing to her feet, she poured forth a torrent of angry denunciation in mixed English and Portuguese.

"How dare you all just assume Eleanor is dead?" she screamed. "She could be stranded someplace and desperate for help and you're all just — just lighting candles for her at Sunday Mass and just — just giving up! And how can you sit there and look at me with that pitying look, like I'm some pathetic little deluded thing to be patted on the head and kept quiet, just because I won't accept that Eleanor isn't just off doing something — it could be perfectly fine — Stop it! Stop *looking* at me like that!"

Tears of frustration were now pouring down her face. She leaped to her feet, knocking over the chair behind her, and ran to the door, trying to choke back the sobs of mixed pain, rage and fear for her friend.

She ran all the way to the Martins house, where she shut herself inside, bolted the door, curled up on the bed and sobbed.

A few minutes later she heard a gentle knock on the door. She ignored it. Another knock came, persistent now, and then she heard LeCourt's voice calling her name. She ignored that, too, and presently she heard the Frenchman walk down her steps and away up the path.

Ten minutes later, he was back.

"Prudence?" he called, after a soft knock.

"Go away," she told him.

"But can you not let me in? I want to be —"

"GO AWAY!" she shouted angrily. "Am I being unclear? What part of 'go away' do you think means I want to socialize right now?"

"OK, OK, I go," he called in the kind of voice one uses to try to soothe a child who is having a tantrum.

And he did. But as his footsteps faded on the porch, Prudence heard the faint murmur of his voice, as if he were talking to someone else.

"You see?" he said — or did she imagine it? "She is…"

And the voice faded as LeCourt passed on down the street away from the house.

About an hour later, Prudence had cried herself nearly to sleep when she was brought back to full alertness by the sound of footsteps outside. She prepared herself for another round of negotiations, telling herself she would be less abrasive this time. "I just need a little time to myself," she would tell him. "Please come and see me in the morning. I will be glad of your company then. But tonight I need to cry and be by myself."

But nobody knocked on her door. Instead, the footsteps

paused just outside, and she heard, very faintly, voices.

"Be sure she does not leave the house tonight," said Raoul's voice. "If she does, come and get me or Marco immediately. But only one of you should come. The other must stay and make sure she does not go down to the quay. I am afraid she may try to sneak out tonight in a canoe to go and look for her friend. We cannot allow that to happen."

Prudence heard the villagers murmur something back to him, which she couldn't quite make out. She was seething again. A stealthy midnight paddle in a strange canoe on a strange river? How stupid did Raoul think she was?

It had never occurred to her to take off in a canoe in the middle of the night. Why would she not wait for day, as she had planned to do in any case? Why would they be worried?

Or — were they afraid that whatever had come over Eleanor would affect her tonight, and that she would sleep-walk out to the quay and get in a boat and disappear, under the spell of whatever had caused first Eleanor's aunt and uncle, and then Eleanor herself, to do so?

That had to be it, she told herself. Raoul was simply watching out for her. It was very sweet of him, really. She would never do the thing he worried she might do, of course, but how was he to know that?

Especially after the performance to which she'd treated the diners in Marcello's that night. Her dawning smile darkened back into a worried frown. What had she said, exactly? All she could remember was shouting and crying. She had been so frustrated. It had been as if everyone in the town had been coached to say the same infuriating words to her until, unable to take it any more, she'd snapped. How badly had she damaged her social prospects in this new place?

She sighed. She would be finding out, she supposed, in the morning. For now, all that could be done was to go to sleep and hope not too much of the detritus of one dreadful day would follow her into the next.

She rearranged herself in the bed and, after some difficulty, finally drifted off to sleep.

Sometime in the night, Prudence became aware of a presence in the room. Slowly she stirred to wakefulness, then sat up in bed, straining her eyes in the gloom. Someone, she saw, was sitting on the edge of Eleanor's bed — sitting there and watching her.

Then she realized that it was Eleanor. She opened her mouth to speak, but no words would come out.

Eleanor smiled at her, a beautiful warm human smile that was at the same time deeply eerie. "Trudie," she said softly, "it's OK. I'm just fine, and you need not worry about me. Remember when I told you, on Captain Bancroft's boat as we came to Carraçao, that I felt I was coming home? Well, I'm home now. You will come and visit me soon, very soon, and I will explain everything to you then. But meanwhile, you must not speak any more of me or of my aunt and uncle to the villagers. Already they suspect who we really are. You saw it in their eyes when we were visiting them, their suspicions. They would be truly afraid if they knew the truth, although they have no cause to be; and people who are afraid do not always behave sensibly."

"What truth?"

"I cannot tell you yet. But within a week you will know."

"Eleanor," she whispered.

"Yes," the spectral figure replied. "It's me."

"Are — are you —"

"No," came the reply. "I am not dead. I'm very much

alive. We will see each other soon. But Prudence"—and here her voice became serious and intense—"one more thing. You can trust Captain Bancroft. Him alone. Other than him only, trust no one. No one. Do you understand?"

"Bancroft?" Prudence murmured. "That cad?"

"He is more than he seems," said Eleanor. "I must go now. Remember: Trust no one."

"Eleanor?" Prudence said, suddenly growing alarmed as her friend's form seemed to fade before her eyes. "Eleanor? ELEANOR!"

The shout woke her up. It had been a dream, she realized—a dream, that was all—and she'd shouted herself awake. The sound of uneasy shuffling on the cabin's front porch told her that her guards had heard her outcry.

Feeling oddly soothed, Prudence lay back down. This time, sleep came easily, and it was dreamless.

Prudence awoke the next morning feeling more refreshed than she had in days. She somehow knew, although it had only been a dream, that the communication that had taken place in it had been real; therefore, there was no need to undertake her risky plan of an early-morning paddle in search of signs of Eleanor. But it was just before sunrise, and there was already enough light to see to write; so she turned to her suitcase hastily to dress herself.

She had only packed one house dress, and that had been so badly mangled by brambles the previous day that she didn't want to wear it. She considered the plus-fours, but decided that if she was going to have any hope of working her way back into the good graces of the town, she'd want to dress as conservatively as possible. So instead she put on a brick-red wool skirt and white cotton blouse with a pair of knee-length black stockings. Slipping her feet into her favorite brown Oxfords, she took her travel journal and pen and went out onto her porch.

There, slumped in the two porch chairs and fast asleep, were the two guards who'd been assigned to watch over her. They were occupying the only two seats on the porch, and she didn't want to disturb them; so Prudence decided she would wander down by the quay and find a quiet place there, perhaps overlooking the river, for her morning journaling.

She stepped carefully past the two sleepers and strolled through the peaceful, deserted streets to the waterfront. There, she sat on the edge of the quay, writing and sketching in her journal and watching the river slowly slide by as the sun slowly warmed up the morning.

She'd been there a little over an hour when she heard footsteps behind her; turning, she saw it was LeCourt, walking toward the *Amazon Princess*.

"Good morning, Raoul," she called to him, and he jumped as if stung by a bee.

"Pru — Prudence!" he called back, in tones that were just a little too hearty. "Are we feeling better today?"

"Well, I am, at least," she replied jovially. "It is a glorious morning. I wish Eleanor were here to enjoy it with me, but that's OK."

"Yes," he said. "And I am very much afraid that we cannot spend any more time in fruitless searching. I am so very sorry."

"Oh, I know," she replied. "That's all right. I'm sure Eleanor is all right."

He looked uncomfortable. Then he said, "Have you had your breakfast yet?"

"Why, no," she said. "Would you care to join me?"

A sudden thought struck Prudence, and her face fell. After the scene she'd made in Marcello's restaurant the night before, would she be welcome back in the place? She knew she needed to apologize to Marcello for her rudeness and for the scene she'd caused. Would that apology seem insincere if it came just before breakfast, when she wanted something from him?

LeCourt seemed to be reading her mind.

"I wonder, Prudence darling, if you would be interested in making a little excursion with me," he said. "There is another village, about a two-hour walk from here, smaller than Carraçao but with a nice little restaurant where we might have a late breakfast. Or — would you like to ride there with me in my automobile? The road is not too very terrible, and we can be there in less than an hour. It might make a good setting for one of your movie scenes, if — er, when *Mademoiselle* Eleanor returns."

"Thank you, Raoul, I would love that," she said.

He gave her a brief quizzical look, but before she could wonder what it meant, it was gone.

R aoul left Prudence to linger over her travel journal while he went to retrieve his car. Soon he was pulling up in it, much to the delight of a small group of village children, who had heard him start it up. It the same tiny coal-black two-seater she'd seen before, obviously very old but well cared for.

"Thank you, Raoul," Prudence said as the Frenchman smoothly assisted her in climbing up onto the high bucket seat, where she arranged herself carefully and tried not to be self-conscious. She felt like rather a spectacle up there.

"It is my great pleasure," Raoul said, as he slid into the

driver's seat. "I hope you do not mind, my automobile is not a new one. It was made, if you can believe of it, in 1909, almost twenty years ago, before the war. It is the only automobile in Carraçao."

"It's a French car, isn't it?" Prudence asked.

"But of course she is French! A Renault, type AX, seven horsepowers."

"I wouldn't think you'd be able to use an automobile here," said Prudence.

"During the rainy season, it is not of much use," said LeCourt. "But when the land is dry, I can drive many places. I could drive all the way to Porto Escuro if it were not for the marshlands there."

LeCourt let out the clutch and the little auto rumbled off the wharf and started up the track through the middle of the village. Soon they were putting at a leisurely pace through the forest, along a path barely wide enough for the car. They nibbled on some food as they drove — Raoul had brought some fruit along with a loaf of *pão francês* to share.

The little car had no windscreen, but Raoul drove slowly enough that there wasn't much wind, and they were easily able to converse. They chatted amiably about various things; but after a half hour or so Prudence noticed that Raoul kept bringing the topic of conversation back to Eleanor. He seemed especially keen to understand why she was suddenly so uninterested in going out and beating through the bushes looking for her.

But by the time they arrived at the neighboring village an hour or so later, he was back to his usual smooth, amiable self, and Prudence once again was feeling the full charm of the mysterious pseudo-Frenchman.

Raoul parked the little car outside the village — so as not to frighten the inhabitants, he said — and the two of them walked into the town.

The neighboring village looked very much like Carraçao, except that it was set back from the river along a large stream, big enough for a canoe but nothing larger than that. In fact, it looked very much like an Indian village, like one of the ones she'd seen from the deck of the big riverboat that had brought her up the Amazon to Porto Escuro, and she wondered if there would be a restaurant in an Indian village. Did the natives eat in restaurants? She wasn't sure.

But Raoul was leading the way to the most European-looking of the village huts, a large structure with a generous porch-like area, and soon they were seated at a table in a room that would not have looked out of place in Belem or Rio de Janeiro. It was completely empty of customers. Behind the understated but civilized-looking bar stood an elegantly mustachioed man, with silver hair and a slight air of seediness, who was obviously not a native. The man smiled at her, and she smiled back.

"Are you hungry, Prudence?" Raoul asked.

"Oh, Raoul, please call me Trudie," she answered. "But no, not hungry, not quite yet."

"Trudie? Short for Trudence?"

Prudence laughed. "No, but I absolutely refuse to be called 'Prudie.' So Trudie is close enough."

"Very well, then, Trudie," he said. "I am going to start my day the right way, with a glass of white wine. The wine is a specialty of this village — it is made not with grapes, but with a combination of Amazon fruits, which is kept as a closely guarded secret. It is delightful, and I say that as a true Frenchman, a man who knows his wines. You must try it."

"That sounds really good right now," she said, "although it's a little earlier in the morning than I like to start my daily bacchanals. But I'll join you."

LeCourt strolled over to the bar, and soon returned with two great crystal goblets of a very pale golden liquid. The two of them settled down with them.

"So, Trudie," LeCourt said, when they were both about three-quarters done with their drinks. "I am so happy to see that you are no longer in such distress about Eleanor."

"Eleanor is fine," said Prudence. The wine was starting to hit her — to hit her harder than she'd thought it would, harder than she'd thought possible. Ordinarily half a glass of white wine would barely have registered with her, but this one had made her quite tipsy. Probably, she thought, it was just because her stomach was mostly empty.

"I know Eleanor is doing just fine," she added. "I'm not worried about a thing."

So saying, she tossed off the rest of her drink with so much panache that some of the golden liquid sloshed out of her mouth and down the front of her blouse.

"Oops," she said.

"Well, how do you know this?" LeCourt said, ignoring her mishap and looking intently at her.

"See, I had this dream las' night, see," Prudence prattled happily. "Eleanor came an' said evvything's fine an' she's in 'er home, whatever that means, but she can't tell anybody from Carra — Carra —"

"Carraçao?"

"C'rasso, yeah. Anyway, she can't tell anybody from Cura — Carra — from here — 'cos they don' like her or something. An' she said I'd be coming to see her soon an' that I shouldn' trus' aaanybody."

"Ah," he said smoothly, finishing his wine. "Now, what

is this city she speaks of?"

Prudence looked confused for a moment. "City? She din't — oh yeah, you're talkin' 'bout the city in my dream! That was two nights ago. I dreamed I was zooming up the river like a flying fairy an' turned in at thish one shpot onna bank an' followed a little footpath an' came out at this lost city, covered with jungle weeds. An' then I woke up, an' it was all jush' a dream. But if Eleanor was in my dream too, maybe she was in that city. Eleanor's lost city. Yeah."

"I see," said LeCourt. "And do you remember where the path was that you dreamed about?"

"Oh yes!" she crowed. "It was right where Cap'n Bankoff stopped the boat yeshterday. Right there. I reco'nized it. But then when Cap'n Banquet took me back to look again a couple hours later, it was gone!"

"Ah. And what did Captain Bancroft say about that?"

"He doesn't know. I din't tell 'im why I wanted to go there. I don' trust — I don't —"

What was that? Something she'd said caught at her rapidly dimming mind, bringing up a memory. Something about trusting people. Eleanor! Eleanor had told her to trust no one except —

She looked at LeCourt, eyes wide with wonder and puzzlement. He looked back at her, a long and cryptic look. Then, just as her fogged-up brain was starting to stir itself to flash a warning, he smiled smoothly and the sinister feeling vanished.

"I think I'll have just one more glass," he said then.

"Oh, me too!" Prudence shouted.

"Coming right up, darling," said LeCourt, and moved smoothly to the bar and spoke to the mustachioed man, and soon was back with two more goblets of golden wine. He set one down directly in front of Prudence.

She picked it up. It was so beautiful, this shining golden wine, so beautiful and so potent. She'd had just one glass, and yet it felt as if she'd had ten or twelve.

That faint warning signal, deep inside her fogged-up mind, was starting to ring again. Something wasn't quite right...but she didn't care. She raised it to her lips and took a long draft, set the half-empty glass back down on the tabletop with exaggerated care, and slid under the table, unconscious.

IX.

THE STRAIT-JACKET.

Prudence awakened slowly, her head throbbing and stomach roiling. The surface she was lying on was hard and unyielding, and the blackness lay all around her like a thick blanket. Nearby she heard a soft splash, as if a frog had just jumped into a pond or river.

She tried to sit up, but she couldn't move her arms. She found that her arms were locked into place around her midsection. Panic seized her. She struggled and screamed for help, wriggling about on what she now realized was the floor of a dark room.

Then a light appeared, and she realized that someone holding a candle had opened a door in the room.

"Sssh, it's all right, Prudie," said a soothing female voice, in Portuguese. "Just relax. Sleep some more. Tomorrow you will be on your way to the nice hospital where you will get the help and support you need to get well again."

"Who are you?" Prudence asked hoarsely. "Where am I? Why can't I move my arms?"

She glared around like a caged tiger, taking in the surroundings that she could now see thanks to the candle. She was in a small room with walls that looked as if they were padded. The only windows were high up, out of reach and out of view. There was no furniture of any kind; only a raised area of padding in the general shape of a bed in one corner. And, looking down at her non-functioning arms, she realized that she was wearing — a straitjacket.

"I am Beatriz," the soft-spoken woman was saying. "You are here because you have been sick, very sick, Prudie. But you are already getting better, and everything is going to be OK."

"Wait a minute," Prudence said, in a trembling voice that showed the effort it was taking to remain in control of herself. "Why am I in a padded room — in a straitjacket? Who — what — you think I'm crazy?"

"Oh, no, no, not crazy, no, no," said Beatriz soothingly. "But you have been very sick. Delirious, in fact. And we thought you might hurt yourself, so we put you in this special room to make sure you were feeling OK. I'm so happy to see you are feeling better, Prudie. Tomorrow you will journey to Porto Escuro to see a specialist, who will see that you are fully cured. Rest now, Prudie. You have a long voyage ahead of you. Rest."

Prudence, having rolled over to one of the walls and managed somehow to sit up, now leaned against it, feeling the heavy wooden underpinnings beneath the layer of padding. Her head throbbed mercilessly as she sat up.

"Could I just — just please have some water?" she asked, in a voice that sounded small and defeated.

The woman said she could, and disappeared for a moment, then reappeared with a glass of water with a reed stuck in it.

"You will have to drink with this straw," she said.

Prudence drank until she couldn't hold her breath any more.

"Thank you," she gasped at last. "What happened? Why am I here? How long have I been — sick?"

"Only just one day," said Beatriz. "You were unconscious when they brought you here, Prudence. They said you were seized with madness in a restaurant in Katakuona and broke many things, and attacked the owner and injured him."

Prudence stared. "I — Cotta-kona? Where — what —"

"Katakuona," Beatriz corrected her. "Rest now, Prudie. You must rest."

And the door closed with a particularly heavy latching noise, leaving Prudence once again in darkness.

P rudence sat there for hours, propped against the wall, as the pain in her head slowly dissipated from an excruciating, throbbing agony to a dull, persistent ache. The darkness became less dense, then turned to pale gloamy dawning, and then to morning. And then, at what she figured must have been about eight o'clock, the door rattled again, and opened to reveal the silhouette of a man.

The man stepped inside. It was Raoul LeCourt, looking worried but compassionate and solicitous. "Ah, Prudence," he said gently. "You are feeling better, I hope?"

"Raoul!" she cried, and tried to leap to her feet, forgetting that she was wearing a straitjacket. The result was a painful, ignominious tumble to the floor, where she wriggled around again trying to find the wall and pull herself back upright.

"Raoul," she wailed, after managing to sit back up, "what is happening to me? Where am I? Why am I here?"

LeCourt gazed at her with tragic sadness. "Ah, Trudie," he murmured. "I am so very, very sorry."

"But — but what —"

She broke off with a sob, and LeCourt let the silence hang in the air for a moment before he continued.

"It was like the episode in Marcello's, when you insulted and abused all the people of Carraçao — only worse," he said. "It was at the restaurant in the neighboring Indian village of Katakuona. You had a glass of wine with me, remember? And then I happened to mention something about poor Eleanor, and you stood up and threw the table over and started screaming that Eleanor was alive and that a horrible vengeance was to be rained down upon the town of Carraçao, and then you started smashing things. The proprietor tried to calm you down but you hit him with a chair. He is still unconscious. And then I tried to calm you down and you clawed at my face — see the mark?"

He pointed to a deep-red mark on his cheek, oozing bright red. She recoiled from it in horror.

"I did that?" she gasped. "I — Raoul, I don't remember any of this! Did I really do such a thing?"

With somber face seemingly carved in lines of tragic, loving sorrow, LeCourt slowly nodded his head.

She was silent for a long moment.

"I'm so sorry," she whispered then. "I'm so very sorry. Is the bartender going to be all right?"

"Yes, he but has the concussion," said LeCourt. "His skull is not fractured, but you gave it a good bump. He will awaken in a few hours. And my visage will heal without a scar. There is nothing permanently done, nothing that cannot be paid for, and I have undertaken to indemnify all the injured parties. You may reimburse me if you wish to, after you are safely home in Los Angeles, but I am glad to be of such service to one who has so brightened my days here."

"Thank you, Raoul," Prudence said, her voice choked and thickened with her gratitude and regret.

"I am pleased to be of service," said LeCourt. "But other damage has been done, that I cannot undo, and you cannot undo it either. The villagers now think you are demon-possessed or possibly a witch, certainly the focal point of a curse out of their legends. We must get you back to Porto Escuro without any of them knowing or suspecting your presence. Your life depends on this."

She nodded, wide-eyed, a nameless dread stirring in her chest just beneath her heart.

"Prudence," LeCourt continued, "it pains me to see you like this. I cannot stand it. I want to take that straitjacket off you. But if I do, you must promise me that you will not try to escape. All the village fears you, and if you were to escape, and be seen by one of them, he would probably try to kill you. I do not know if I could stand it if you were killed, Prudence. Can I trust you? Will you give to me your promise?"

Prudence nodded, a tear sliding silently down her cheek from one of her fright-widened eyes.

Raoul stepped over to her side and, approaching Prudence, lifted her gently to her feet. Then he untied the long sleeves of the garment and she wriggled out of it with a combination of relief, revulsion, and half-suppressed panic. She let the straitjacket fall to the floor, as if afraid to touch it voluntarily, and moved as far away from it as she could.

Raoul watched her with something like nervousness for a moment; then his features melted into a gentle smile. "I see that I can indeed trust you," he murmured. "I am very glad."

"What happens to me now?" asked Prudence, in a tiny voice.

"You must remain here today, *chérie*," said Raoul. "I have made arrangements for you to go to Porto Escuro tonight, after everyone in the village is asleep. The villagers say that you are demon-possessed, and I fear that one of them might try to kill you, even while you are under my protection, if he saw you. So, we will take you down to the quay after midnight tonight. Meanwhile, we wait here, and I will make you as comfortable as I can.

"When you arrive at Porto Escuro, I have arranged for one of the staff psychiatrists at the Sisters of the Sacred Heart Charitable Hospital to tend to you. You will spend a week, perhaps two, in their nerve-calming gardens and spas, until Dr. Ruis determines that you are all better. After that, it would be best if you were to return to the United States."

"I — I can't ever return here, can I?" Prudence said.

"No," said Raoul. "They think you are a witch. I will give you my delivery address here in Carraçao, and ask that you will send to me a letter when you are returned to Los Angeles, and upon receiving it I will send to you your camera gear and film."

"Thank you, Raoul," Prudence whispered.

For answer Raoul took the shivering Prudence in his arms, held her close and kissed her tenderly upon the lips again. It was not a welcome move. Deeply and subtly terrified, Prudence was in no mood for romance. But she was acutely aware that Raoul was her only friend, now that she had forfeited the acceptance of the village.

Like most outsiders, Prudence had lived her whole life with the full knowledge that the love of others was always conditional. No matter how firmly she might appear to be a part of a community or family that had adopted her, there would always be a line she could cross that would cause them to reject her, to spit her out, to draw a line with her in the cold outside and themselves safe within.

It was not much of a leap for her to become convinced that she had crossed that line with this new community, which had the previous day seemed so warm and welcoming. And now her only friends were Eleanor, who was missing — and Raoul, who was gently pressing his lips onto hers and — oh, how she didn't want to do this, but if she rejected him, would he —?

She tried to make herself relax into his kiss. He was a good kisser. She remembered how dreamy he had been a few days earlier, on the porch of the Martins house — but then she hadn't been terrified.

Remembering that kiss helped, and she felt herself starting to soften a little in spite of the terror. But then his hand started moving up the small of her back, as if he might be preparing to undress her, and that she could not allow. Reluctantly, she pushed gently away from him.

"Oh, Raoul," she murmured. "I'm so sorry. I'm just so frightened. It's all just so awful. May I at least have a chair to sit in, and a book to read? It will be such a long day, hiding out in this padded room doing nothing."

Raoul said that she might, and smiled sympathetically at her and withdrew. And was it her imagination, in the dim light, or did he look a little hurt?

The chair, which he soon brought, was a small and rickety one, but better than nothing; and he brought three books: a copy of Joseph Conrad's *Heart of Darkness*, a tattered collection of the tragedies of William Shakespeare, and a three-year-old copy of *Weird Tales* magazine. But it was still too dark to read, so she sat there in her chair, leaning against the padded wall, and wished her headache would subside.

She yearned to escape, to run, to be gone from this place. Had she really done what Raoul said she had done? How could she have? It seemed so out of character for her, even if she had been out of her mind, to do something like that: trash a bar, owned by a stranger whom she did not even know, for no reason at all? And call down curses on a village full of people who had been fast becoming her friends?

She racked her brain afresh, wincing as the effort brought back the throbbing headache, which had almost subsided. The last thing she remembered was drinking a toast to Eleanor's return. They'd been in that bar in the Indian town, the one she'd trashed. She'd been drunk — surprisingly drunk; the local fruit wine was clearly heady stuff, as Raoul had warned her; she couldn't really even remember how many glasses of it she'd had. She recalled chatting amiably about something (what had it been? Something about Eleanor) and Raoul smiling benignly at her as she babbled. It was probably her dream. That had to be it.

A voice cut through her thoughts, so clear and crisp that it almost sounded real: "Remember," it purred. "Trust no one."

"Eleanor!" she gasped. "Eleanor . . ."

She rose and started pacing the floor, still wondering what she had done and what she should do. In her thoughts she clung to Raoul as the only person she knew, the only person she could talk to. But at the same time, she had never felt so isolated and alone. She thought achingly of Camila and Ana and Amanda and — who was the other? Gabriela, that was her name. Now she would never get to join them at Ana's house for bridge. She wondered briefly if she would ever see them again, then realized that of course she would not; they all thought her a witch.

That felt a little funny. None of the ladies she'd met, who had invited her over for bridge, seemed like the type to believe in witchy nonsense. Even old Kylla, and Old Man Paulo — elderly representatives of an earlier time in the Amazon — seemed more levelheaded than that. Could they really be as stereotypically superstitious as that?

Apparently they could.

Prudence sat there, imprisoned in the padded room, as the day dragged on, its monotony relieved only twice when Raoul brought in meals and ate with her, seated on the floor. She tried to sleep on the stiff padding that served for a bed, but it was too uncomfortable and her mind would not stop racing. She tried to while away the time reading the magazine Raoul had left for her, but she started with a story called "The Rats in the Walls," and the it did not improve her mood. She picked up *Heart of Darkness* — she had already read it, many years before, but sometimes a re-read can be a comfort. She quickly realized such would not be the case with *Heart of Darkness*. With its alien Congo jungle and its deadly river and its mad, malarial character Kurtz, it was just too close to her present circumstances. She ended up with the Shakespeare in her lap, re-reading *Julius Caesar*.

Finally, as darkness started to gather in her little padded room, she laid the book down and simply sat there in the chair, gazing at the door, waiting for it to open.

Hours later, it finally did. Raoul entered, followed by a burly villager whom she recognized as Marco Morais, the taciturn man who seemed to be Raoul's regular sidekick.

Morais' eyes flashed angrily when he saw her, and she wondered why. Then he pushed past LeCourt, almost rudely, and snatched the straitjacket up off the floor, where it had lain since she'd cast it off the day before. He looked at Raoul.

"How did she get out of this?" he demanded.

"It is all right, Marco," Raoul said soothingly. "She can be trusted, as you see. I allowed her to be out of the strait-jacket while she was in our room here. If she had escaped or damaged your property in any way, you know I would have reimbursed you for it."

Morais looked only slightly mollified. He tossed the garment disdainfully at Prudence's feet, and his hostile eyes met hers again. "Put it on," he said.

His voice was curt and commanding, the voice one might use if talking to a dog. Prudence felt a hot flush of anger, and opened her mouth to speak; but before she could do so, Raoul took the floor.

"Marco!" he said, more sharply than she had yet heard him speak. "*Mademoiselle* McMarion is ill. It is rude and churlish of you to speak like that to her. Should she damage your property after you provoke her so, I should certainly refuse to reimburse you."

He turned to Prudence. "But I am very much afraid you must put it back on, dear," he continued, in his usual tone of smooth kindliness. "Just for the journey. If one of the villagers were to see you unrestrained...."

Prudence shuddered. Then she shuddered again as she picked up the horrid thing and wriggled into it. She turned her back so that LeCourt could tie off the sleeves for her.

Morais stood beside him and stared sullenly.

Then they left the little madhouse-cabin and made their way down to the quay in the dark, and although no villagers were around to see her, Prudence nonetheless felt silent tears of humiliation streaming down her cheeks. She felt like a criminal being paraded through the streets to the jailhouse.

All was still and dark in the riverside town, but down by the quay she saw light and activity on the *Amazon Princess*. As they approached, she could hear its steam engine hissing quietly, and the crackle of wood burning in the firebox.

Their footfalls on the wooden dock brought Captain Bancroft out, and he stepped off his boat to meet them. When his eyes met Prudence's, they widened in surprise, and dropped down from her face to take in the straitjacket; when he brought them back up to meet hers again, they were narrowed and suspicious, under a deeply furrowed brow. Then he turned to LeCourt.

"What the hell is this?" he growled.

LeCourt merely favored him with an icy smile, then turned to Prudence.

"Now, Prudence darling, do be careful," he told her. "If you should fall in the river while wearing that straitjacket, we should have great difficulty finding you in time, and you could never swim."

He turned to Bancroft, who now was standing there with arms akimbo. "And *Monsieur* Bancroft," he said, "I have this letter for to be delivered with her to the Sisters of the Sacred Heart. It is sealed; it is confidential and important. Deliver it only into the hands of Dr. Ruis, the director of the facility there."

Bancroft mechanically reached out and took the envelope. Prudence could see his jaw working, and his eyes were narrow slits.

"Also please to understand that it is very important that the straitjacket only be removed by the medical professional who will be helping *Mademoiselle* McMarion at Porto Escuro. Please not to allow her to remove it during the journey to —"

"Well, you're welcome to make your own arrangements to transport your prisoner, then," Bancroft interrupted curtly. "Nobody steps aboard my boat wearing a straitjacket."

"She has to wear the straitjacket," Morais said, speaking directly to Raoul in a decisive, commanding voice.

Raoul nodded, then turned to Rick. "I'm afraid that I must insist that —" he started, but his words trailed off as Bancroft turned his back on him and stepped back on board the boat.

"*Monsieur* Bancroft? *Monsieur* Bancroft!" he called, with rising volume and obvious frustration. Bancroft paid no attention. He disappeared into the pilothouse and a moment later they heard a loud, hissing blast as he released the steam pressure from the boiler. Then he blew out the candle in the pilothouse and stepped back on the deck and glared down at the two men on the dock.

"Get the hell out of here," he growled. "Nobody tells me what to do on my boat. You want somebody to haul Miss McMarion to Porto Escuro in a straitjacket, you're talking to the wrong man. Meanwhile, it's the middle of the goddamn night and I want to get some sleep. Good luck figuring it out."

"But we have a deal," said Morais.

"Yes," said LeCourt. "I am prepared to hold you to the deal we made."

"Our deal does not involve you dictating dress code on my boat." Bancroft was actually snarling now. "You dirty

bastards are about three words away from getting permanently blackballed. Then you'll have to get your own
goddamn boat and drive yourself around on it, LeCourt,
or get that cheap musclehead of yours" — he jabbed a finger
at Morais — "to do it for you. When you do, you won't find
me trying to tell you how to run it or what your passengers
are allowed to wear."

Even by the faint light of the deck lamp, Prudence
could see LeCourt turning scarlet. He opened his mouth,
but at that very instant, something deep inside her seemed
to click, and she suddenly felt it was incredibly important
that she get on Bancroft's boat immediately. Adrenaline
tingled in her limbs as she gulped in air, racing to speak
before LeCourt could make his reply.

"It's OK, Captain Bancroft," she said. "I will wear the
straitjacket."

Or, rather, that's what she tried to say. What actually
came out of her mouth — it almost felt as if her mouth had
been hijacked by some deep, cryptic level of her subconscious
mind — was this:

"Oh, Raoul! I gave you my word that I would not try
to escape. Do you not trust me to keep my word?"

In the momentary silence that followed this outburst,
Prudence wondered where it had come from. It hadn't
occurred to her to say such a thing until she actually was
hearing herself say it.

Whatever deep pocket of her subconscious had
produced it, though, had clearly been on the ball. As soon
as it was said, she could see that it was the perfect thing to
say. LeCourt gasped as if punched.

"I — but — er —" he stammered. "I mean — I guess it
would be all right for her to not wear the straitjacket. If
you insist. I — that is — the hospital psychologist —"

"Good," grunted Bancroft, curtly cutting off the stream of stammered attempts to qualify the permission. "Take that thing off and let her climb aboard, and then pay up."

Raoul untied the straitjacket with noticeable reluctance. The faint alarm bells that had started ringing in Prudence's head when she first realized that Raoul proposed to leave the straitjacket on her for the voyage had been growing progressively louder. She wriggled free of it with the same sense of dread and revulsion as previously, and left it where it lay on the dock, stepping around it like the corpse of a venomous snake.

The *Amazon Princess* was her sanctuary. If she could get both feet on board that boat, she would be OK. If she were stopped short of that goal, if even one foot remained on the dock this night, she was forever lost. She knew this as surely as she knew her own name, yet she had no idea why, or how, or what "forever lost" might mean. She only knew that everything depended on getting aboard that boat. And she had to do it before Marco Morais figured out how to prevent her from doing so. Already she could see that he was opening his mouth to say something.

"Step aboard now, miss," Bancroft was saying. "Right foot first. Get out of the way, there, gunsel."

This last was addressed to Morais, who had stepped past LeCourt to position himself between Prudence and the gangway. He leaned over, picked up the straitjacket again, and stood there looking at her, obviously preparing to intercept her when she tried to board.

So she leaped like a gazelle over the boat's rail, just as she'd seen young Alberto Ribeiro do the previous week when he was running from the angry captain of the *Swathmore*, coming down with a heavy thump on the deck of the boat beside the cabin. And the moment her feet touched the deck, she felt such a flood of relief suffuse her body that she staggered and dropped to one knee. Tears of relief started from her eyes.

"Get back out here," Morais was shouting after her. "I'm going to take you to Porto Escuro myself."

Ignoring Morais completely, Bancroft stepped up to her side and helped her to her feet. "Make yourself comfortable," he said, helping her to a seat on the observation deck. Then he turned to face the two men on the dock. "LeCourt, pay up."

"I think we are going to make a different arrangement, thank you, *Monsieur* Bancroft," said LeCourt coldly. "Prudence darling, please to come back onto the dock now."

"We have ze deel," Bancroft sneered in a fake French accent. "I am prepared to 'old you to our deel."

LeCourt looked uncertain. Morais looked furious. Bancroft grinned at them.

"I tell you what," he said then. "I've never done this before, but I'll let you pay me when I get back. Of course, I know you will pay me, since until you do, my services will be unavailable to you. We'll be casting off now."

"No you won't," grunted Morais. "LeCourt, give him his money. We're canceling the voyage and paying you in full." He turned his face toward Prudence. "Get off that boat. Now."

There was a moment of silence. Then Bancroft spoke, very slowly and deliberately.

"I don't know you very well, Morais," he said. "But I don't like you. You bring this woman to me trussed up like a chicken, and when I insist that she be untrussed, for some reason that's a deal breaker for you. Not only a deal breaker, but you're willing to forfeit six hundred *reais* to walk away with nothing. In my book, that's suspicious behavior."

He was silent for a moment. Then he turned to Prudence. "What's your pleasure, sweetheart?" he said, with what seemed to Prudence like deliberate harshness. "You staying on board, or going back on shore?"

Prudence just looked at him. He must have seen the terror in her eyes, because his own softened considerably and he flashed her the ghost of a reassuring smile.

She tried to say, "I want to stay on your boat with you," but all she could manage were a few gasps that sounded like sobs. For an answer, she was reduced to hand signals — pointing to the deck of the *Amazon Princess*.

Bancroft nodded once, then turned to the two on the dock. "You heard — er, you saw the lady," he said. "She doesn't want to come ashore."

"I'll go with her, then," said Morais.

"The hell you will," said Bancroft.

"Marco," said LeCourt. "Stop. Why are you doing this?"

He turned to Bancroft. "I wish to pay you now," he said. "I do not like to be owing money to someone. It is all right, Marco, do not make a scene, you will wake the entire village."

This last was directed at Morais, who had stepped toward the deck of the boat as if intending to board it and seize Prudence by main force. Morais stepped back, visibly seething. Bancroft, who had stepped toward him with fists knotted and forearms bulging as he did so, stepped back and relaxed a little.

"Marco, please to give Captain Bancroft the straitjacket," said LeCourt. He sounded, to Prudence, as if he were trying to restore the illusion that he was in a position of authority over Morais. "She will need to have it on when you deliver her at the hospital."

"Good to know," grunted Bancroft as Morais threw

the hateful thing onto the afterdeck.

Prudence moved around the observation deck to put as much space between herself and the two men on the dock as she could. The thing that had started stirring in the back of her mind when she learned about the straitjacket was coalescing slowly into something dark and suspicious, centered around Raoul LeCourt. Somehow, Marco Morais' sudden and sinister assertiveness had changed everything. Was he really an assistant, or was he actually in charge? Did he have something to do with Eleanor's disappearance? Why was it so important to him that she be in a strait-jacket — so important that he had tried to cancel the voyage over it?

Bancroft, meanwhile, had cast off the lines and given the dock a shove, and the *Amazon Princess* was drifting away from the quay. "Thank you for your business, LeCourt," he said, in a coldly businesslike tone. "See you again someday."

And with a curt nod to Morais, who merely stared stonily back at him, Bancroft moved to the pilothouse, and Prudence heard the hiss of steam as the riverboat began to move — very slowly, for the boiler pressure was still low — out away from the quay and into the black, tranquil river.

X.

THE DELIVERANCE.

The light of morning awakened Prudence and she sat up with a start. Bancroft had left her there, slouched on the surprisingly comfortable throw-cushions of the settee. She looked around and saw that the little riverboat was anchored in the middle of a broad, flat expanse of river; the shore was a good half mile away on either side. She must have fallen asleep before Bancroft had anchored, because the last thing she could remember was the little riverboat plunging forward into a primordial darkness that seemed to swallow up the light of the boat's carbide lamps. She figured Bancroft must have just gone far enough downstream to be away from Carraçao before weighing anchor for the rest of the night.

She caught a whiff of coffee and knew that her taciturn companion was already up and about. Swinging her legs down onto the deck, she stood up and stretched, filling her lungs with clean air. She felt as if she'd just awakened from a days-long dream. Of the events that had transpired since she and Raoul had sat down in that strangely modern restaurant in the Indian village of Katakuona, her memory had a syrupy, torpid quality, like memories of a bad dream. She reflected back on them. What was it that made them seem so wrong, so unnatural, so — so evil?

Her thoughts turned to the captain, Mr. Bancroft. Although she had been profoundly unimpressed by him right from the beginning, she had a real sense now that he had rescued her, even if he had only done it for the money. Even now, far away from the scene and with a new day dawning, there was no doubt in her mind that he had saved her life. She no longer knew what to think of Raoul LeCourt, but his sidekick, Marco Morais, seemed positively sinister. And Morais had been almost desperate to get her off Bancroft's boat once she'd gotten on — so much so that he'd been willing to fork over the full fare for nothing.

That was interesting. If Bancroft were really as mercenary as he seemed, would he not have simply kicked her off the boat, collected his money and gone back to sleep? But instead, he had insisted on delivering her as per the original deal. Perhaps he wasn't quite as mercenary as she had thought.

He'd been happy to collect the six hundred *reais*, though.

There was a sharp hissing sound from the front of the boat, and she heard machinery turning deep beneath her feet. They were getting under way, she realized. So she stood up and made her way to the bows, where the pilothouse was.

Stepping inside, she found Bancroft there before the pilothouse window, hand on the wheel, puffing meditatively on one of his massive, nasty black cigars.

"Morning," he grunted, when he saw her approach. Taking the cigar out of his mouth, he carefully removed the glowing ember with his folding pocketknife, blew through it to clear out all the smoke, and set it down in the ashtray.

"Good morning," she said, then paused, unsure of what she wanted to say.

"Feeling a little better?" he said. "You were in rough shape last night."

"Yes, and yes," she said. "Much better. But I'm still so confused about — so many things."

"You and me both, sister," said Bancroft. "You hungry?"

"Ravenous," she said. "But mostly thirsty. Thirsty, and I've had this throbbing headache for days now. I don't know what it could be. It started in that restaurant with Ra — with Dr. LeCourt, and just never stopped."

Bancroft looked sideways at her, a cryptic, quizzical sort of glance that made her feel like she was being judged. But it lasted only for a moment. Then he turned and stared straight ahead at the river, lips pursed, apparently lost in thought.

Then he turned to face her again.

"I can't leave the steering station in this part of the river," he said. "We'll be stopping to nosebag in a few hours — I eat my lunch early — but if you want to grab something to tide yourself over, the galley is through that door. Make yourself at home."

That seemed uncharacteristically generous of Bancroft, she thought. Then she remembered the six hundred *reais* and realized he was being well compensated for this trip.

She nodded her thanks, then climbed through the companionway hatch into the galley. There, she found a tap from the water tank, and drank cup after cup of clear water. Then she found a box of pilot-bread crackers and took two pieces, and climbed back up into the pilothouse with them.

"All set?" Bancroft said. "Two hunks of hardtack? Is that all you want? There's some tinned meat in there too. And cheese, and real bread. Help yourself."

"This will do until lunch, thank you, Captain," she said. "You can light your cigar again if you like. I don't mind the smoke. But you were very kind to put it out for me."

Bancroft grunted, a guttural noise that somehow sounded appreciative, and reached for his cigar again.

"Don't let it get around," he said, with a small, wry smile. "You'll ruin my reputation if you tell anybody."

"That you did something considerate?" she shot back, flashing him an answering smile that was not unmixed with relief. "Don't worry, your secret is safe with me."

She wanted to thank him, to tell him that she probably owed him her life, but she thought it would just sound ridiculous. So she stepped out of the cabin and made her way back to the afterdeck.

It was about three hours later that Bancroft tied the riverboat off to a small, primitive dock that seemed to have been built on rickety pilings in the middle of nowhere. It stretched out into the river, and at its other end lay a small footpath that led off into the forest.

Bancroft tied the boat off at the very end of the dock and disappeared into the galley. When he reappeared, he was carrying two cans of tinned beef, a half loaf of stale-looking bread and a box of hardtack. Then he excused himself and trotted up the dock and disappeared into the forest.

He reappeared about five minutes later with an armload of fruits of various types. "The Jaragua tribe keep a little garden here," he said, in response to her look of surprise. "It's not a trading relationship, we just do nice things for each other whenever we can. So they don't mind me raiding their garden once in a while, as long as I don't put too big a dent in their stocks."

Prudence selected one of the fruits and bit into it. It was delicious. Juice running down her chin, she said, "Why don't they serve these at Marcello's?"

"Marcello has no idea those even exist," said Bancroft. "I don't even know what they're called. But they sure are good. It pays to know the right people. Try these, too. *Cupuaçu*, they call them."

The two of them ate in silence for a little while. It was a silence that grew steadily less awkward and more companionable, until Prudence forgot herself enough to start making small talk.

"So," she said, "am I the only cargo on this entire voyage? And what are you going to do with me?"

"Yes," said Bancroft, sounding a little uncomfortable and maybe defensive for the first time. "LeCourt paid me for the entire voyage down the river just to deliver you to Porto Escuro. Apparently you are then going to be delivered into the care of the sisters who run the asylum there. Funny, you never struck me as the least bit loony, but LeCourt says you're nuts."

"Asylum? Loony? What?" said Prudence. "You're — you're joking, right?"

"Nope. Oh, he didn't say it in those words. But that was the basic gist. He said this patient — who turned out to be you — seemed perfectly normal, but then would suddenly snap. He was really eager to get you out of Carraçao right away. Woke me up and offered me six hundred *reais* for the trip, as you know. No cargo, just you. It seemed a little odd, but you know me, I'd never turn down that kind of dough."

"But you did turn it down, when I showed up in a straitjacket."

Bancroft laughed. "Oh, no, I didn't," he said. "I wasn't going to give him a refund. He'd either pay the money and abide by the rules of the ship, or pay the money and not get anything for it. We already had a deal; I got paid either way."

Prudence stared at her toes. Something about this didn't make sense. Actually, none of it did.

Bancroft looked at her and nodded. "It's weird, isn't it?" he said. "You're only one woman. How dangerous can you be? Why wouldn't he just wait for the next regularly scheduled run down the river? You paid me for a round trip; it would be totally free. Instead, he digs deep and gets you on a special run, just you and me. And then he makes that huge fuss about wanting you in a straitjacket. I'm gonna be honest with you, Miss McMarion, I don't understand it. And I don't much like it, either.

"You know what bothers me the most?" he continued. "The straitjacket. I can't understand that. How big of a threat can one woman be, that she needs to be straitjacketed for the entire trip? And it's only when I made it clear that you weren't going to be wearing that thing on my boat that he started trying to back out."

"He told me it was for show," said Prudence. "That if anyone from the village saw me unrestrained, they would…."

She trailed off, choking back an unexpected sob.

"Would what?" said Bancroft. "String LeCourt up by his thumbs for treating you that way? You bet they would.

You've made a pretty good impression on Carraçao, Miss McMarion. They like you a lot more than they like Raoul LeCourt."

"But he said — Raoul said — Dr. LeCourt said they thought I was a witch."

Bancroft's staccato laugh pealed out over the water like a distant burst of gunfire. Then he grinned at her, a real open friendly smile, the first time she'd seen anything like it on his face. "Forgive me," he said. "I shouldn't laugh at you. But it's the 1920s, Miss McMarion. There's no devil-witchy-shrunky-heady witchdoctor juju in Carraçao."

"But — well, Raoul said I went into some kind of crazy spell and called down some kind of curse on Carraçao and trashed a bar and clobbered the bartender with a chair," she said. "And he said he was sending me to Porto Escuro to get help. To get better. But to tell the truth, I don't remember any of those things. I remember having a sort of breakdown at Marcello's, and it was embarrassing, but it didn't seem like it was that big a deal, not big enough to have to sneak out of town wearing a straitjacket. I just don't understand it."

"Well, if there was a reason to have you snuck out of town in the middle of the night wearing a straitjacket, I don't know what it could have been," said Bancroft. "It sure wasn't for *your* protection from the villagers. More likely it was for LeCourt's. They like you, Miss McMarion. They were actually worried about you, they still are. You had that outburst in the restaurant and then you disappeared. Your friend Camila was really worried, came to me to ask for help finding you. She had no idea you were in LeCourt's — in his care. They thought maybe you'd gone off after your friend and a caiman got you or a school of piranhas. I really should have stayed in town long enough to let her —"

He broke off suddenly, an odd look of guilty worry crossing his face. Prudence didn't notice. She was looking at her toes, a sinister unease stirring in the back of her mind.

"Then Raoul really was lying to me," she murmured. "He really did — was —"

She was stopped by a thought that suffused her with horror. It was the recollection of Raoul's hand, reaching up from the small of her back as he kissed her, in an obvious prelude to undressing her. She had never been so grateful to have resisted a man's advances as she was in that moment.

Bancroft was looking at his toes. The guilty look had modulated into a look of focused, concentrated worry, like that of a man on the horns of a dire moral dilemma wondering what to do. Then he shook himself briefly and shrugged.

"Well, it's none of my business anyway," he grunted, reaching for the water jug.

Prudence, who had actually started to warm up to the taciturn riverman, felt her lips tighten as she turned away from him.

Still, she reminded herself, he had saved her life. Somehow she was convinced of this. She had no idea how she knew it, but she did. If she had been thirty seconds later getting onto Bancroft's boat, or if he had been just a little less firm in his response to that horrible thug Marco ....

B ancroft lingered for a while at the little dock in the middle of nowhere, relaxing in the pilothouse with the rest of his massive stogie.

"I usually leave first thing in the morning, rather than in the middle of the night," he explained, as he applied a match to the inch-thick cylinder of evil-smelling black tobacco. "So we're a little ahead of schedule. We'll be getting to our nighttime anchorage around seven o'clock tonight, I guess."

Prudence tried to stick it out, clinging to the companionship even though Bancroft had become taciturn almost to the point of rudeness, and seemed almost to be actively trying to encourage her to leave; but eventually the smell of the horrible cigar drove her out into the fresh air of the observation deck.

She was out there when, with a shudder and a sigh and a hiss of steam, the little riverboat got under way once again. Bancroft had to come out of his pilothouse to cast loose from the dock, but he barely even looked in her direction. His face was clouded and troubled; he looked like a man lost in thought, and rapidly reaching a conclusion that he did not like. It wasn't an unfriendly look, merely preoccupied; but its main aspect was that of a scowl. She opted to stay out of his way and avoid speaking to him.

But then, just as he was making his way back toward the cabin, she caught a flash of movement from the shore — at the end of the dock.

She peered at the riverbank, wanting to be sure. She saw nothing further. Yet suddenly she couldn't shake the feeling that eyes were upon her.

She hurried to the pilothouse to ask Bancroft about it.

"Oh, sure," he said in reply, jetting another dank cloud of black foulness into the well-polluted air of the wheelhouse. "That would be the Jaragua. They like to keep an eye on the river. Don't worry, I get along very well with them. We won't be bothered."

She exited the cabin and went back toward the observation deck. Just then the sun, shining down on the foliage at the end of the dock, flashed on the surface of something convex and made of glass. She paused for a moment, peering intently at the foliage again.

She still couldn't see anything.

But she would have given a great deal to know if the Jaragua tribesmen used binoculars.

XI.

THE REMEMBERING.

The rest of the day unrolled lazily, but Prudence found it very boring and lonely out on the back deck beneath the broad sunshade. And every time she entered the wheelhouse, Bancroft would look up from what appeared to be deep thought, and pull out one of those horrid, foul black cigars. So she spent most of the day by herself, meditating on the beauty of the Amazon and wishing sadly and occasionally desperately that Eleanor were there to enjoy it with her.

They anchored for the night at another broad part of the river. Captain Bancroft was, if anything, even more taciturn than before, limiting his conversation to the bare minimum and hurrying off to the wheelhouse as soon as he was finished eating. Prudence was left, bored and lonely, to wander back to the observation deck and sit there in the dark. The softly stirring air occasionally brought a whiff of Bancroft's foul black cigars to her nostrils.

Finally, she slipped into her cabin and climbed into her bunk to sleep.

The next day dawned crisp and beautiful. Prudence opened her eyes and realized that, for the first time in years, she actually did not want to get out of bed. The day stretched out before her, looking not like a vast smorgasbord of possibility as it usually did, but like a vast wasteland of dullness and loneliness. She would sit by herself on the observation deck. She would nibble at pilot bread. Was there still any fruit? That could give her something to look forward to, at least.

She heard and felt the boat getting under way. Either she had slept unusually late, or Bancroft was starting unusually early. Maybe both.

Finally she climbed out of her bunk and pulled on her clothes — the same brick-red skirt, white blouse and black stockings she'd been wearing since the morning of her fateful automobile ride with LeCourt — and stumbled out onto the deck and around to the wheelhouse.

Standing behind the wheel, Bancroft grunted a greeting and nodded at the door to the galley. Then he turned his attention back on the river, ignoring her completely. She entered the galley and got out a handful of pilot biscuits and filled a tin cup with water.

Bancroft poked his head in the door. "I'm making coffee," he told her curtly. "Want some?"

"Oh, yes, please," she said.

He grunted again and withdrew.

Prudence gnawed on a pilot biscuit and considered. Bancroft seemed like he was being deliberately distant, like he was actively trying to push her away. Why would he do that? He'd been companionable enough on the first day, as they were getting under way at least. But now, he seemed to be carefully avoiding contact with her.

The coffee, when he brought it, was strong and black and scalding, and just what she wanted. She smiled gratefully at him as she accepted the cup, but he would not meet her eye. He grunted an acknowledgement of her thanks, and withdrew to his steering station so quickly that she wondered for a moment if she smelled bad or something. She quickly dismissed the thought; nobody who smoked as many cigars as Bancroft could possibly have a working sense of smell. But it was odd, and demoralizing. And Prudence was pretty thoroughly demoralized to begin with.

By lunchtime she was convinced he was actively avoiding her. He didn't call her for lunch; she simply noticed that it was about noon and came forward to ask about it, and found him in the wheelhouse, in a cloud of dank gray smoke, gnawing on some pilot biscuits. He didn't even look at her, just stared out the front window. Feeling uncomfortably like an intruder, she slipped into the galley, grabbed a handful of the hardtack biscuits that she was rapidly coming to hate, and returned to her post on the observation deck.

The scenery slid by, magnificent as always, as a growing dread started to coalesce inside her. She didn't know why, but somehow she just knew that this silent treatment she was getting from Bancroft was ominous. It was like the attitude she imagined a prison guard must have toward an inmate condemned to death—there was a sense that he did not want to get to know her too well because he knew something she did not—something bad.

That night, she decided, she would give her best effort at breaking through that icy defense. He would have to sit down with her for supper. He couldn't just eat it on his feet while steering; it would be dark.

The day dragged on, seeming to last a dreary eternity. Finally, the little riverboat came around a bend in the river and arrived at another one of those little docks in the middle of nowhere. This one was even longer than the other had been, stretching a good three hundred feet out into the river, and it was in considerably worse shape.

Bancroft came out of the wheelhouse to tie the boat off, and looked impressed when Prudence stepped up to help.

"Hey, thanks," he said, seemingly in spite of himself.

"For what?" Prudence replied. If she could just force him to converse with her, she thought, maybe she could break through....

"Well, I'm not used to high-class passengers being willing to lend a hand," he said.

This was a good start; it was more words than he had spoken to her all day. She smiled, and clumsily tied the stern line off with a large, sloppy "granny knot." Stepping up behind her, he quickly retied it. She noticed this as she was moving toward the bow.

"Did I not tie the knot right?" she asked.

"It's OK," Bancroft said. "Everything's jake now."

"But I want to know how to do it right. Can you show me?"

She saw the reluctance in his eyes, but he nodded curtly. "Sure," he said, and, walking to the other cleat, took the dock line and wrapped it around it.

"Twice around, and then you make a loop, see? And pull tight."

"Can I try?"

"Sure."

She untied the line, then wrapped and looped and pulled.

"That's perfect," said Bancroft. "You look like an old mariner. I mean — oh, great cat, that did not come out right. I mean — "

Prudence laughed, for the first time in days. It started out as a chuckle, then snowballed until she was doubled over, howling with mirth. Bancroft was laughing, too, but a little tentatively.

"I knew what you meant," she assured him when she was sufficiently recovered to speak. "And thank you — for the compliment you intended it to be, not the insult it accidentally sounded like."

Bancroft was still smiling a little. "That really was a boner, wasn't it?" he said.

Prudence stepped back onto the boat. The ice seemed to have been broken. But if it were to stay that way, she'd have to keep the conversation moving. And if he clammed back up, she'd never be able to figure out why he was being so ominously taciturn.

"Why are these docks all so long?" she asked. "It seems like it would be better to be close to shore."

"No," said Bancroft. "It's for security. Very few dangerous animals will go more than a few dozen feet out on a floating dock. But this one in particular is extra long because there's a road that passes within about five hundred feet of it, over that way — a dirt road, barely more than a walking path, but they sometimes bring wagons with supplies on it. So there's always a greater danger of bandits and such. I sleep a lot better at night knowing I'm a hundred meters offshore."

"Who maintains the docks?" asked Prudence.

"Oh, I do," said Bancroft. "It's not that hard. The dock is in sections, floating on old oil drums. It's anchored out at the end on a piling that I had sunk in the river by a friend from Manaus who owed me a favor."

"And there's a road nearby," Prudence remarked innocently. "That sounds like it would be convenient for certain kinds of freight."

Bancroft looked at her, a sharp look that quickly moderated into an amused smile.

"Miss McMarion," he said, "I think we're going to get along just fine. Now, let's have a bite to eat."

Dinner aboard the *Amazon Princess* was the same dull fare as lunch had been — stale hardtack and canned beef. But Bancroft also brought out a bottle of red wine, and she gratefully accepted a large tin cup full of it. Bancroft happily decanted the rest of the bottle into his own mammoth tin cup and they sat down to eat.

Over dinner, Prudence was relieved to find that the dam had burst; the ice had broken. In fact, she was a little surprised at his loquaciousness. He had spent the entire day, and most of the day before, avoiding her presence — driving her out of the wheelhouse with monosyllabic conversation and great gray clouds of evil-smelling cigar smoke. Now, with a veritable lagoon of red wine in his hand and no work to do, he seemed to relax into an almost amiable sociability.

"So, what brought you to this backwoods ritzburg in the first place?" he asked, looking at her curiously.

She glanced up from her beef, which she was eating with a fork straight from the tin. "Making a movie," she said.

"Well, yes, I knew you were making a movie. But why here?"

"It was Eleanor's idea," she replied. "She'd always wanted to come back here and make a movie about Carraçao. She loved — I mean, she loves this place."

"Mmm. What's your movie about?"

Prudence told Bancroft the plot of the movie they'd been shooting: about Steve Cordite, and the treasure map, and the cursed gold and the thieves who were eaten by caimans after overloading the boat, and the tragic death of Maya followed by Steve's repudiation of the treasure. He listened in appreciative silence.

"Wow," he said. "A real rock-'em-sock-'em adventure story. I'd like to see it if it ever gets made."

"Well, I guess it won't be, now," she said gloomily. "I've been chased out of town on a rail. Who knows how long this psychologist, this Dr. Ruis, will detain me. Anyway, whether it's a day or a week, either way I guess I can't ever go back to Carraçao."

Bancroft suddenly looked very uncomfortable. He opened his mouth to say something, changed his mind and closed it again. Then he looked around as if groping for something to change the subject to, and finally stared out the window at something across the river in the trees. Then he started gathering himself as if preparing to leave the table.

"Plus," Prudence continued, not noticing Bancroft's odd behavior, "Eleanor was the producer. She was financing everything. I don't have the resources to make this movie on my own."

"That's interesting," Bancroft mumbled distractedly, still staring at the bushes by the end of the dock. Then he looked at his wine cup, still half full. Then he took a big drink, settled back down in his chair, turned, and looked at her again.

She would later learn that this moment was the closest he came that night to walking away. Had it not been for the wine still remaining in his cup, he would have stood up and, murmuring an apology, excused himself and returned to the pilothouse and to his monosyllabic taciturnity — and thereby sealed her doom. But getting up from a table and leaving a conversation with his wine half finished, or taking it with him, would have been too rude even for Bancroft; so he stayed.

Instead he took another big drink of the wine, to hasten the moment when he could make a graceful exit; and he tried to change the subject. "Is this the first movie you've made?" he asked.

"Yes," said Prudence, who for the time being remained blissfully unaware of all of this internal drama. "My first independently produced feature film. And I wrote the photoplay myself."

"Photoplay?"

"Yes, the story, the script. It's called a photoplay. Like a stageplay for a movie camera."

"You just one day decided you were going to buy a bunch of cameras and go into the movie business?" said Bancroft.

"Not exactly," said Prudence with a little laugh. "First off, I work for a small studio, so I know what I'm doing. Eleanor and I had agreed to cut my boss in on the project in exchange for him helping us with distribution, so there's that. But me, I come from a long line of show-biz people. My parents were Vaudeville performers. They met in Dawson City, up in the Yukon, during the Gold Rush in 1899."

"Well," said Bancroft, "that's before my time, but I've heard plenty of stories about it. Did they make you a part of their act?"

"Yes, after I got a little older," she said. "I've been on stage in front of crowds since I was four years old. Then I started writing plans and storylines for shows, I was maybe eleven or twelve at the time. Daddy found one and said we'd perform it the next weekend, and we did, and we never made so much money before as we did that weekend. And after that, Daddy had me write all the shows."

"That's interesting," said Bancroft again — but this time, he did not sound in the least distracted. "So why are you not a Vaudeville girl now? You've got the looks for it."

He delivered this compliment in the most natural, straightforward manner possible, and not even Raoul LeCourt could have been smoother. She wondered if he'd been looking her over. She herself did not think she had the looks for Vaudeville. Her neck was too thick, her face was too round, her hips were too broad and her waist was too short — for starters. But she sure wasn't going to respond to his complement with an argument. "Thank you," she said simply. "But Vaudeville wasn't going to work for me as well as I wanted it to. The main reason is, I'm not tall enough. You kind of need to be statuesque."

"You're not that short," said Bancroft. "You're what, five-five?"

"Five-four-and-a-half," she said. "They want girls who are five-eight; that's the ideal height. If you're between five-six and five-nine, you're good to go. Shorter or taller, and you just don't get the good parts."

"Like Elean — like Miss Martins?"

"Eleanor is five-ten. She's actually a little too tall. But she makes up for it with style and poise. No Vaudeville impresario would turn her away, trust me on that."

"I thought Vaudeville girls were supposed to be tall, tan and terrific."

"That's showgirls you're thinking of — dancing girls, basically. Vaudeville is different. When you're on stage, you know, being much shorter than your leading man isn't good, but towering over him like some scary Amazon is worse."

He nodded. "So, what did you do then?" he asked.

"Well," she said, "by the time I realized Vaudeville wasn't going to be my racket, the war was on, and pretty soon the U.S. got sucked into the whole mess just like Daddy always said we would. I volunteered to go overseas to do shows for our soldiers. Daddy didn't want me to go. He said if anything happened to me he would never forgive President Wilson for it."

She took a big sip of her wine and stared at the tabletop for a moment.

"So, did something happen to you?" Bancroft said, in a surprisingly gentle voice.

"I guess you could say that," she replied. "You know, it was such an adventure. I should have had the time of my life, if it weren't for the fact that so many of my new-found friends kept — not coming back."

She sighed wistfully and looked out the window for a moment.

"I was sixteen years old," she said. "These lovely boys would come try to put the moves on me, and I'd push them off gently like we were trained to do, and they'd go back to the front, and — and I learned never to ask what happened to them after that."

"That's a rough thing for a sixteen-year-old kid to have to deal with," Bancroft said.

"Yeah," she said, in a softly melancholic voice, and took

another sip. "It got rougher. But the war finally ended. Thank God."

There was another moment or two of silence, and now it was Prudence's turn to look around the room for a change of subject.

"Well that's my war story, or one of 'em at least," she said then, with forced cheerfulness. "After that, though, I was through with Vaudeville. I still wrote scripts, but I never went back on the stage. But that was OK, because something else was starting to happen, and that was radio. I was involved with radio from the very start, back when it was still a big old complicated mess that only people with great patience could put up with."

"I remember that," said Bancroft. "I never had much patience for that sort of thing, and being tied to a radio rig with headphones drove me bats. So it wasn't my scene."

"Yeah," said Prudence. "Well, it sure was mine. I loved it. And in time, it got better, and I got better, and in '26 I was writing for a variety show called The Bull Durham Hour with Tom Mix. You've never heard of it, I bet. Tom's studio — I think it was Fox — found out he was moon-lighting with us and sent him a letter, and then it became The Bull Durham Hour with Tim Mox, and the studio sent another letter, and we were all let go. And that was the end of that.

"Every staff member associated with the Bull Durham Hour got picked up at NBC," she continued. "Everyone but me."

"Oh, I see," said Bancroft. "And why was that, do you think?"

She looked at him sharply. "I've no idea," she said crisply. "But I was the only woman. Everyone else was a man. My best guess was, they didn't think a broad could do the job, and they couldn't be bothered to give me a shot at proving 'em wrong. So I went off to the West Coast and looked up Tom. I figured he'd maybe put in a good word for me, at least."

"Tom?"

"Yes, Tom Mix. He remembered me and made a phone call and got me a job at I think the weirdest studio in town, a sort of low-budget animation shop run by an autocratic little chain-smoking funnyman named Walter Disney. Ever heard of him?"

"Nope," said Bancroft. "Unless — does he do cartoons?"

"Bingo. Best known for Alice's Wonderland and more recently Oswald the Lucky Rabbit. Although there are some legal issues going on with that right now that I can't talk about. I actually still work for Mr. Disney, and I'm going to need my job back when I get back to Los Angeles."

Bancroft looked uncomfortable again. He opened his mouth as if to say something, and then once again closed it and looked down at his feet, looking thoughtful.

Again, Prudence didn't notice. "Mr. Disney is — I couldn't ask for a better boss, really," she said. "He's a slave driver, don't get me wrong, and brother, let me tell you, he is a top-shelf tightwad. But when I went to him and asked for a leave of absence so I could go shoot a movie in the Amazon, he only asked me one question."

"What's that?"

"It was, 'Can I buy in?'"

Bancroft's eyebrows shot up. "That's very interesting," he said, swinging around and looking at her intently. "So Walter Disney is a partner in your movie?"

"Right."

"That means he is going to have a great deal of interest in what happens to you, and your film," he mused.

"Actually, yes, but, well, kind of," said Prudence. "Because part of the deal was, if it failed or we decided not to shoot it, Eleanor would buy him out. We cut him in so that we could get distribution. But now Eleanor is — might be —"

"Right. But — right," said Bancroft. "So what are the chances you might lose your job over this?"

"Oh, that won't happen," said Prudence. "First off, he gets his money no matter what. They have it all in writing. If Eleanor really is gone, her estate will pay him.

"But even if he didn't, I don't for a minute think he'd fire me over it," she added. "Mr. Disney really is a good man to work for. I joke about him being a Chesterfield-smoking Mussolini, but he's actually a very good boss. The best, as far as I've seen."

Bancroft looked lost in thought. Then he seemed to come back to himself, and took a big drink of his wine, which he'd been neglecting, and asked if she had any plans for when she got back to Los Angeles.

"No," she murmured. "I guess I'll just go back to work."

"Any family there?"

"No," she said, taking another sip. "Daddy died right after we got back from France, right after the war. Dropped dead in the middle of a show, that's … why I quit Vaudeville. Mother lives in Florida now, with my sister. And I —"

She looked at him. She was really feeling the wine right now. She was feeling something else, too — an urge to tell him an old story, a story she'd only told a few other people, a story she hadn't even told Eleanor yet. And the words of Eleanor, from her dream, were suddenly echoing anew in her ears: "Remember: You can trust Captain Bancroft. Him alone …. "

By now the sun had gone completely down, leaving only the light of the candle to see by. She turned and smiled up at his face, which in the candlelight looked hard and craggy but also, in an odd way, sensitive. It was also looking distracted again. Had she been a little less affected by the wine, she would have noticed that his attention was not entirely on her story, and she would have assumed — incorrectly, as she would later learn — that it was because he was bored by it, and she would have courteously ended the conversation so that he could get back to his wheelhouse and box of cigars and she could get some rest.

But the wine was strong, and her defenses were all down. She opened her mouth to speak.

"I told you about the soldiers in the war, who met me and went away and died," she said, in a softly melancholic voice that had an immediate effect on Bancroft's craggy face. "I got to be pretty good friends with one of them. Jonah was his name, Jonah Willits, from a little town in northern Missouri. We all had calling cards, us show-biz girls, with our pictures on them, and we could sign them and give them out. I gave Jonah one of mine, and I wrote on the back of it my address back in the States so that he could look me up after the war was over. And he asked if he could cut a tiny piece of my hair to keep with it."

A brief silence hung in the air before she continued.

"He went back to the front, and two weeks later the war ended. All the way home I planned how I was going to look him up and go visit him. It was too early to talk about marriage, and I was only seventeen when the war ended. But if it hadn't been, I would have been ready to. I could not wait to get home."

She lapsed into silence again, bracing herself against the flood of old memories that were stirring back to life inside her.

"When I arrived, there was a letter waiting there for

me," she said — she was almost whispering now. "He had written it and addressed it and sealed it up in an envelope in his inside uniform pocket with a note clipped to it asking that it be mailed to me if — if he —"

She swallowed hard, and closed her eyes for a moment, and pulled herself together. When she spoke again, the soft, vulnerable melancholy was gone from her voice, and she was smiling briskly at Bancroft.

"I'm very sorry, Captain Bancroft," she said. "I guess I took you a little farther down Memory Lane than I'd planned to. It's funny how things happen to you, and the wounds can stay so fresh."

"Yeah," Bancroft said softly. "Funny."

"And that's why I live alone in Los Angeles," she finished lamely.

"He must have been a helluva man for you to still be carrying a torch for him ten years later," Bancroft said, in a tone of voice she'd never heard him use before. It was husky, almost emotional.

"I don't really know," she said. "I never really got to know him well, if you think about it. But, well... it's silly, isn't it?"

She smiled at him again and arose from the galley table. "I think I'd better retire for the night," she said. "Thanks for the conversation, Captain. It's been a lonely few days. It's very nice to have someone to talk to, other than Dr. LeCourt."

"Please," Bancroft said. "Call me Rick."

"Rick. Goodnight, Rick."

"Goodnight, Miss McMarion."

She wanted to tell him to call her Trudie, but she thought it might be just a little too forward, so she just smiled at him and started to withdraw from the galley, making for the door that led past Rick's cabin and out to the observation deck, where her cabin was. As she did, the boat gave a little dip, which caused her to sway slightly under the influence of the wine.

Bancroft, who had been stretched out in a relaxed way on his chair, suddenly surged to his feet and shot past her and out the cabin door, fast and silent as a striking panther.

"Who's out there?" he shouted, and she saw that his big black revolver was in his hand. She hadn't seen him draw it; it had seemed to just materialize there.

Then something whistled, and she saw him duck, and a big knife flew past him and stuck quivering in the floor at her feet.

She shrank back instinctively, then sat back up, peering back through the cabin door to where Rick had gone. Then two bright flashes, like twin lightning strikes, silhouetted Rick on the dark deck, and she saw a third flash blossom on the shore at the same instant. After that, there was a splash, and a gurgle, and silence.

But Prudence knew, from that flash of light on shore, that someone was hiding in the bushes with a gun. Hiding and waiting for a clear shot at her or at Rick.

XII.

THE GUN-FIGHT.

Prudence stared out the window of the galley into the pitch-black moonless night. Somewhere on that dark shore, beyond the end of Rick's smuggling pier, a man was lurking with a gun, probably a rifle. Lurking and waiting for someone to show a light or a silhouette, or —

Suddenly realizing her own peril, she ducked back down below the window. The rifleman would be able to see the light in her window. That meant the next person who walked into the galley would be picked off.

And just as suddenly, she realized that Rick didn't know about the shooter on the shore. His eyes had been full of the fire coming out of his big black pistol. He hadn't seen the flash on the shore, the flash that Prudence had seen. Sooner or later, he would silhouette himself against something and —

Prudence dropped to the floor and crawled over to the big knife, still jutting out of the floor. She yanked it free. Then she crawled to the table, took the candle down, and skewered it on the knife, as close to the base as possible. Holding the knife as far away from her body as she could, she quickly lifted it above the window facing the spot on the shore where she'd seen that flash — moving quickly, and trying to simulate how a person would move if she had just picked the candle up off the table and was about to go outside with it.

Broken window glass showered the floor of the pilot-house, and the sound of a rifle shot bellowed across the still river. In spite of herself, Prudence dropped the candle, and it went out in a shower of sparks on the cabin floor. A second later, the darkness was lit with another flash of fire as another bullet slammed into the woodwork behind her, closely followed by the sound of another rifle blast.

Then she heard four more shots from the observation deck. Bancroft was returning fire. A strangled yell sounded from the distant shore, telling them one of his shots had gone home.

She heard Bancroft's feet pounding on the deck, hurrying toward her. A tiny, faintly glowing ember nearby in the darkness told her where the candle was, and she stepped forward to pick it up before it faded, crouching low, glass crunching under her shoe soles. She stuck the candle back in the holder just as Rick entered the galley.

"What're you doing with that candle?" he hissed sharply.

"Drawing fire from the guy on the shore," she whispered back. "Job done. Is there any boiler pressure left?"

"Should be a little bit," he replied. "Go stoke up the fire, but keep the curtains drawn tight. We gotta get out of here."

"Sure. Are we untied from the dock?"

A vicious whispered curse was her answer, and he started for the door.

"Stop," she hissed. "I'll get it. You get the boat moving."

"There's a man on the beach with a high-powered rifle," Bancroft hissed back. "I'll be goddamned if I'm letting you go out there and get shot."

Under ordinary circumstances, Prudence would have noticed his sudden concern for her welfare. She would remember and think about it later, but for now, she was fully focused on other things.

"Listen, you dumb sonuvabitch," she hissed. "I don't know how to run this boat. You do. If one of us is going to get hurt, it should be the one who can't drive the boat, so the other can bring the injured party to a doctor instead of just wringing her hands over his bleeding body and wishing she could drive. Got it? Now shut the hell up and start the engines before we both end up dead."

His eyes flashed at her, and even in the almost-nonexistent light she could see the admiration in them. She'd remember that later, too. For now, there was time for just one thing.

Gripping the knife the unknown assailant had thrown at Rick, she stealthily made her way to the foredeck. Her ears, though still ringing from the close-quarter gunfire, were working again, and she could hear a crackling sound as of someone stepping on a branch. Clearly the gunman on shore was not dead. The slightest noise would surely bring another shot.

Then she was at the forward line. A quick swipe of the knife — which felt great in her hand and was viciously sharp — and the bows of the boat were free and drifting away from the dock. Beneath her feet she felt the thrum of the steam plant starting to turn over. She padded as stealthily as she could to the observation deck at the stern to repeat the process.

As her sharp knife bit into the line, a flash like lightning lit up the night sky, and the rifle on the shore roared like thunder. In the blaze of its light, she saw the entire boat illuminated for an instant before being plunged back into darkness. She knew that she herself would have been visible to the shooter in that flash, clear as day.

He must have fired at random, she thought, hoping to see his target by the light of his muzzle flash. Now she could hear the sound of someone frantically working a rifle bolt, and knew a follow-up shot was coming in less than a second. She threw herself down prone on the observation deck, head toward the flash, making as small a target as possible of herself.

"Rick!" she screamed. "Go! Go! Go!"

Something slammed into the woodwork nearby, toward the back of the boat, as the night sky was lit up again; the bellowing roar came a fraction of a second later. Again came that frantic clatter of someone working a bolt, and some-thing clipped the canopy over her head as a third shot blasted its defiance — and a fourth, which raised a great splash off the stern of the boat.

She heard the bolt working again, but this time it was followed by a sharp click. The gunman was empty. Surging to her feet, she hurled the knife as hard as she could toward the place where the muzzle had flashed, then sprinted to the pilothouse.

"Firebox," Bancroft said when he saw her. He was steering the boat; she knew he was able only to guess which direction he ought to be heading, probably based on where the muzzle flashes had come from.

Without a word, she hurried over to the firebox and started feeding pieces of wood into it. The flames licked up hungrily.

The gunman fired three more times. Prudence heard one shot strike the boat, but by now they were a good distance from shore, and the gunman was having to aim each shot at the spot he thought he remembered from the muzzle flash from the previous shot. Finally, perhaps realizing he was doing nothing more than illuminating Rick's way for him, the gunman gave up.

But now a new danger loomed. Without the rifle shots to light his way, Rick had no idea where the boat was going — and, its firebox nicely stoked, it was moving faster and faster.

"What are we going to do, Rick?" Prudence asked, trying to keep her voice steady. "You can't see where we're going, can you?"

"No," he said shortly. "In a minute I'll go out and light the carbide lamps, but I can't do that now because we're still in rifle range."

"So what can we do?"

"Hope and pray we don't circle in and hit the shore," said Rick shortly. "Every now and then I can see the treeline where it meets the night sky. I'm trying to use that to steer by. But…"

Prudence looked at him. The light from the boiler fire was gleaming on the butt of his revolver, which he had distractedly stuck in his pants pocket. Looking at it gave Prudence an idea.

"Give me your pistol, Rick," she urged, "and I'll go out on deck and give you a couple muzzle flashes. You'll at least be able to see if we're heading for the bank."

"You'll draw their fire," said Rick dubiously.

"Aw, Ricky, I didn't know ya cared!" she quipped, and dexterously extracted the pistol from his pocket with two fingers before he could stop her. "It's empty, isn't it? Where are your cartridges?"

Rick reached into his pocket. "You are a lot of trouble, Prudence," he said, sounding simultaneously exasperated and impressed. "I mean, Miss McMarion."

"Do call me Trudie," she told him. "And don't worry about me. I think I can avoid getting hit."

She filled the pistol with fresh cartridges and climbed around to the deck of the boat. Then, as she was starting to raise the pistol high over her head and off to one side, she reconsidered, and, kneeling down, held it low over the water at the bow of the boat. She knew the flash would silhouette the entire boat, but lacking a bright point of light at which to shoot (not to mention a silhouette of herself standing up in the bows) the rifleman might get less of a clear shot.

She pulled the trigger and cursed as the bullet splashed into the water, showering her with spray.

But the flash illuminated the bank of the river just in front of the boat, a few dozen feet away. She'd fired just in time; thirty more seconds and they would have been stuck on the beach.

Rick immediately cranked the rudder over to the right, trying to avoid he bank. As he did so, there was another flash from the rifle on shore, and she heard a bullet hit the bank ahead of them with a sharp splatting noise; Rick's sudden change of direction had taken them out of the bullet's path. Then came another shot, and another. She waited, pistol in hand, grateful to the fool on the riverbank for the light he was supplying in his no-hope attempts to hit something he couldn't see a thousand yards away.

And now the boiler was heating up. Still slowly, but with increasing speed, the *Amazon Princess* continued down the river, with Prudence firing judiciously as they went, until Rick was able to steer the boat safely around a bend in the river, out of sight of the rifleman, who was now at least three-quarters of a mile behind them.

Then he cut the power and came out on deck, an electric flashlight in his hand. Prudence handed him the pistol as he emerged.

"Thanks, Prudie," he said, tucking it away in its holster.

"Not Prudie. Trudie," she said firmly. "Long story. But please, don't call me Prudie."

For some reason, this struck Rick as hilariously funny, and he laughed so hard and long that he had to clutch at the handrails for support. Prudence looked at him, smiling a quizzical smile that he could not see because it was so dark, and wondered how it was that she could have come to like him so much better in just a little over twenty-four hours.

Soon Rick had a pair of powerful carbide lamps blazing, hanging from specially positioned hooks at the front of the boat, and they lit the way before them as well as they could hope. And shortly after that, the little riverboat was on its way — slowly and cautiously — down the river and away from the gunman.

Now that the immediate danger was past, Prudence felt an enormous weariness wash over her. She was standing next to Rick at the steering station in the wheelhouse, staring out into the murky darkness, when it hit her, and it caused her to stagger just a bit. She reached out to the pilothouse wall, and heard the broken glass crunch under her feet.

"You doing all right?" Rick asked, reaching out to steady her.

"Yeah … so sleepy," she murmured. "You going to keep going all night?"

"No, I don't think so," said Rick. "Those carbide lamps will be good for another half hour before I have to refill them, and that's long enough to get us to a part of the river that's about two miles wide. I'm anchoring off in the middle of that. Anybody wants to take a shot at us from a mile away, I say, let 'em."

"Oh goody," said Prudence. "You think we lost 'em?"

Rick chuckled wearily. "I think so."

There was a brief silence.

"I can handle this, Trudie," Rick said then. "You go lie down. You look exhausted."

"I am exhausted," she said. "But I'm staying up until you get the boat safely anchored. You might want my help. Who knows?"

He looked at her in the candlelight for a moment. "I might, I guess," he said.

He smiled at her then, and seemed to want to say something more, but instead he turned back to the wheel without a word. But she saw him reach forward to the little shelf that ran under the windows and set down something that he had been holding in his left hand. It was a cigar.

And half an hour later, the boat safely anchored on an expanse of water so vast they couldn't even see the shore with the carbide lamps, Rick and Prudence mumbled an exhausted goodnight to one another and disappeared into their respective cabins.

XIII.

THE UNMASKING.

The next day, Prudence woke up late — late for her, at any rate. She couldn't know for sure without a clock, but it looked like it was at least seven.

She climbed out of her bunk. She had been too exhausted to dress for bed — not that it would have mattered, since her pajamas were packed away in her suitcase, back in Eleanor's relatives' house. Raoul had not brought her suitcase to the dock; all she had with her were the clothes she had been wearing when she'd gone with Raoul to the nearby village, three days before — and, of course, the straitjacket, which Bancroft had folded neatly and put in her cabin, but she was certainly not going to wear that, not even with the sleeves cut off.

Of course she'd slept in her clothes… what else could she do?

The boat was not yet under way, but a whiff of wood smoke as she walked out onto the deck told her that Rick was already building steam for the journey. She made her way to the back of the observation deck and sat down, drinking in the morning and wishing she had a change of clothes. Did she dare try to wash her things in the river now, while Rick was busy in the pilothouse?

She decided that no, she dared not. A vision of Rick rounding the corner and seeing her there in her underwear, her backside sticking up in the air as she leaned over the rail to wash her stockings in the river, flashed before her and left her shuddering. She'd have to figure something else out. Maybe she could do some laundry in the boat's "head."

It was a good decision. A few minutes later, Rick did in fact round the corner at the side of the cabin, and if she had risked stripping and washing her clothes in the river, he would have gotten a real eyeful.

Rick seated himself on the opposite side of the settee. He was holding the two big tin cups that they'd drunk wine from the night before; this morning they were full of black coffee. He reached forward with one and handed it to her.

"It's not very hot," he said. "I thought you'd be up a while ago."

"Me too," she mumbled, rubbing her eyes with her free hand before taking a healthy swig of the strong black brew. "Rick, Raoul didn't bring any luggage with me, did he?"

"No," said Rick slowly. "No, he did not." He paused for a moment. "I've got a spare toothbrush. Brand new. You're welcome to it. What else do you think you might need?"

"Well," she said, "I've been in these clothes for three

days now. I need to wash them. I thought about doing that in the bathtub in the head, but I didn't know if that would be OK."

"That's what I do," said Rick. "Laundry goes in the tub with me and I scrub on it a bit while I'm washing up. It cleans up pretty good. But then I have to hang it out to dry afterward, and you've got nothing to change into."

"I don't mind wearing wet clothes."

"No need to do that. I'll lend you some of mine."

He got up, leaving his coffee behind, and ducked into his cabin. A moment later he emerged with a light khaki shirt and a shapeless ball of fabric.

"I think you'll be able to wear my shirt, but there's no way any of my trousers will fit around your hips," he said. "This is a bathing suit, the old-fashioned kind that goes most of the way to your knees. You'll look silly in it, but I promise not to look at you or laugh, and I think it's the best I can do. Anyway, it's just until your skirt dries out. And if you wait to bathe until we get under way, it'll be pretty easy for me to just stay up front in the wheelhouse until everything's dry and back to normal."

Prudence eyed the bathing suit dubiously for a moment, then met Rick's eyes. "Thank you," she said. "It'll work."

The two of them sat for a while in silence, sipping their coffee. Rick looked as if he wanted to say something, but couldn't quite bring himself to do it. Finally, his coffee finished, he stood up.

"I'd better get us under way," he said.

Prudence took the things he'd left for her and went into the head for her combination bath and laundry. The air was already comfortably warm, but the water in the tub felt ice cold; she wished she'd thought to ask Bancroft for a pan of water from the boiler, just to take the edge off.

Upon emerging, still shivering, from the bath, she found the bathing suit positively would not fit over her hips, so she gingerly squeezed the water out of the wool skirt as thoroughly as she dared and put it back on, wishing she had her plus-fours instead. Rick's shirt, though, fit just fine.

Feeling hungry now, and wanting another cup of coffee, she went forward to the wheelhouse, where she found Rick happily perched behind the wheel on his stool in a cloud of foul cigar smoke.

"Uh-oh," he remarked when he saw her. "Looks like the swimsuit didn't fit. Sorry about that."

"That's all right," she said. "It's a nice warm day. May I — do you mind if I get some more coffee, and maybe some hardtack?"

"Go ahead," he said, carefully removing the ember from the end of his cigar. "I think there's one more *cupuaçu* in there, too. You're welcome to it."

"Thanks," she said, and ducked into the galley door. Soon afterward she emerged with the coffee and pilot biscuits. She noticed that he'd opened a window to clear the cigar smoke out, which seemed a little silly considering two of the other window panes had been shot out. Nonetheless she opened her mouth to thank him. But before she could get the words out, he spoke.

"You saved my life last night," he said.

"Did I?"

"Yep, you did, and I think you know it, too. I had no idea there was a man on the shore with a rifle until you drew fire from him with that candle-in-the-window trick. He would have been able to wait there until I got myself silhouetted against the cabin window or something, and then, pow. How did you know he was there?"

"He fired a shot at the same time you were shooting

at the man on the deck," she said. "You probably couldn't see because of the flash from your own gun."

"Why didn't you just tell me there was somebody on the shore?"

"I thought — it's silly. But I thought maybe he didn't know we knew he was there, and if I could get him to shoot, you'd be able to see where he was. Whereas if he heard me yelling to you that there was a man on the shore, he'd be more careful."

"That's not silly. In fact, it worked. I got lucky and hit him with one of those shots. Did you hear him yelp?"

"Yes. He must not have been hurt badly, though."

"Right, it didn't seem to slow down his rate of fire much," Rick acknowledged. "And it was only a pistol bullet. Still, it was better than a miss, and it wouldn't have happened if I hadn't had a muzzle flash to shoot at."

"The man on the deck," Prudence said then. "Did he — did the —"

"Caimans got him, I think, yes," said Rick. "But I was worrying about other things at the time. He might have made it to shore, I don't know."

"Well," she said, "in any case, you certainly saved my life from him."

"I guess we make a pretty good team," Rick replied with a grin, and there was something tentative about the grin that brought the blood to her cheeks in a genuine, full-blown, bona-fide bashful-girl blush for the first time since the Great War.

"I guess we do," she said, with a demure smile. "But Rick, why do you think they attacked us? Was it Indians?"

Rick shook his head. "I know all the tribes within a hundred miles of this river," he said. "You can't do what I do without having those connections. They know me and they like me. I regularly bring them stuff as tribute for using their river. I treat them with respect and I defend them from people who don't, and they know it and they respect me for it. No, it's not Indians."

There was a moment of silence. Then Rick spoke up again.

"I'd like to tell you who I think it was," he said. "But I think you won't believe me, and you might think — oh, to hell with it. I'll be direct with you, Trudie. I think it was Raoul LeCourt."

She looked up at him in surprise, and saw he was almost physically braced for her response.

"That's — ridiculous," she stammered unconvincingly. "You can't — I mean — I —"

She lapsed into silence for a moment, then looked up at him again. "Where do you get that idea? Just because you don't like the man?"

"Look," he said. "I know you like him, and I know you know I detest him. And I can't think of any reason why he would want to — oh, hell. I just — there are things I need to — to tell you about him."

Prudence was silent for a moment. She was thinking of Marco Morais barking orders, and of the straitjacket that lay neatly folded on a shelf in her cabin.

"He's not really French, you know," she said. "Maybe he's not really a doctor, either."

"Oh, he's a real doctor, all right," said Rick. "I've seen his diploma. Some institute of nervous disorders in France."

"Nervous disorders?" Prudence said. "Raoul is a nerve specialist?"

"I think so. Mostly he works as a general practitioner around here, though. Not a lot of call for psychiatrists on the Amazon. But… there is an insane asylum in Porto

Escuro, mostly full of syphilis patients."

"You mean the Sisters of the Sacred Heart sanitarium, where you're supposed to be delivering me?"

"It's not a sanitarium," said Rick, in an oddly hard voice. "Its official name is Sisters of the Sacred Heart Home for the Feeble-Minded and Insane."

Prudence gasped.

"And you're not being referred to them for a couple weeks of relaxing and water-taking," Rick continued. "You're being involuntarily committed. By Dr. Raoul LeCourt.

"Listen," he said then, his voice softening. "This is all going to be a big shock to you, on top of everything that's happened. And me and my big mouth, I just unloaded a bunch more just now, when I'd planned to try to explain more before I — anyway, I have got to talk to you about some things. About this trip, and about Raoul LeCourt, and about the straitjacket and the insane asylum and last night — and — and some other things. We're going to be arriving at Porto Escuro at around five o'clock today, so we have some time, but before we get there, we need to talk, you and I."

Prudence realized her mouth was hanging open. She closed it with a snap.

"Spill," she said, in a voice like oiled steel. "Spill it all. Now."

Rick turned and looked at her for a split-second, then gave her a grim and mirthless smile.

"All right," he said. "I'll start in the middle of the story, since I don't know what else to do. On Monday, LeCourt came down to the boat and told me he had a transport job for me. Said he needed a patient transported to Porto Escuro as soon as possible. This patient, he said, was a mental case, and had afforded him a rare opportunity to practice his skills as a nerve specialist. The patient was suffering from a strange pattern of breakdowns, very dangerous, needing help very badly. I said I wasn't going to Porto Escuro for another week, and he'd have to wait; but LeCourt said he wanted this done as a special run, and he was ready to pay for it. And you know me, I like getting paid for things."

"OK," said Prudence, slowly.

"He says he wants the patient picked up at one in the morning because she's more tractable at night," he continued. "I say, fine, for the right price I'll pick her up whenever you want. So he says, fine, we'll be there at one tomorrow morning with six hundred *reais* for the passage.

"So, one o'clock comes along, and I'm all steamed up and ready to go, and he shows up with you."

Rick looked off into the distance for a moment.

"You know, I'm a bit of a hard-boiled character," he said. "About an eight-minute egg, me. I'm no angel. There's a reason I live here, in the middle of nowhere, far away from the reach of North American and European law enforcement. I am, or have been, a smuggler, a bootlegger, a thief, a no-questions-asked arms dealer, and even a killer. Not a murderer, you understand, but a killer just the same. The point is, I'm not squeamish. But there was something about the way they brought you down here, all trussed up in that straitjacket and looking somehow — somehow broken — something about that whole thing made me draw the line, right there, on the spot. I was not going to be any part of something that involved you trussed up like livestock and, it looked like to me, psychologically beaten into submission."

He lapsed into silence, looking like a man who's said a little too much. Prudence was silent, too, turning the story over and over in her mind. Raoul a psychologist ... but he'd never told her so. Wouldn't he have told her that, when she was being held in that padded room, if nothing else to assuage her terror? Had she been in his office, there, in that padded room? And—

A horrible new thought struck her, and she raised her eyes to meet Rick's. He seemed to know just what she was thinking. He nodded.

"A nerve specialist would know just what to give a lady to cause her to act like a lunatic, wouldn't he?" Rick said. "If, that is, he wanted her safely put away in a Home for the Feeble-Minded and Insane."

"He told me I was only going there for a week or two, to see a doctor he was referring me to," she said. "But he also told me it was a sanitarium. A garden of rest. Not an insane asylum."

"Not only is it most definitely an insane asylum," said Rick, "it's an insane asylum with a really bad reputation. Oh, it's solid gold among the mainstream Brazilian society in Porto Escuro and other outposts of civilization, but if you ask the Indians on the river here, or any of the ex-patients there, you get a very different story. Depending on what instructions LeCourt had given for your treatment, I knew you could be there for six months, or you could be there forever.

"And even if you were released in a week or two, you probably wouldn't still be all in one piece," he added. The odd hardness was back in his voice; he sounded almost savage now. "Rumor on the river, and I have this from sources I trust, is that the Sisters don't share the usual Catholic skepticism about eugenics. They sterilize most of their patients before they're released."

He paused for a moment. Prudence stared in horror, unable to speak.

"All of which wasn't really any of my business," he went on, his voice softening again; "or so at least I had been telling myself. But then came last night, and you saved my life. After that, minding my own business wasn't really an option any more.

"I was up about half the night thinking about this," he continued. "I put down a lot of my success, such as it is, to a couple of basic things: I mind my own business, and I take care of my friends. So now I'm in a pickle. Those two things are in opposition. You don't seem crazy to me, but hey, maybe the doctor knows something I don't, and in any case, not my business, right? Except that he's sending you to an institution that I know some very unpleasant things about. An institution I could never deliver a friend to.

"And that's a problem because we've been under fire together now," he said. "We're comrades now. Friends. So there was no way around it. I had to know what that letter said."

"Letter?"

"Yes. The letter LeCourt gave me to give to the people from the asylum. I was to deliver it... unopened."

Rick drew a ripped-open envelope out of his back pocket and handed it to Prudence. The envelope had been opened, obviously, by sticking a finger in it and ripping it through the top. Wedged into it was a letter, and Prudence caught a glimpse of the green of American currency.

Eyes open wide, she unfolded the letter and read:

Dear Mother Dolores,

This letter relates to Miss Prudence McMarion, who is being delivered into your care today. I have been working with Miss McMarion for several months now. The madness that is progressively taking over her consciousness has gotten markedly worse, and worsens daily. I have made many attempts to control it with medication and with therapy, but recently an incident occurred which has made it impossible to ignore the need for an immediate involuntary commitment to a high-security facility such as that of the Sisters of the Sacred Heart.

Miss McMarion, in the grip of psychosis, made an attempt upon the life of the proprietor of a restaurant in Carraçao, then rampaged through the facility like an angry bull. She was stopped only when I stealthily injected her with a sedative. Since then, in custody at my office, she has occasionally lapsed into rages in which she calls down the curses of demons on the town and on us at my office, and commands everyone within earshot to join her in rituals of devil-worship. As you can imagine, this has the superstitious natives very excited, and as a result her life is in danger if she remains here in Carraçao.

She goes for long periods of time seeming perfectly sane. Do not be fooled by this. She can, at any time, be triggered by the most innocuous things into a murderous rage.

Under no circumstances should she be considered for release from your facility until she has gone at least two years without a relapse.

Sincerely,

—RAOUL A. LeCOURT, PH.D., M.D.

P.S. On an unrelated note, enclosed is a personal donation intended to help the Home continue its vital mission. Thank you for all the good things you do.

Tucked into the envelope with the letter was a tidy stack of crisp, new hundred-dollar bills — dollars, not *reais*. She counted them rapidly. There were fifteen of them.

She turned her eyes to meet Rick's, feeling utterly numb. Rick met her eyes impassively at first, and then slowly a sardonic smile creased his features.

"That's just what I thought," he said. "Now, I knew LeCourt was a bad egg, but I really never imagined he'd be capable of something like this."

Prudence said nothing. She couldn't speak. She still felt numb, but her eyes had begun to smolder. A tear slid down her cheek… a tear of rage. Rick watched the whole involuntary performance with that same sardonic smile, leavened with a growing note of approval. Then he got to his feet and turned back to face the river, and reached for his cigar again.

"Take your time," he told her. "I expect you'll want to think this through by yourself, out on the deck, and I really need the rest of this cigar. When you're ready to make plans, come back to the wheelhouse and we'll talk."

Prudence left the wheelhouse and moved back toward the observation deck, almost in a daze. She sat down on the settee and just tried to absorb everything. Raoul, the man who a few days earlier she had thought she might be developing romantic feelings for, was trying to get her committed to the deepest, most impenetrable part of a madhouse located in the deepest, most impenetrable part of the Western Hemisphere — and held there against her will for at least two years, and probably surgically mutilated to boot. But why? Why would he secretly take this strange attitude toward her, a woman he barely knew but had twice kissed with real and unfeigned passion, and had even once (as she thought) tried to seduce? And she hadn't rebuffed him forcefully; she had left him with plenty of opportunity to think his romantic advances might not be unwelcome… hadn't she? He couldn't be acting out of the spite of a spurned would-be lover. So, why?

It just didn't make sense.

And then there was the strange late-night attack on the boat. Had he been behind that? She got the distinct impression, somehow, that whoever had attacked the boat had been after her, not Rick. And the only person she knew of who had somehow expressed a desire to be rid of her was Raoul. But why would he have attacked her when he was already shipping her off to the madhouse?

She got to her feet and trotted forward to the wheelhouse, bursting in upon Rick in his cloud of foul cigar smoke, and asking him what he thought of this.

"I'd say," he said, stubbing out the end of his cigar in the ashtray, "most likely he would have done that because there was fifteen hundred dollars in that envelope, and he figured if he could take care of us the old fashioned way he wouldn't have to part with it. Or maybe he just decided that he couldn't trust me to do what I said I was going to do. Remember that huge fuss his sidekick Morais kicked up, wanting you off the boat because I said no to the straitjacket?"

Prudence shuddered. She remembered, all right, and even now in the cold light of day she still was convinced that she had never been closer to death than she had the instant before she'd leaped onto Bancroft's boat.

"You saved my life that night," she said. "I will always believe it. If you'd backed down and let Marco take me off your boat, I'd be dead right now."

"Lot of that going around, that life-saving stuff," he grunted. "Listen, I forgot to tell you one thing. I found this on the back deck this morning. I'm pretty sure it was dropped by that knife-thrower I shot last night during all that excitement."

He reached into the corner and brought up a long,

slender reed. "It's a blowgun, with curare-tipped darts," he said. "None of the tribes around here use them, but of course every European knows the Amazon tribes use these all the time, right?"

"Oh!" said Prudence. "So you think they were going to kill us and frame the Indians?"

"You chirped it," said Rick. "Problem was, you can't step on my boat without me knowing. He wasn't expecting me to be coming at him the instant he got on board. He didn't have time to get this unfamiliar gat out and blow a dart at me, so he went for his knife instead."

"Nice," said Prudence.

"Anyway, I think it was you that they were after last night," he said. "But no way would they have let me live to tell anybody what had happened. They wanted us both dead, and for it to look like an Indian attack.

"But what I really don't understand is, why was LeCourt ready to spend fifteen hundred dollars plus six hundred *reais* to get rid of you? Do you have any idea why he would want you out of the way that badly?"

"Well," said Prudence very slowly, "I've been thinking about that too. And I can't figure it either. But I just keep thinking that it must have had something to do with Eleanor's disappearance."

Rick was silent for a moment.

"Tell me what the last thing you remember doing with LeCourt was," he said.

"Well," she said, "let's see. We drove to that other village, about an hour away. We were going to have an early lunch at the little restaurant there. We each had a glass of this delicious golden wine that Raoul said was a specialty of the place, and —"

She stopped, frowning. "I don't remember much after

that," she said. "It gets really hazy. I remember at one point looking at my glass and wondering why it was only half gone, when I was feeling so very drunk already. I assumed, when I woke up the next morning, that I must have had more, to have gotten so sozzled, and just don't remember. But as I think about it…."

"So you're thinking he might have drugged you with the wine," said LeCourt.

"The more I think about it, yes," said Prudence. "And then he started asking me all sorts of questions about Eleanor and then I told him my dream."

"What dream?"

Prudence told him, again, about the dream of the strange abandoned city.

"But the funny thing is," she added, "I recognized that spot on the riverbank, from my dream. When we were out looking for Eleanor, I saw it. I saw that very spot."

"You dreamed about a spot on the river, that you'd never seen before," Rick said dubiously, "and then you saw it while we were out looking for Eleano — for Miss Martins, the very next day?"

"That's right, yes," she said. Then, as he continued looking at her, she went on: "I know it sounds really weird and improbable. And maybe I was somehow mistaken, maybe my memory is reshaping itself somehow, I don't know. But I recognized the spot. It was the spot where we looped back to look at the caiman."

Rick burst out laughing. "So that caiman, you made that story up?"

"Right. And remember how ardently Raoul did NOT want us to investigate it? He almost seemed desperate. He —"

Prudence froze, the smile vanishing like a candle blown

out. She was remembering the look LeCourt had given her — that fleeting flash of a look he'd given her through the pilothouse window as they were turning away from that spot on the river. It had been like looking into the face of a desperate husband contemplating killing his wife for the insurance money.

Rick had stopped laughing too. He was looking at her expectantly, and she realized he'd just asked her a question. She hadn't even heard him speak.

"I'm sorry, what was that?" she said.

"Did you tell him?" Rick's voice was low and crackling with intensity. "Did you tell him about that spot being in that — dream of yours?"

Prudence stared at him for a moment. "I — I think I did," she said, slowly and with a dawning horror. "Yes, I think I did."

They stared at each other for another moment, wide-eyed. Then Rick pivoted on his right heel like a street fighter turning to meet a new opponent, and seized the wheel in both hands and started spinning it.

"What are you doing?" said Prudence.

"I'm getting us turned around," said Rick. "We are going to find out what the hell this is all about."

"Don't do it," said Prudence. "Not yet. When we don't show up at the asylum, they'll figure out that we're onto them. They know we escaped from their ambush, Rick."

Rick nodded, and turned the wheel back in the other direction.

"You're right, of course," he said. "I hate to waste a moment of time, but if we don't follow through with our trip to Porto Escuro, they'll know. Plus, it's getting late in the day anyway.

"Listen, Trudie, we're going to be arriving in Porto

Escuro around five o'clock this afternoon. About four thirty I want you to pull up the panel on the floor of my cabin and climb into the hole you'll find there. Try to be as quiet as you can. I'm going to tell them you jumped overboard and tried to swim for shore, and a school of piranhas tore you up."

"Piranhas? Not a caiman?"

"Nope. Caimans are much more dangerous at night, but they don't often attack during the daytime. Piranhas, this time of year, are a real nuisance, they're hungry as hell and they'll go for anything. Locals know better than to swim in the river during the dry season, and if they end up in the water they know to move as easy as they can because the splashing attracts them like chum to a shark. An outsider like you, though, won't know that, and…."

"Got it. Piranhas. If anybody asks me what ate me, I'll remember to tell them it was piranhas."

He smiled. "Anyway, be prepared to spend about two hours in there," he said. "Maybe more if anything goes wrong. Bring whatever you need to get comfortable."

XIV.

THE HIDING-PLACE.

Prudence went to Rick's cabin and, after a short search, found the locker panel set into the floor. She quickly discovered that it wasn't a cabinet — it was an access hatch to the bilge of the boat. The ribs of the hull, spaced about every foot or so, looked like they would be extremely uncomfortable to lie on for two hours; and, as if that weren't enough, there were about four inches of greasy bilgewater sloshing about between them, black and slimy and disgusting.

Prudence looked around for something to line the bottom with. She could use a blanket, but it would wick the water up into itself in minutes. She decided to return to the wheelhouse and ask Rick for help.

"Rick," she said, when she arrived, "do you have something you could lay over the ribs down there so I'm not lying in that water?"

"Oh, yes, of course," he said. "I should have thought of that. We'll stop and cut some sticks to make a sort of floor."

This was soon done, and a blanket lain over the sticks to provide some padding, and Prudence climbed in to try it for size. It was very tight, and, after Rick put the cover on it, very dark. But she was not going to complain.

"You know, you don't have to do this," said Rick. "You could wait for me upstream a little ways."

"Maybe I should do that," she said slowly, "but there are animals in this forest that I'm afraid of."

"Too bad we didn't think of this yesterday," Rick remarked. "I could have dropped you off with some friends in the Nuboki tribe. Well, it's too late now, I guess."

"Yes. And we can't backtrack, can we? They'd get suspicious if you arrived a day late."

"I think they would," he said. "But I can leave you on a nice little clearing with a pistol and a camp chair to wait for me."

"And what if you're delayed, and can't come back until morning?" she said. "You'll be arriving at five, right? If you're delayed more than an hour or so, won't it look a bit funny to insist on still leaving port when there's only an hour or two of daylight left? And I can't spend a night here in the open by this river. You'd come back to find me missing or dead or half-eaten."

Rick nodded. "Good point," he grunted. "But you wouldn't be half-eaten. You'd be all the way eaten. Animals around here don't go in for half measures."

Prudence shuddered a little. "Yes, I noticed that."

By now it was almost noon, so they ate a quick lunch before continuing — tinned beef and pilot crackers again, this time with no fruit, with more red wine.

Prudence spent the rest of the afternoon in the pilot-house with Rick. In marked contrast to his behavior the day before, Rick never touched his cigars the entire time she was there with him, and was clearly enjoying her company. Increasingly, she was enjoying his. His taciturnity and churlishness seemed to have vanished completely, and he now seemed almost garrulous.

She chatted about animation-studio projects she'd worked on during her time at Disney's studio, some of which he'd actually seen; he talked about his life on the river, and interesting projects and cargoes he'd hauled. She tried once to get him to tell her about his pre-Amazon-River past, but he sidestepped her question so smoothly and firmly that she did not pursue it.

"I'll tell you about that part of my life someday, Tru, I promise," he told her, a little guiltily, after it became clear that she wasn't going to press him further. "I know it's not fair. You've told me some deeply personal things about your past, and I should be telling you things about mine. I just can't. Not yet."

Disappointed, and with her curiosity whetted, she tried to reassure him that she didn't mind.

"Sure you do," he said. "I would too. I'll tell you everything soon. I promise."

They ate their dinner a little early, since Prudence wouldn't have much chance to eat or drink for some time; and, hoping to take a bit of the edge off of what looked likely to be a very uncomfortable few hours, she had a particularly large helping of Rick's red wine. All too soon, it was four-thirty in the afternoon, and time for Prudence to go into her hiding place below decks. Reluctantly, she crawled into the hole and lay there, facing upward, waiting for Rick to put the lid down.

He paused before reaching for it, looking down into her eyes.

"Listen," he muttered. "There's a possibility that the nuthouse people will get a magistrate to order the boat searched. I'll do whatever it takes to make sure that doesn't happen, but if it does, you'll be dragged kicking and screaming off to the asylum, and I'll be hauled off to the city joint, and we might never see each other again."

He broke off eye contact, looking across the cabin at nothing in particular, as the silence hung heavy for a moment. Then he looked back at her.

"If that happens, I — I want you to know — look, we've only really known each other a couple of days, right? But I feel — I — oh, hell, never mind. I just want you to know that I will do whatever it takes to keep you out of that asylum, or failing that to bust you out and get you back to Los Angeles. No matter how long it takes and no matter what I have to do. I — you —"

Prudence had opened her mouth to speak, but no words would come out. Then, overcome by an impulse that may have been augmented by the wine, she shot her little feminine hand out like a striking cobra, seized his shirt front, and pulled his face down into the bilge and onto hers.

The kiss that resulted was completely unlike the one Raoul LeCourt had bestowed upon her just a few days before, which she still felt dirty for having participated in. Where Raoul's had feathered over her lips with an almost professional tenderness and sensuality, the kiss she now bestowed upon Rick Bancroft was raw and elemental and fierce, and he returned it in the same spirit. She kissed the man she had hated forty-eight hours before with the frank, unrestrained passion of a woman who knows it may be her last kiss.

When Rick lifted his face from the bilge, his eyes were shining with a light that Prudence had seen in a man's eyes only once before — during the Great War.

He opened his mouth. She reached up and put her finger on it.

"Don't say it," she whispered. "Don't say anything. If there is any chance this is going to be the last time I see you, I want to remember you just like this."

Rick recovered a little and smiled at her. "Goodbye, Tru," he murmured. "I hope I see you again in a few hours. If not —"

"Don't," she whispered. "Don't say it. I hope so too. Goodbye, Rick."

Bancroft reached for the hatch cover then, and the Stygian blackness of the bilge closed in around Prudence. But as she lay there, listening to the deep thrumming of the propeller shaft and the constant swish of water rushing past the hull, she smiled with a deep contentment. She knew there was no place on Earth that she would rather be right now than tucked into this dank, smelly hole, alone in the dark with her thoughts.

Well, maybe there was one other place.

Many minutes later, she heard the distinctive low-pitched, flute-like moan of the *Amazon Princess's* whistle, followed shortly by the sounds of progress slackening, and she knew they were coming into the port of Porto Escuro. She could feel the hull responding to Rick's footsteps as he ran about the deck getting mooring lines ready, and then the steam engine and propeller shaft went still, and she felt the hull bump gently against the dock.

Now she could hear Rick's footsteps as he trotted around the deck, securing the lines. Then she heard a murmur of conversation outside; Rick was talking to somebody. Then she heard him stepping off the boat — she felt it swinging gently to and fro after his weight came off — and walking away up the dock.

What could he be doing?

Perhaps, she thought, he had to check in with someone to report her as having been "eaten." She lay there quietly and waited.

The dock they were tied off to was obviously a busy one. She was surprised at how much she was able to hear when people walked by the boat on the dock, even though she was well belowdecks and behind a tight-fitting hatch panel; apparently Rick had left the cabin door open, probably for air.

Rick was gone for only a few minutes. When he returned, she heard and felt him step back onto the ship, and his footsteps moved along the deck toward the cabin in which she was hidden.

"I'll have to step away for a few minutes," he muttered, seemingly to himself, while bustling around the cabin overhead. "I've let the harbormaster know I'm here and that I've got to report your death. That should take no more than twenty minutes and then we'll be —"

"Ahoy!" called a voice from on the dock. "*Senhor* Bancroft?"

Rick hurried out of the cabin and stepped onto the deck. "Yes?" she heard him reply.

"We'll need you to come with us to the magistrate," the voice answered. "Right now, please. We have a warrant for your arrest."

"Excuse me?" Rick rasped.

"From an incident a couple weeks ago. You are accused of having assaulted Edward Cromwood."

"Who the hell is that?"

"The captain of the barkantine *Swathmore*. Do you remember now?"

There was a moment's silence. Then, "OK, I'm coming. Give me a minute to get my things."

"We'll send someone to get your things later," said the voice. "Right this way, please."

She heard his footsteps moving away toward the edge of the boat, and then receding down the dock.

Prudence lay there, trying not to panic. Would Rick be thrown in jail? Would he be there for days? What should she do?

At first she thought it would be best if she were to wait for nightfall and then try to slip ashore unnoticed. But where would she hide? She knew no one in Porto Escuro.

No, she would have to stay aboard the boat. She would wait until nightfall — she could lift the hatch cover a little bit and see if it was still light — and when it was dark, she would get up and slip into the galley and eat and drink. She would have to be very careful not to make the boat rock as she moved about. She would eat, and drink, and use the bathroom; and then when morning came, she would have to get back in her hiding place in the floor, and stay there all day… she could do that.

But then how could she answer Nature's calls? She couldn't possibly go twelve hours without urinating. She would have to lie in there and — and soil herself.

No! Wait! That was it. She would lock herself in the "head." There would be little room to move about, but she could bring food and drink, and the toilet would be available when she needed it. She would stay locked in the head until Rick was released from jail and returned to the boat, be that a day or a week. No one else would come aboard; why would they?

She felt much better then. It was stuffy and uncomfortable there in the cramped space, but she had a workable plan, and she had sunset to look forward to.

With a sigh of relief, she relaxed a little. There were, she knew, a good three hours yet before it would be dark enough to climb out. It would be very boring waiting in the floor for so long, but she could while away the time by thinking about her movie and trying to overhear snippets of conversation from people walking by the dock.

About twenty minutes went by, during which she overheard snatches of several conversations. Then came the voices of two men, who stopped on the dock right outside the captain's cabin.

"...right here," one was saying, speaking Portuguese with an accent she couldn't place. It was a man's voice, oily and nasal and with a cruel edge that she could detect even muffled through the woodwork. "Yes, it looks like they have arrived. Marco told me she would be in a straitjacket, so she should be pretty easy to handle. Even if she finds out where she's really going, nobody is going to listen to a woman in a straitjacket screaming, no matter what she says. Ahoy! Captain Bancroft? Permission to come aboard?"

This last was shouted out loud. There was no response.

"Well," the voice said, "this is strange. Bancroft was specifically instructed that under no circumstances was he to leave the prisoner alone. It looks like he has done just that. We'd better go collect her."

"What, you mean board Rick Bancroft's boat without

his permission?" said another voice, this one reedy and tentative. "We'd better not. Let's wait for him to get back."

"I got a bad feeling about this," said the first voice. "I'm going aboard. She should be in one of the cabins. Unless maybe Bancroft ironed her."

"Ironed her? With a clothes iron?"

"No, idiot, with shackles. As in put her in irons. Wait here."

She felt the boat dip a little as the man stepped aboard.

"Lenny, you better watch out," the second man called out, sounding close to panic. "If he catches you —"

"Shut up, you little runt," snarled the oily-voiced man. "Keep your eyes peeled. If you see Bancroft coming, kick the boat three times. I'm going to search the boat."

"OK, Lenny," said the other, very nervously.

She felt and heard the unseen man walking across the observation deck to the cabin doors which faced it, and she heard the latch on the door of the cabin she'd slept in. For a minute or two she heard him rummaging around in there. He seemed to be taking his time and being very thorough. Now she was glad Raoul LeCourt had put her on the boat without any luggage, because there would be nothing in there to indicate she was still on board.

Except —

"Christ, Luiz, I found her straitjacket!" hissed Lenny. "It's all folded up neat and tidy here in the passenger cabin. It doesn't look like she's worn it for days!"

"Well, um, maybe she has two," said Luiz.

"You stupid idiot. Who has two straitjackets? It's not a fashion accessory. Something funny is going on here. I think Bancroft is pulling a fast one. I'm gonna search the captain's cabin. Remember, three kicks if you see him comin'. I can talk my way out of it if he catches me snooping in the passenger cabin, but I don't want him catching me going through his personal stuff."

Prudence's eyes stared fearfully into the darkness as she heard the man called Lenny's heavy footsteps just over her face. She heard him opening cabinets and drawers, occasionally muttering a curse or an exclamation of surprise. She wondered what he was finding.

Then she heard him walking back toward the door. But as he reached it, he paused for a moment.

"That's funny," she heard him mutter to himself. "Perfume?"

She knew it wasn't; it couldn't be. She had no perfume, and she'd just bathed and washed her clothes earlier that — oh! That was it! It was the soap!

Her heart pounded as she waited to hear if he would renew his search. If she heard the door handle turn, she'd know she was safe. If not —

The floorboard creaked. Then a footstep, and another, and another. Lenny was walking back into the room, and she could hear him sniffing the air as he came.

Then, through the cloud of claustrophobic panic that was settling over her, a flash of inspiration cut through like a bolt of lightning. She stretched her foot out beyond the little deck of sticks that they had built, found one of the boat's heavy ribs — and kicked it. Three times.

The results were very satisfactory. With a guilty curse, the man bolted out of the room and leaped off the deck of the boat, leaving it rocking gently in the water behind him. Prudence knew that if Bancroft had really been coming back to the boat, that rocking would have been a dead giveaway.

She heard the murmur of quiet conversation, followed by an angry shout: "What do you mean you didn't kick it?

You did! I heard it!"

The conversation died down again into murmurs that she couldn't understand. They seemed to be standing by the bow of the boat, far from her hideout. Then she heard the footsteps approaching again.

"Got it?" the cruel-sounding man was saying. "Lean against the boat just like this. That will keep it from banging into the dock and giving any more false alarms. If," he added, his voice breaking into a sneering tone, "if that's what it really was."

The boat dipped again, and the man was back on board. Prudence held her breath as his footfalls approached the captain's cabin again, and then breathed a sigh of relief as they continued past its door and made their way around to the bows. He was looking in the pilothouse.

A few minutes later, she heard Lenny's footsteps coming back, moving quickly this time. "She's been eating with him in the galley," he told his companion. "I'm telling you, Luiz, they're up to something. Keep a sharp eye out. I'm going to look some more in the captain's cabin."

He walked back across the observation deck and she heard his feet stepping into the cabin again. Panic seized her. She knew she should wait until the last possible instant, but she couldn't stop herself. She stretched her foot out and again kicked the rib three times.

She heard Lenny jump and run out of the cabin again. This time, the conversation occurred right next to the cabin door, and she heard it all.

"Goddamnit, Luiz, is this another one of your tricks?"

"Tricks, boss? What'd I do?"

"You kicked the boat again!"

"No, boss, I swear I never did!"

"Well, then, you let it hit the dock."

"No, Lenny, I held it out like you said! I swear to God I did!"

There was a long silence. Then: "One more false alarm and I'm going to beat you so hard you'll beg me to put you out of your misery."

This line was hissed out with both venom and volume. Then Lenny got back onto the boat. He made a beeline for Rick's cabin again — and this time, Prudence controlled herself. She would only kick if she heard him actually reaching for her hidden hatch cover.

He searched for another minute or two. Then she heard a swish, and she realized he had pulled away the carpet that lay over the cover of the hatch behind which she lay, trying to quiet her breathing and listening to the throbbing hammering of her panic-stricken heart.

She was discovered.

In desperation, she stretched out her foot to buy just a little more time, with one last false alarm…if Lenny would buy it. But as she drew her foot back to give the rib its kick, she heard three distinct thumps, coming from somewhere else on the boat.

It was the signal! Luiz was giving the signal! Could Rick be coming back? Was he out of jail so soon?

But she quickly realized things were going to be different this time. Lenny paused only for a moment.

"Goddamnit," she heard him mutter. "I'm gonna kill him."

And he started fumbling at the hatch again.

Again came those three thumps, more urgent this time. Lenny was paying no attention now. She saw a flash of light as his fingers gained the underside of the hatch. Less than a second now…she thought about that kiss, with Rick looking down into the hatch. That would be the last one she'd get from him, probably forever, she thought.

A sad smile crossed her face as Lenny pulled up the hatch.

XV.

THE REBIRTH.

As the man called Lenny pulled up the hatch under which Prudence McMarion lay, the entire boat shuddered under three heavy blows. Lenny, startled, fumbled the hatch cover, and it dropped back closed with a crash. Prudence held her breath so any dust that might have been knocked off would not make her sneeze. Lenny, with a curse, started fumbling at the hatch again.

Then she heard another voice.

"Hey! You there. What the hell are you doing kicking my boat like that? Oh no you don't, you get back here and explain — why, you little bastard!"

What followed was the unmistakable sound of knuckles on flesh, audible even through the woodwork to Prudence. The sound came again, and then there was a muffled crash, as of a body falling heavily to the deck.

It *was* Rick. He was back.

Lenny seemed to have stopped moving. Prudence assumed he was crouched down in the cabin, hoping not to be discovered.

There was a pause. Then she heard Rick's voice, raised in a shout: "Hey sonny! Want to earn a quick *mil-reis* coin? Run find a policeman and bring him to my boat just as fast as you can!"

Lenny's feet, positioned just about right over the top of Prudence's face, shuffled his feet a bit. Then he stood up and stomped to the door of the cabin.

"I'm no burglar," he shouted. "I'm here looking for my cargo. Don't you dare call the cops on me."

"DeKock?" It was Rick's voice, but Prudence hardly recognized it. It quivered with rage. "What the hell are you doing on my boat? If you're not a burglar, why are you burgling my private quarters? Oh, no you don't, don't move. And throw that gun in the river."

There was a splash. A second later, she heard a groan coming from the dock.

"I get it now," Rick said then, in a voice less choked with rage, but still hard and steely. "This little runt was your lookout. That's why he was kicking my boat. Well, it looks like I'll have two of you for this officer instead of just one. Funny, if you would'a just hunkered down in there and waited for the cops to come arrest your friend, I probably never would have known you were in there."

"Where the hell is the woman I'm supposed to pick up?" Lenny shot back, apparently trying to brazen it out. "I see she's not wearing her straitjacket. Where have you got her hidden? What are you trying to pull?"

"You can get that information from the police, like

everybody else," Rick snarled. "Speaking of which — hello, officer. Yes, sonny, here's your money. Thanks for being so quick. Burglars. The little guy was watching for my return, the big guy I'm holding the gun on was — well, right where he's standing right now, rifling through my cabin."

"Come on out, you," said a new voice, and she heard Lenny's footsteps crossing the deck.

The men moved toward the bow of the boat, apparently to inspect the hull for damage from Luiz's frantic kicking. She heard the murmur of conversation there for a few minutes, but all she could make out was Rick's voice saying, "Of course I'm pressing charges! What kind of stupid question is that, DeKock?"

Several minutes later the voices moved close enough for her to hear again. Rick was talking:

"…tell the sisters that my services are no longer available to them, as long as Lenny DeKock is still working for them," he was saying. "And one other thing. She left this behind when she jumped overboard. It appears Miss McMarion searched the wheelhouse while I was asleep, or in the head, or something. My orders were to deliver it unopened to the sisters, or their medical representative. Miss McMarion appears to have opened it, and found its contents very interesting. I certainly found them interesting. Had I known what this letter says about Miss McMarion's mental state, I would never have agreed to transport her.

"Oh, and by the way, there were originally fifteen of those hundred-dollar bills. I had to nick two of them to bail myself out of jail. Call it, if you will, a service fee."

"So, when did you say she jumped?" said a new voice, a cultivated-sounding native Brazilian.

"Around ten o'clock this morning," said Rick. "I heard a splash, looked behind me, saw her trying to swim to shore.

I came around to chase after her, but she was making a hell of a splashing commotion in the water and you know, it's the time of year when they're really hungry. I knew what was going to happen. I yelled at her to stop splashing but… it was too late."

"Jesus," said the new voice. "So they tore her apart before your eyes?"

"She was a couple hundred yards behind the boat," said Rick. "I couldn't see much. The screams were pretty bad, though. I've been around, Joey, and I was in the war. I've seen and heard some pretty awful things. I've never heard anything like those screams."

A new set of footsteps was now heard coming up the dock. "Oh good, I'm glad to see you boys," said Rick. "Just stack them on the observation deck, right there, that's perfect."

Heavy footsteps tipped the boat, and she heard thumps and grunts of strain. Someone was obviously loading boxes on board the *Amazon Princess*.

"Beautiful," Rick said then. "What do I owe you boys?"

The muscles in Prudence's legs started cramping as the footsteps receded. She flexed her leg muscles, first one and then the other. Please, she prayed, let it be over soon.

Then the voices were back.

"Shame about the girl," said the cultivated voice — Joey, Rick had called him. "We're going to have to file a report and I'll need you to sign the death certificate as a witness. You're staying the night, aren't you?"

"I'd better not," said Rick. "I have to get that sugar back upriver for the general store right away; they're almost out. Is this something I can do on my next run? I'll be back in a week."

"No, not really," said Joey. "The American embassy is

very demanding in cases like this. I really need you to sign off on this before you go, and I can't get it ready before tomorrow morning. But I can set it up for eight in the morning if you like, and you can just sign and go. You won't be able to get very far upriver tonight anyway, you know."

There was a long pause. Then Rick replied: "I know. I'm just worried about DeKock's goons coming back. I'm going to take the boat and anchor it in the harbor for security. But I'll be back here at eight o'clock sharp to meet you. Will that work?"

There was a mumble of assent. Then Rick stepped back aboard the boat, and she heard footsteps retreating on the dock.

Rick stepped to the cabin door and peered in. "Fifteen more minutes," he said. Then he closed the door and she heard him walking around the boat, obviously casting off the mooring lines. A few minutes after that, the engine started to turn over — slowly and anemically, since there wasn't much steam up — and the propeller shaft made its familiar grinding noise.

About ten minutes later, the engine sounds stopped, and she heard a splash as if an anchor had been dropped.

More time went by: ten minutes, twenty minutes — it all seemed like an eternity to Prudence now. Her left calf was stiff and cramped. She wished Rick would hurry.

Then the panel door rattled and she saw a gleam of candlelight; and by it, she saw Rick's fingers working under the door of the hatch. He pulled the panel away and, as a wave of fresh air washed gloriously over her, she looked up into his worried eyes.

"Keep your head down, Tru," he murmured. "I guarantee they're watching us with telescopes from every angle they can get to right now. I've got the cargo set up blocking the view through the cabin door, but they'll see you if you come near a window. Sorry to have to do this, but we can't leave until morning."

"I know," she whispered. "I heard. Thank God I didn't wait upstream for you, I'd be spending the night."

"Nope. You wouldn't. But the two of us would probably be running from the law by tomorrow morning. So, yes."

"Rick? Who is it that owns the *Swathmore*?"

Bancroft frowned. "Wealthy local merchant, probably the most powerful man in Porto Escuro. His name, believe it or not, is Sílvio da Silva. He owns several sailing ships, all of them with English names and English captains, but he's as Brazilian as they come.

"I'd better get going now, before someone gets suspicious," he said then. "I'll bring some food back here for you on the sly in about an hour," he said. "Here's the wine cabinet, here. Help yourself. I'm going to go forward and make a big show of smoking a cigar. I'll see you in an hour or so."

"Check. Listen, Rick, that oily man — DeKock, I think you called him — he knows about this panel in the floor. He almost had it open when you came back."

"Good, thanks for telling me," said Rick. "We'll move you somewhere else under cover of darkness tonight. For now, just stay in here, keeping below the window level. I'll be back in an hour or so."

"Rick," she said, as he turned to leave. "Rick. You were —"

"Don't say it," Rick shot back, with a playful smirk tugging at the corner of his mouth, and turned to go.

For the next hour she lay on the floor of the cabin, stretching her stiff muscles and wishing she had a book to read. Then Rick came back, slipped her a tin of beef from his pocket, took a bottle of wine from the cabinet and with a word or two of encouragement, retired to the wheelhouse.

Another hour went by. Twilight came, and with it Rick returned to the cabin, smelling of cigar smoke, the still-mostly-full wine bottle in his hand.

"Can I sit up now?" she whispered.

"Not just yet," he said. "They'll expect me to sit up for a few minutes with the candle burning, so I'll do that, pretend to be writing some stuff. When I blow out the candle, the coast is clear."

He took about another ten minutes by the candle as she sat on the floor looking up at him, holding the cup of wine he'd poured for her. Then, as the twilight faded into a faint gloaming in the distant west, he blew out the candle, and she climbed gratefully up off the floor and sat down next to him, and he reached out in the darkness without a word and touched her face and drew her to him and kissed her again, and again.

R ick made no attempt at further intimacy that night, for which Prudence was grateful; although her attraction to Rick Bancroft was powerful and growing, she would never have forgiven herself if she'd yielded to him so soon. She knew that he wanted her as well, but was holding back. Maybe he shared her worry about letting things move too fast, or perhaps he simply didn't want her to think he was the kind of man who would take advantage of a woman in a vulnerable situation.

In any case, she spent the night in his bunk — he absolutely insisted that she take his bunk, while he slept on the cabin floor, and in the morning when she awoke he was already up.

"I brought you coffee," he said. "I had to bring it when it was pitch dark outside, so it's cold; but it's coffee."

She took it gratefully and sipped. It was actually still fairly warm. The sun was only just starting to rise.

"Now, we're going to need to have you get back in the floor again," said Rick. "I changed my mind about moving you somewhere else. There is nowhere else except the chain locker up front, and I can't put you in there until we weigh anchor."

Prudence shuddered. "What about the head?" she asked, almost desperately. "Can I just lock myself in the head?"

"Too risky," said Rick. "What if Joey asks to use it? What if I have to use it? Out on the river, a man can just sort of go on the other side of the boat and do his business, but in port that sort of thing is frowned upon. And I don't think either one of us would be comfortable using the toilet together."

That made sense, and Prudence reluctantly said as much.

Rick nodded. "Trust me," he said. "It's the best we can do, and you'll be in no danger. If nothing else, I'll just open up the steam valve and we'll run for it. You better believe I'm carrying a full head of steam when we go back into the harbor there at Porto Escuro.

"I'm due to sign those papers as having witnessed your death at eight o'clock," he continued. "The boiler's heating up now. By nine, we'll be on our way back up the river and you can get back to normal, if there is such a thing after you've been declared dead."

He paused for a moment.

"Maybe getting declared dead is what I should do," he said thoughtfully. "Then I could finally stop —"

He started, and looked at her, almost seeming surprised

to see her there. "Oh, never mind," he said briskly. "I'll get things going. Sunrise is at about six-thirty, so you'll have to stay low after that. Around seven-thirty we'll bundle you back into the hole for just one more hour and a half before you're — free."

He looked envious. She reached out and laid a soft hand on his rough forearm as he turned to leave.

"Rick," she said. "Rick darling, don't ever feel any pressure to tell me anything you're not ready to talk about, OK? I'm not going to press you to explain what you just said, about getting declared dead, although I do hope you'll tell me someday. But I want you to know this: I don't care. I really, really don't. You told me you were not a murderer — I wouldn't care if you were one. That's all."

Rick turned to face her and — as much as he could in the murky darkness — looked her right in the eyes.

"Yes, you would, Tru," he said gently. "Because if I were a murderer, I wouldn't be me."

She smiled at him. "That's right, you wouldn't, would you?" she said. "I think we understand each other."

He looked at his feet awkwardly, looked at her, smiled encouragingly and disappeared, closing the cabin door behind him. She settled down on the cabin floor to wait.

A little after seven-thirty, Rick returned to the cabin and helped her back into her floor locker. With dread in her heart, she reluctantly climbed in and waited as Rick gently placed the panel back in its grooves.

This time, she knew she would only be in the floor for a little while. But the time dragged on even more slowly than it had the previous night. She listened to the sounds of the boat as it forged through the water and then thumped against the dock.

On the deck she heard Rick and Joey chatting briefly

as Rick signed the papers certifying that she was dead. Then, there were cheerful farewells on both sides, the boat rocked again to Rick's footsteps, the propeller shaft creaked back to life, and she knew she was almost free.

A dozen minutes passed, seeming like so many hours to the impatient Prudence. Then a flash of daylight dazzled her as Rick picked up one end of the panel, and an instant later he was pulling the whole thing up.

It was over. She was free.

Feeling like Persephone returning from the land of the dead, Prudence stepped out into the bright sunlight of a brilliant Amazon morning. The rainforest was once again gliding by them as they steamed along the river, and it somehow looked cleaner, brighter, fresher, its colors more saturated than it had before. She felt as if she'd just been reborn, reborn into a completely new life. And—in this new life, she was no longer from Los Angeles, or New York. This was her home now. Snakes and all.

On the little table in the cabin were their two tin cups, full, beside a stack of hardtack biscuits and a half-empty bottle of wine.

"It really is too early in the morning to start drinking already," said Rick. "But I wanted to celebrate somehow."

XVI.

THE SHADOW IN THE DEEP.

ick and Prudence spent the morning steaming upriver at the *Amazon Princess's* maximum cruising speed. Prudence spent some time on the observation deck, basking in the overwhelming sense of relief; then she went forward to keep Rick company in the wheelhouse.

When she stepped inside, Rick was about halfway through one of his big cigars. He hastily removed it and set about preserving it for future smoking in the usual way.

"You can smoke your cigar, Rick," she told him. "I don't mind."

"You sure?" Rick replied, a little guiltily.

"Of course!" she said with a laugh. "Two of the windows have been shot out. I think the air in here is going to stay fresh no matter what."

He hesitated. "Maybe later," he said.

They watched the scenery gliding by in silence for a few moments. Then Rick turned toward her.

"We need to do some serious thinking right now," he said. "Lenny DeKock is probably already out of jail. He's got the resources to bail out. But it was very unlike him to do something like board my boat without permission. For whatever reason, somebody is desperate to get you out of circulation."

"Who is that man, anyway?" Prudence said. "I've only seen his feet, when he almost uncovered me. But his voice is just unbelievably creepy."

"Yeah. He's one of the local expats I warned you about, back when we first met," said Rick. "Probably the worst one of us all. I'd run across him before, back when I was running — er, when I was working in upstate New York. He's a South African mercenary. A real piece of work. I don't know who he's working for, but you can bet your last shekel he's not working for the Sisters of the Sacred Heart, even if they might think he is."

"That's funny," said Prudence. "I wouldn't think there would be too many South Africans in a place like Porto Escuro. Our local production manager is a South African too: Leonard Stevens."

"That is a coincidence," said Rick, "but there are plenty of South Africans running around. Most Americans just think they're Australian."

"So for some reason they've hired an exotic mercenary to help take me out," Prudence said thoughtfully. "I don't know what Lenny DeKock charges, but he can't be cheap. So Raoul spent six hundred *reais* on you, fifteen hundred dollars bribing the sisters, and whatever on Lenny. All just to get rid of little old me."

She was silent for a moment, then continued: "I just know — whatever is going on has something to do with Eleanor. We've got to get to that place in the river from my dream, and follow that path. I think we'll find Eleanor if we do."

"Well," said Rick, with a touch of his old flintiness creeping back into his voice, "I don't believe in any of that spooky-spiritty oui-ja crap, you know. But I'm game. It's as good a lead as any other we've got. And it is weird that you dreamed about it."

Prudence looked into the distance for a moment.

"Rick," she said, "what you have done for me is more than enough to repay the debt, if you want to call it that, of saving your life. Without Eleanor to back me up, I barely have enough money to book passage home. But I just don't want to —"

"Hey! Trudie! Stop that!" Rick said crisply. "Look, I know, I have a reputation for being a stingy, money-grubbing bastard. Let me tell you, honey, it's well earned. I actually take pride in it. But I take care of my friends. I don't make money off them, I don't send them bills, and I don't want to hear another word about you paying me anything, and you'd better not even try to give me a nickel. Someday it'll be your turn to be there for me. Right now it's my turn to be there for you."

She looked at him gratefully and nodded.

The rest of the day passed without incident — except for one thing. As she was reclining dreamily on the observation deck, Prudence noticed that the river water was unusually clear in the portion of the river they were moving through. She leaned over the rail and gazed down into its green depths, wondering if she'd be able to see fish there — maybe even some of the piranhas that were, at that very moment, being officially blamed for her own untimely death.

There were a few small fish, flitting across her field of vision — pancake-shaped fish about eight inches long; they might have been piranhas; she didn't know. But as she watched them, she noticed something funny. The dark shadow of the boat, flashing across the depths of the water, did not seem to be falling on the fish as they swept past. She could see the shadow distinctly, moving at the exact same pace as the boat, appearing to sway from side to side as the light was bent by the intervening waves.

But as each little fish swam into the shadow, it remained brightly illuminated by the sun.

And then she realized that the sun was not in a position to cast the shadow she was seeing. So — what was that long, black, shadowy *thing* down there, moving at precisely the same speed as the boat? She stared, fascinated. It was vaguely boat-shaped, but long and —

A small scream escaped her lips and she scrambled back into the boat, away from the gunwales. She had recognized the shape, and realized that the slight side-to-side movement was not from the shimmering effect of the waves. It was the steady side-to-side movement of a water snake. But she had never imagined that any snake could ever be that big. And it was pacing the boat so precisely that she was sure they were being stalked.

She raced to the wheelhouse, where she found Rick already coming out.

"What was that?" he said, looking worried and relieved. "I heard you scream. I was afraid that maybe —"

"There's a snake stalking the boat!" she gasped, still frightened. "A huge snake, as big around as the boat almost.

Moving through the water at the same exact speed as us. I thought it was our shadow in the water at first."

Rick frowned. "That can't — show me!"

Prudence led him to the rail. But the *Amazon Princess* had just entered into the downstream outflow of an especially muddy tributary stream, and the water they were cruising through was an opaque tan color now. They could see only a few feet into it.

Rick gazed into the water for some time. Then he turned and looked at Prudence. "I'm glad it wasn't something more serious," he said. "When I heard you scream, my first thought was that you'd fallen overboard and I was going to have to watch the piranhas eat you for real. They're thick in this part of the river."

Prudence shuddered. Rick looked back into the water, then turned back to her.

"Trudie, have you ever heard of something called a Yacumama?" he asked then.

"No, I — oh! Oh — yes. Yes, I have heard of it. The old woman who saw Eleanor paddle away told me about it. The giant snake!"

"Right," he said. "Nobody really believes they exist except the Indian tribes. Me, I believe the natives. The Yacumama is supposed to be shy, and I've never heard of anyone ever having been eaten by one. But... are you sure it was a snake you saw?"

"Only a snakelike body that disappeared into the darkness behind the boat," she said. "I couldn't even see the head. I don't know, I don't know — maybe I was just being silly."

Rick looked at her for a moment. "All those people telling you you're crazy, and now they've got you distrusting yourself, huh?" he said. "Well, I'm not buying it. If you saw a snake, you saw a snake."

"I — it just seems like it can't be," she said.

"Hey, this river is full of things that we don't know about," said Rick. "Also, nobody ever died from assuming there *was* a tiger lurking on the trail, but plenty have died from assuming there *wasn't*. If there's no real reason to think you were wrong, it's probably safe to assume you're right."

"And a giant snake is stalking our boat?"

"Sure, why not? I have to run back to the wheelhouse. Come back with me if you like."

She hurried behind him into the wheelhouse and settled down into her chair as he made the course correction. Then he turned toward her.

"Whatever it is, it's not a threat to us as long as we're not in the water," he observed. "And this time of year, I'm pretty sure it's the last thing we'd have to worry about if we *were* in the water. But trust me, if there was a snake out there attacking eighty-foot riverboats, I'd know by now."

That sounded very reasonable. But she still had little desire to go back out onto the observation deck again, and no desire at all to lean over the rail.

They anchored for the night a little way downstream from the spot where they'd been attacked by the rifleman, in the same wide section of the river in which they'd anchored after the attack.

"That dock is just way too close to the road for my comfort," Rick explained, "and obviously the word is out. I'm not eager to give our gun-toting friend a second chance."

Prudence made no objection. If anything, she wished they could have stopped a little farther away from the scene of the midnight skirmish.

They got under way earlier than usual the next morning, just after dawn, following the usual hardtack breakfast; they were all out of "real" bread, Rick's stock of tinned beef was starting to look thin, and they wouldn't have any fruit until the following day, when they'd be stopping by the dock near Rick's Indian friends' garden.

But now as they approached the other dock — the long one that Rick had built for smuggling purposes, at which they'd been attacked — Rick slowed the boat to a crawl.

"What's that in the water over there?" he said, pointing with the unlit cigar in his hand.

"It looks like a pith helmet," said Prudence. "Should we pick it up?"

"Yes," said Rick. "It's got to be from one of the two mugs who attacked us the other day."

Rick picked up a long whisker pole from where it lay by the cabin-top handrail and gingerly approached the dock, where the helmet lay lodged against the boards. Carefully he hooked it and pulled it toward the boat. Soon he had it on the observation deck, where it lay rolling around in a small puddle of river water as he stowed the whisker pole once again.

As Rick put the pole away, Prudence picked the helmet up and looked it over. Inside the hat band was a name: "Emil Capett."

"Emil Capett, Emil Capett," Rick muttered to himself, drumming his fingers on the cabin top. "Where do I know that name from? Emil Capett…."

"He's not from Carraçao, I'm pretty sure," said Prudence. "If there were another American in Carraçao, I'm sure I'd have heard about it."

"There is another American, but he keeps a low profile," said Rick. "But his name is Hy Jones, not Emil Capett…

he's another M.D., works with LeCourt. But, it seems to me I've heard the name Emil Capett, and I can't think of where."

"How does the name feel to you?" Prudence asked. "Good, neutral, or bad?"

"Huh?" said Rick. "Is this more spiritty oui-ja mystical bunk, Tru?"

"No," said Prudence, "it's not spiritty oui-ja mystical bunk. I'm not a spiritty oui-ja mystical kind of girl, and after you get to know me better you'll figure that out. But when I can't remember where I've heard a name, I can usually remember the emotions associated with it. Like if you say Mussolini, I might not remember who Mussolini is, but I'd have a kind of cold thuggish feeling hearing the name. See what I mean?"

"Oh," said Rick. "Yeah. I don't know. I think it's probably bad. It's not a man I know, more like a name I've heard about."

The rest of their journey passed without incident, and the next day they stopped for supper a few miles downstream from Carraçao and rode there at anchor until nightfall. Rick was waiting for the moon to come out over the water; it would be a slender new crescent that night, shedding just enough light to enable them to see the channel.

When the time was right, they slipped past the dark outlines of the village of Carraçao with the steam plant just barely ticking over. Even so, Prudence thought the boat was impossibly noisy. But it was two in the morning, and everyone in Carraçao appeared to be fast asleep.

Rick turned the power up again after the city was well behind, and when they came to a broad lagoon, they dropped anchor and retired to their cabins.

The next day dawned clear and bright once again on the river. Prudence, feeling nearly her old self, got up just before dawn and sat on the observation deck with a notebook and pen borrowed from Rick's cabin — she'd transfer the info to her travel journal later, if she ever got it back. Not that there was much in that journal. It seemed as if she'd opened that little book a hundred times over the course of her journey, never writing anything in it but the date. Now she'd make up for that with a detailed journal entry of the events of the past few days.

Prudence noticed that they were anchored in the middle of the lagoon where they'd gone to film the caimans. That had been less than two weeks before... but she remembered it dimly and hazily, like the memories of another life.

Somehow the dozens of lazy caimans already gliding around the boat made her feel safe. Caimans were earthly monsters, known quantities — unlike the huge ghostly snake she thought she'd glimpsed stalking their boat. But already she was starting to doubt the evidence of her senses once again. Rick might have believed it was a snake she'd seen, but the more she thought about it, the less likely it seemed to her. Would not those little fish have frantically skittered out of the way if they saw a snake like the one she thought she'd spotted? And yet they were flitting past as if the snake didn't exist. So, perhaps it didn't.

Rick's cabin door rattled and he emerged, blinking sleepily, his pajama pocket distended with the weight of the revolver he apparently habitually kept in it. "I'm not used to people getting up before me," he grumbled. "I'm usually the first one on deck."

"Well, I'm the earliest early bird I know," said Prudence, "so, better get used to it."

"I hope I get the chance to," he shot back, with a mischievous smirk. "Guess I'll go start the boilers."

"Want some help?"

"Nope, I got this. You relax and enjoy your morning time. I'll be back with hot coffee in about forty minutes. If you need me, you know where to find me."

Prudence's heart swelled within her as she realized that Rick was deliberately and consciously leaving her alone so that she could enjoy her solitary quiet time. No man had ever done that for her before without being asked. In fact, she had once even broken off an engagement to a man specifically because he would not respect her morning meditation time. It was a decision that had horrified her mother, but she had never for a moment regretted it.

She settled in and started writing.

True to his word, Rick was back forty minutes later with two mugs of steaming hot coffee, along with a handful of hardtack biscuits and a couple of fresh fruits from the Jaragua tribe's garden. The two of them sat on the observation deck in companionable silence eating their breakfast.

"You really should let me upgrade your galley a bit for you, Rick," Prudence remarked. "Mealtime doesn't have to be like this, you know. The fruit is wonderful, but hardtack is tough to live on."

"I suppose," he said, sounding embarrassed. "I think I have some canned beans in there. Maybe we can mix it up a little at supper."

They finished their repast and cast off a few minutes later, the boiler having heated up to a nice temperature. From there it was just an hour or so to the spot Prudence had seen in her dream.

When they got there, Rick anchored the *Amazon Princess* near the shore, then banked the fire carefully so that it would maintain steam as long as possible.

"I don't know what we're going to find here," he told Prudence, "but one of the many possibilities is that we might be forced to run for our lives. If that happens, I mean to be ready to run fast."

XVII.

THE SUNKEN RIVERBOAT.

**W**ell," said Prudence as she stepped into the *Amazon Princess's* little lifeboat-dinghy for the trip to shore, "now is the time for me to face my fear of giant snakes."

"Oh yes, the giant snake," said Rick distractedly. "Don't worry about him, Tru. If he was in the habit of snatching people out of boats, don't you think we'd know about it by now?"

"Well, no," said Prudence soberly. "First Eleanor's aunt and uncle, and then Eleanor, have been apparently taken out of boats and eaten, or at least that's what everyone thinks. Their boats drifted down to the village covered with tooth marks. Everybody thought they were caiman bites, but maybe they were snake bites."

The silence hung ominously for a second. Then, "Hold

that thought," Rick said, and jumped back onto the deck of the *Amazon Princess* and ducked into his cabin.

When he emerged, he was holding a small silver revolver by the barrel. He handed it over to her, butt first.

"It's not much of a gun, but it's a gun," he said. "It's a five-shot .32. I've got some extra bullets for it; do you want 'em, or should I hang onto 'em?"

"You keep them," she said. "But thank you, I'll definitely take the gun."

Rick took the boat's bow painter loose and, holding onto it, stepped gingerly into the dinghy and settled down onto the center thwart. Prudence, far up in the bows, looked out toward the shore and clutched the little revolver tightly. The path had reappeared, she noticed — the wall of vegetation that had covered it on the previous visit had once again vanished — or had she imagined that, too?

She felt the little rowboat surge forward as Rick dug the oars into the water. She leaned out over the bow and, in spite of herself, looked down into the river. There, far below her, she could see… but wasn't that just the shadow of the rowboat reflected in the river's depths? She couldn't tell. This time there were no fish.

Shadow or snake, whatever it was wasn't showing any inclination to eat them. Prudence loosened her grip on the pistol a little and looked out at the shore of the river as Rick's practiced strokes moved them closer and closer to land. He was rowing backward, facing the direction of travel so that he could see where he was going.

As they approached the shore, Prudence realized that everything about it was familiar from her dream — even things that she hadn't remembered. There was the small tree girded with fruits that she now recognized as *cupuaçus* — but she hadn't known what they were until Rick had brought the fruit in from the Jaragua tribe's garden and told her what they were.

And then there was something that was not familiar from her dream. It was by the spot where she'd seen the markings in the mud, or thought she had. It was now covered with brush. But nearby, just inside the vegetation line where it had been hidden from view, lay a paddle made of golden varnished wood.

Eleanor, she knew, had been here before her.

Rick saw it too, and he was looking at her, very puzzled. "You say you saw all this in a dream?" he said.

"Yes," she said. "This, and the path, which leads to an ancient stone city."

"The path? What path?"

The route Rick had picked in bringing the dinghy to the shore had taken them to one side of the path, and from where they sat just then, it wasn't visible. For answer, Prudence pointed to the spot at which she knew it debouched, visible now only as a slight break in the foliage. In that spot, as they drew closer, the slender game trail came into view through the screening leaves and branches, as if conjured by her pointing finger.

"OK," he muttered, touching his forehead as if to make sure it was the same size and shape as before.

In spite of herself, Prudence laughed at him. "I told you, I'm not a spiritty-oui-ja mystical kind of girl," she told him. "If I tell you something spiritty is going on, well, it is."

"OK, that's fair," said Rick. "Let's go see how spiritty this is going to get."

A few minutes later, Rick had the dinghy securely tied to an overhanging tree branch, and was helping Prudence step out onto the grassy shore.

Something made a rustling sound nearby, and Rick turned his head, looking worried. "What was that?" he said.

"A frog maybe?" said Prudence.

"Maybe," he said, peering through the dense shoreside foliage. Then a long, slender green snake dropped down almost at his side, and he leaped back with a curse as it slipped down the tree to escape.

"Stupid whipsnake," he muttered. "OK, let's go."

They walked to the path, and Rick bent down to inspect the mud of the riverbank near where the trail started. "Trudie, come look at this," he called.

Prudence came and looked.

There, in the mud left by the receding waters of the river, she distinctly saw a footprint. It was a small, feminine print that had obviously been made with a pair of low-heel Oxfords, of the type very tall girls often wore in Los Angeles.

"Eleanor," she whispered.

"That's how I'm reading it."

They looked at each other for a moment, and then without another word turned to follow the trail up the hill.

They soon discovered that the trail didn't lead straight up the hill. It first followed along the shore of the little tributary creek that ran out by the strangely-shaped mahogany tree. And as they followed it, they soon came across a fork in the trail; one side went up the hillside to their left, and the other ran down to the creek. Looking out over it, Prudence could now see that it was not a creek, but a small lagoon of sorts.

"Say, Trudie, can you see that thing sticking up out of that oxbow pond?" said Rick suddenly. "Right over there. Does that look like a steamboat to you?"

Prudence looked carefully. The lagoon was narrow and

the forest canopy completely covered it, so there wasn't much light. But the more she stared, the more clearly it was an old steamboat. Its hull seemed to be wedged in the mud at the bottom of the pond, the waters of which looked to be just a few feet deep at that point.

"How would a steamboat get here?" she asked, puzzled.

"This used to be the river," Rick explained. "It used to run right through this glade here. Then one winter during flood season the river cut across the neck of this bend around here, and left it high and dry. It's called an oxbow pond. Around here, oxbow ponds are a good place to find schools of starving piranhas when they get cut off from the rest of the river. The damn things get so desperate they'll literally jump out of the water to try to bite you and drag you in."

"Oh," said Prudence. "I wonder what boat it is. It really looks like one, now that you mention it."

"I'm going to run down and take a look," Rick said. "I'll be right back."

"Isn't it piranha season?"

"You oughtta know," he joked. "But don't worry, I'm not going near that water."

Prudence waited at the junction of the trails as Rick made his way down to the edge of the oxbow pond. When he got there he turned and called up to her.

"It's definitely a steam yacht," he called. "Looks like the type they were building in about 1885. No way it's been in this spot for forty years, though. It was probably ten, fifteen years old when it sank. Also, this pond is teeming with trapped piranhas, so don't get any ideas about exploring it."

"Say, Rick," Prudence called back, "there's something painted white in the bushes about twenty feet to your left."

"Is there?" he replied. "Let me see here..."

He thrashed his way through the bushes, making as much noise as possible to encourage any coral snakes and other dangerous nasties to get out of the way. Soon he was clearing the underbrush away from a long, open dinghy.

"I guess that answers that question," he said jovially.

"Rick, from up here on the trail those branches look like they were laid over that boat on purpose to hide it," Prudence called down to him. "Be careful, it may be booby-trapped."

"I take it this wasn't in your dream?" Rick called back.

"No," she said. "So maybe you're right, and it's just a coincidence."

"Maybe," Rick replied. "But there's not much else to see or do here. Let's — whoa, what's this?"

He bent to pick something up, then abruptly stood up. "Let's go, Tru," he said briskly.

Prudence put her hands on her hips and watched him as he thrashed his way through the foliage, until he got about halfway up.

"What was that?" she demanded, suspiciously.

"Just an old boot," he said, a little too casually.

She eyed him with suspicion as he continued to make his way up through the underbrush toward her. Then she stepped off the trail and made her way toward him. He moved to block her.

"Rick," she said, and impatience seasoned with a hint of anger flickered in her voice as she perceived that he intended to try to stop her. "Rick, I saw the look on your face. Rick, it's sweet that you want to shield me from whatever that thing was, but I am not some corset-wearing, laudanum-sipping Gibson Girl who faints when gentlemen use coarse language. What did you see down there?"

"It's — it's a boot," said Rick reluctantly. "With — with foot-bones still inside."

Prudence shuddered in spite of herself. "How old do they look?"

"Old enough. At least ten years. Let's get moving."

Prudence glanced again at the rowboat, started to turn away — and then wheeled back to stare at it.

"Whoa," said Rick. "Why the double-take?"

"Take a look at those marks on that old rowboat, Rick," she whispered, pointing a trembling finger.

Rick looked. Then he ran back through the underbrush for a closer inspection. Prudence followed him, and this time he did not try to stop her.

"They're tooth marks," she whispered, as he pulled aside the fronds. "They are, aren't they? Just like the marks on Eleanor's boat. Only — only they're deep. Like they actually crushed the boat."

It was true. The rowboat looked as if it had been smashed like an eggshell by something with huge teeth.

Rick stood up and gazed out through the dim light toward the wrecked steamboat, several hundred feet away.

"Trudie," he said, "does it look to you like that steam yacht has tooth marks on it, too?"

Prudence squinted, trying to make out the marks on the weathered old hulk. "I can't see," she said.

"I'll bring the rowboat around and have a closer look when we get back," he said.

His voice dropped to a whisper, which she only just barely caught: "If we get back..."

Prudence suddenly turned. "We'll look at it later," she said. "Right now, I don't want to know if a giant snake attacked a full-size riverboat. There's nothing we could do about it, and if it's true it could only make us less able to respond to whatever is going to try to kill us next. Let's go."

With Prudence leading the way, the two of them plunged forward once again through the forest, and soon they gained the path once again. It was a narrow one, just as in her dream, little more than a game trail. The branches were close at each side, so they had to walk single file. Overhead, animals and birds jabbered and screeched and hooted. She felt the trail's familiarity starting to pull her along, and she picked up speed until she was almost running.

Prudence could hear Rick breathing hard, trying to keep up with her. She somehow knew exactly where she was going, and the next time the path split into two forks, she darted up the left-hand fork before she even realized she'd made a choice.

"I hope — you know — where you're going, Tru," Rick panted. "'Cos I'm lost."

"Don't worry," she shot back, her voice smooth and unhurried, although she was breathing hard too. "I got this. I'm running on spiritty oui-ja power."

Then, before Rick had time to come up with a witty riposte, she abruptly stopped short. Rick — who was, as he would later red-facedly admit, shamelessly admiring her backside rather than looking where he was going — blundered headlong into her from behind.

Prudence started to fall forward. Rick reached around to catch her, and pulled her back upright; and the two of them stood there, his arms around her waist and her hands resting on his forearms, gaping at the scene that lay before them.

They had reached a spot in the forest where the path opened out onto a meadow. And a few yards into the meadow, a sheer wall of weathered granite rose up out of the ground, crenellated and garnished with vines and moss.

The two of them stood there for a moment staring up at it. Then Prudence stepped forward out of Rick's arms and walked confidently toward the wall.

Rick followed, feeling a little like a bewildered puppy. She turned to the left when she reached the wall and started walking parallel to it, across a bed of grass that looked almost like a well-kept lawn. Soon she reached a great arched doorway, black and ominous, with heavy stone doors standing open on the inside, that pierced the wall about three hundred yards away from where they'd left the forest.

Without a moment's hesitation, as if impelled by some outside force, and with Rick following dubiously and nervously behind, she plunged ahead through the archway and into the dreamed-of hidden city.

XVIII.

THE TEMPLE.

Just inside the doorway, Prudence stopped again. This time, Rick was ready for her, and managed to avoid a collision.

The wall they had passed through enclosed a space far bigger than it had appeared from without — bigger, and open to the sky, taking up the entire side of the little hill facing the river. Inside was a field of curiously short, even grasses, almost like a lawn that hadn't been mowed in a couple weeks. Through the center of it ran a wide avenue that led about a quarter of a mile up the gentle slope of the hill to where the first of a cluster of vine-covered buildings stood; then it passed between these buildings and appeared to end in front of what looked, in the distance half a mile away, like a sort of ziggurat.

Prudence stared. The whole scene seemed somehow

familiar — but that was probably just because the whole scene looked so much like what she'd expected to see. The inside of the city looked very much like some of the Spanish paintings she had seen depicting the Aztec cities they'd found in Central America, only with considerably more open space. It was also, she noticed, not nearly as crumbling and overgrown as she had expected it to be. The walls were weathered, but not crumbling. They were covered with vines and branches of overhanging trees, but the vines looked decorative, like ivy growing on the outside brick walls of a college lecture hall, and the trees that were there looked as if they'd been planted, not sprouted. And although she couldn't see them from where she stood, Prudence was fairly certain that all the roofs of the buildings were intact. And then there were those grasses, looking almost as if they'd been mowed.

A few years earlier, when Prudence had first moved to Los Angeles, she'd left her modest house in New York vacant for a year, deeming it imprudent to sell it without knowing if the move was permanent. She'd contracted with a local service to maintain the place while she was gone. They had cut the grass and repaired the damage from that winter's ice storm, but the flowerbeds had gone unweeded and the hedges had gone untrimmed, and when she'd returned the next year to put it up for sale it had looked — not abandoned, but certainly vacant and definitely unloved. This city gave her the same impression.

But perhaps that was just because it was so robustly built. The walls of the buildings she was looking at, which she'd at first taken for blocks of cut stone, on closer inspection appeared to be made of large gray kiln-fired bricks, ten or twelve inches square, stuck together with a substance like mortar — something she hadn't thought ancient South

American civilizations knew how to make. The walls looked to be at least two feet thick.

They were standing before a broad avenue that led down the middle of the city, directly bisecting it, lined with large buildings or villas. The avenue sloped slightly uphill. And at the end, close by the wall on the other side, stood the ziggurat-temple thing; it resembled the Chichén Itzá ruins in Mexico, of which Prudence had seen pictures in a tourism brochure once. It appeared to be smaller, and to lack the grand central staircase.

Rick stepped up beside her and stared. Her hand sought his, and she pointed down the boulevard to the temple. "That's where we need to go," she said. "Right down there."

"OK," he said, in a sort of hushed whisper. "Say, Tru, have you noticed — no, that's just silly, never mind."

"What is it?"

"It's just that standing here looking over this city, I feel somehow different. Like when we walked across that threshold, something changed."

"Now who's being all mystical and spiritty?" Prudence shot back, her eyes teasingly seeking upward for his.

"No, seriously. It's as if gravity had changed a little bit, just a little, and I'd gotten five pounds lighter or heavier. But it's not that. I don't know what it is, but I don't like it."

"I know. Don't be afraid. I don't know what it is either, but when we find Eleanor, I'm sure she will tell us."

He looked away, looking uncomfortable.

"What is it?" she asked.

"I just — nothing. Never mind. Lead on."

The avenue was mostly clear, with grasses bunched here and there, none over ankle deep. They had gotten about halfway down its length when Rick abruptly stopped, touching Prudence's elbow as he did.

"Trudie," he whispered sharply. "Look at this."

He pointed to a patch of bare earth, between tussocks of grass. Distinctly, in the dust, they could see the outline of a man's boot track.

The two of them looked at each other, wide-eyed. They were not alone in this strange ancient city.

"Eleanor," said Prudence. "She could be in danger."

Again that uncomfortable look from Rick, and abruptly Prudence realized what it was: he thought Eleanor was dead, and that all they would find would be a moldering corpse.

She opened her mouth to reassure him, but he was already gesturing toward the distant temple.

"Let's go," he said. "But quietly."

They proceeded up the boulevard now at the fastest pace they could manage without making undue noise. When they got closer to the temple, they found that there was indeed a central staircase, but it was cut into the stone fronts of the tiers, rather than built up over the top of them. It was also not very wide — just five or six feet.

The moment she set her feet on the staircase, Prudence knew where she was going. She had been there before, in her dream, which she hadn't fully remembered until just now: a smooth stone dais, with Eleanor lying atop it, in a trance... Prudence pounded up the stairs, taking them two at a time, as Rick hustled after her.

"Eleanor!" she cried, as she reached the top and entered the temple. "Elean —"

She stopped again in her tracks, and this time Rick didn't even come close to stopping in time. The two of them tumbled to the stone floor in a tangle of arms and legs.

Rick leaped to his feet to help her up, but she just sat

there on the stone, staring in blank disbelief across the room.

"Did I hurt you, Tru?" Rick said.

"No," said Prudence, in a tiny voice. "Eleanor is gone. I think we're too late."

For at the other end of the room stood the dais Prudence had seen in her dream, with Eleanor lying asleep or entranced on its top. Only now, it was bare.

A fter a moment, Prudence raised her head and looked into Rick's puzzled eyes, wiping the tears from her own.

"Eleanor, in my dream, was on that dais," she said in a very small voice, pointing. "She was lying on it in my dream, and when I approached she raised her head and smiled at me and that's when I woke up. But now she's not there. And I feel — I just know that means something has gone wrong."

Rick nodded. "I've wanted to talk to you about that, Trudie," he said, "only I didn't know how I could. But if we do find Eleanor here, there's a chance she'll be — that is — well, you know."

"Dead. Yes, I know what you mean. All I can say is, if she were dead I would know. Don't ask me how. But she's not dead. I just sense that she's in trouble and needs our help. It's a feeling that's been growing in me since just before we saw that boot track. Then I forgot about it when I remembered my dream, but seeing Eleanor not here, I just know we have to do something… I just don't know what."

"Well," said Rick, "there's dust all over this place. Let's look for footprints."

"Good idea," said Prudence. She moved over toward

the dais, eyes on the floor, as Rick followed.

They quickly discovered a dense cluster of footprints in the dust, looking like the same boot-track pattern that they'd seen in the boulevard.

"They lead through that doorway behind the altar, or whatever that is," said Rick, pointing the trail out to Prudence.

Prudence looked closely. "I don't see any women's footprints," she remarked. "Where could Eleanor be?"

"Maybe one of them —" Rick started, but stopped short of voicing his thought.

"Carried her out?" finished Prudence, with a look of dread.

"Let's go find out," said Rick briskly, and, pulling his big revolver out of his belt holster, he started following the tracks.

The tracks led into a dark hallway that wound around behind the altar and terminated at the top of a set of stone steps.

"Here's where we have to be a team," Rick said. "I want you to take the pistol, and I'm going to hold the flashlight. That way, if somebody gets the drop on us, they'll shoot at the light, and you'll be free to return fire."

"No," she hissed. "I'll take the flashlight. I'll draw the fire. I'm no good with a pistol."

"Look," Rick whispered back harshly. "If I were the kind of man who uses his — who uses a woman for gun bait, you wouldn't want anything to do with me. Luckily for both of us, I'm not that kind of man. Now take the goddamn pistol."

Prudence wanted to continue objecting, but her sense of urgency was strong and she somehow knew they couldn't afford to delay. Reluctantly she took the pistol from him.

"But why don't you keep this, and I'll use the one you lent me?" she asked.

"That little .32? It's pretty weak for this kind of work. Keep that in your pocket for the emergency I bet we're about to have."

"No, I'll use it, and you hang onto your big one," she said firmly, handing it back to him. "It'll be better for two of us to be able to shoot back than just one."

"Something in that," he muttered, taking the gun back. "Let's go."

Flashlight held high in his outstretched left arm, Rick led the way down the stairs.

The staircase they were on was long. It seemed to go on forever. Prudence wondered if it went all the way back down to the street level, or if it actually went below. Just as she was concluding that it must go farther still, it terminated in a single door — a regular, modern door, with a knob and lockplate. It looked very out of place there, at the bottom of that ancient stony-block staircase. Rick carefully put his hand on the knob, trying to keep it from rattling; then he opened it and pushed through.

The two of them now stood looking into a large shoe-box-shaped room, well lit by the sunlight pouring through a bank of windows, unglazed but with heavy stone shutters swinging on hinges made of what looked like bone, facing out into a courtyard on one side.

Rick pocketed his no-longer-needed flashlight, but kept the gun out and ready for use. They looked around. The room was full of very modern-looking equipment.

Rick padded forward with a smooth and silent gait like that of a jaguar; Prudence followed him on tiptoe. When she recognized the equipment, she gasped. It was a compact hand-powered letterpress, and it was surrounded by stacks and stacks of paper money.

She picked up a bundle of bills about an inch thick, secured with a rubber band. It was U.S. currency, or appeared to be — all one-hundred-dollar bills.

Rick picked one up as well. He was chuckling.

"This must have been a hard lesson for someone to learn," he said merrily. "Counterfeiting hundred-dollar bills. That's rich."

"I don't know," said Prudence. "It might not be such a bad idea. I can't remember the last time I saw a hundred-dollar bill, other than those ones in the letter to my nuthouse. If they were printing fives or twenties, and the forgery wasn't perfect, I think I'd know."

"Maybe so," said Rick, riffling through a stack of the bills. "I think I'll take these with me as a little souvenir. It suddenly makes a lot more sense why LeCourt's donation to the Sisters of the Sacred Heart was in hundreds."

"You think this is LeCourt's operation?" said Prudence.

"I'm sure of it. It explains everything: his big-spending ways, and his desperation to get rid of you after you told him about that dream that brought you right to the door of his outlaw hideout. He knew it was a matter of time before you hauled off and followed your dreams, and when you did, he would be busted. This also explains why his sidekick Marco Morais was so hot to get you off my boat when it turned out you wouldn't be in the straitjacket. He got cold feet, worrying that if you weren't tucked away in your cabin all wrapped up in a loony-suit, you'd talk me into turning around and doing exactly what we're doing now."

"So he tried to take me off the boat so he could shut me up in a more traditional gangster style," Prudence said.

"Yep. You told me you figured that by not letting him do that, I'd saved your life. I think you're right, I did."

"But why would they go to so much trouble, printing fake money all the way out here?" said Prudence. "Why not do it right in Carraçao? It all seems so unnecessarily elaborate."

"Actually," said Rick, "the more I think about it, the more perfect it all is. This place is not too far off the river. The people in Carraçao have these legends about it, which I'll tell you all about sometime; I always thought it was just legends, but apparently they really exist—in any case, they're not going to come snooping around. And if you have a light enough boat, when the water's a little higher, you can pull it up into that oxbow lagoon with the sunken steamboat and the dead guy's foot, and nobody will ever find you in a million years. You can make a million dollars in fake money in one shot, then bring it out and start pushing it. Brilliant. If, that is, you can find somebody dumb enough to take a fake hundred-dollar bill."

"What's that smell?" Prudence asked suddenly.

"Hot lead, I'm sure," said Rick. "Printer's type."

"That doesn't make sense," she said. "We have a print shop at Disney's place, and this doesn't smell anything like Linotype lead. Plus, why would you be casting movable-type plates when you're printing dollar bills?"

"Say, you're right," said Rick, on the alert again and looking around the room. His eye fell on what looked like a portable furnace and crucible, tucked away in the corner by one of the open windows. He padded over to look at it; Prudence followed.

The furnace was off, but the whole kit still radiated heat. Next to it lay a medium-size gas bottle of the type used by welders.

They peered together into the crucible, and gasped at what they saw in it.

Inside the crucible was a heavy gold diadem, from which a number of large jewels had apparently been pried, half-melted into a pool of liquid gold. Someone had been melting it down — apparently to disguise the origins of the gold it was made from — and whoever it was had not long been gone. Beside the crucible there was a jumbled pile of gold objects — cups, plates, pieces of jewelry, and miscellaneous other things — that had obviously been intended to go into the pot next.

Prudence felt her eyes oddly drawn to the object nearest the crucible, the piece that had obviously been next intended for the melting pot. She picked it up. It was massive headdress, looking vaguely Egyptian, shaped like a great serpent that wound around the wearer's brow and finished with a fierce-looking crocodilian head just over where the wearer's brow would be. The head looked like that of a caiman, only shorter and somehow intelligent-looking.

She stared at it. It looked somehow familiar.

"Is this —"

"A Yakumama?" Rick said, finishing her thought for her. "Sure looks like one to me."

Prudence started to set the piece down. Then, spurred by a whim that felt almost as urgent as a command, she stepped to the window and dropped the Yakumama headdress into some overgrown vines below. It landed with a brushy thump.

"What did you do that for?" said Rick.

"I — I don't know," said Prudence.

Rick shrugged slightly, then gestured with his pistol at the pile of gold things. "I know all the local styles, and this is one I've never seen before," he said. "There's at least a million dollars' worth of gold here. Probably more like two or three. Here, hold this pistol, would'ja?"

Prudence tucked her own little revolver into her pocket and took Rick's big black one from him. He reached down into the pile and pulled out a large goblet.

"Solid gold," he muttered.

"Why do you think they shut the melting machine off?" she asked, looking into his face with a puzzled expression not untinged with worry.

"Ran out of gas, looks like," said Rick. Then he reached down and touched one of the rubber tubes leading from the gas bottle. "Actually it looks like a line break. Probably filled the whole room with gas. I bet they evacuated out of fear they'd blow the whole works to the moon."

Suddenly Prudence had a sickening realization. She grabbed his forearm. "They just left!" she whispered furtively. "The melter-thing is still hot. They'll be back any minute. We've got to get out of here before they come back! Quickly, Rick, this way!"

She turned toward a doorway that led out into the courtyard. But as she did so, a soft and sinister sound rang out in the room — a sound with a significance far out of proportion to its volume. It was a businesslike, well-oiled triple click. It came from the doorway from which they'd entered the room.

The two of them slowly turned to see Raoul LeCourt standing in the doorway, his left arm in a sling and his right hand gripping the butt of a very large revolver, which he had just cocked.

XIX.

THE DANCING-LESSON.

"Well, well, well," LeCourt was saying. "Welcome to my treasure room, old friends. You have no idea how delighted I am to see you here. Prudence, sweetheart, why don't you be a doll and just lay that pistol down by your feet there, and kick it over toward me? Gently, gently."

He was speaking without any trace of a French accent now. Actually, he sounded very much like a waterfront tough guy, and Prudence thought she probably had been right when she'd flippantly remarked, many days before, that he was likely from the Bronx or New Jersey.

Prudence laid the pistol down on the floor and kicked it gingerly over toward him. No heroics now, she thought. Maybe later, but not just yet. She glanced over at Rick.

Rick was smiling the sardonic smile of a man who

doesn't hold his own life particularly dear. "Mr. Capett, I presume?" he said.

"The same," the fake-Frenchman replied. "Emil Capett, or if you prefer, Emilio Capetti. How'd ya learn my name?"

"You left your hat behind in the river the night I put the bullet in your arm," said Rick, with a steely smile. "Speaking of which, you can have that .38 there, the one you took from Miss McMarion. It's my gift to you — souvenir of the day you got shot with it."

Capett's lips tightened. "For a guy looking down the barrel of a cocked Colt, you got a big mouth," he said. "Do me a favor, keep talkin' like that, give me an excuse to start takin' off pieces of your face. I owe you an arm anyway. An eye for an eye, right?"

"Oh, I get it, you think I'm making fun of you," said Rick. "Nope. I'm not. You don't want the .38, that's fine, but if it was me I sure would. I've been shot three times now, and I own two of the guns that did it, and the third one is at the bottom of the Bering Strait. Memento Mori, or whatever, you know?"

Capett peered suspiciously at him. "Well, you know, it's gonna be my gun now anyway."

"Right," said Rick. "Look here, Capett, we haven't always gotten along so well. I think that's because you played the part of the greasy French ladies' man to perfection. But I don't see why we have to be enemies here. I think I can — er, I mean, I think we can help you in some pretty significant ways with your project here. For instance, is that your boat on the bottom of the oxbow lagoon?"

"No, my boat is anchored close to the beach, and it used to be your boat," Capett shot back. "And after I put a bullet in your ear and throw your body in the lagoon for the fishes to dispose of, that'll be official, won't it?"

Rick laughed easily. "Come on, Capett, you're not fooling me," he said. "A guy who can pull off that expat-French-doctor swindle on a whole town for two and a half years, no way a guy like that is dumb enough to think the best way to keep a lid on a secret hideout like this is to murder a high-profile local businessman and then be seen driving his boat around like nothing happened."

Capett looked uncomfortable for a moment, and Prudence wondered if in fact he had been thinking that. The thought almost made her giggle. Then, with a shock of horror like a wet towel in the face, she realized where Rick was going with this.

"You don't want that," Rick was saying. "Dealing me in is going to cost you guys so much less than rubbing me out. And looking at the amount of gold you've got here, I think you can afford to. How many guys you got working with you?"

For a moment Prudence wondered if Rick might be bluffing. Would he really? Throw in his lot with this — this evil pirate, who had just gotten done trying to get her thrown into the bleakest, blackest hole on the continent, to be imprisoned and abused and probably sterilized — would he really just leave all that behind for a fat slice of dirty money?

But money — money was his weakness, she remembered. For all the positive traits he'd shown over the past few days, she knew he remained a profoundly mercenary man.

"Rick!" she gasped. "Rick, you can't mean it!"

Rick turned and looked at her with eyes glowing with excitement. "You've got to be kidding," he said. "Come on, Miss McMarion, be reasonable. I understand that Emil here tried to do something really awful to you, but you

understand why, don't you? You're going to let your resentment over his trying to put you in the cooler for a year or
two prevent you from getting in on something that could
make us all millionaires? Seriously?"

He held her eyes as the shock and dismay in them
crystallized into wounded betrayal and then hardened into
ice-cold fury. "Come over here and I'll tell you," she said
in a low, very unfeminine snarl.

Rick turned to Capett. "She'll come around," he said
smoothly. "She wants money to make her movie. Sooner
or later she'll realize that partnering up with us is the only
way she's going to get it. I'd stick her in a locked storeroom
to cool off and think about it for a bit. Meanwhile, let me
tell you what I want out of this. How many guys do you
have?"

"Three," said Capett. His attitude had softened somewhat, and he clearly was seriously considering the propo-
sition. "Until that fight on your boat a few nights ago, there
were four. I have to admit, you're pretty good with that .38.
But I woulda got you if I hadn't tried for the shot at the
dame when she picked up that candle to follow you out of
the wheelhouse."

Fierce joy shot through Prudence when she heard this.
He doesn't even know I tricked him, she thought. *He just thinks
he missed.*

"Yep, you sure would've," said Rick mildly. "I had no
idea you were even there until you started squirting lead at
her. But, water under the bridge, right? Anyway, so you're
splitting the loot four ways? Fine. I don't want to do any
work other than my regular services as your boat guy, so I
won't ask for a fifth. But I'd like a tenth, and I think you
should offer Miss McMarion a tenth as well. Don't you
think so, Miss McMarion?"

Prudence's reply was very short and consisted of two very unladylike syllables. Capett actually looked a little shocked.

"Lock her up," Rick said, waving dismissively. "She'll come around."

"And what do you suggest that we do with her if she refuses to cooperate?" Capett asked.

Rick looked at him with mock exasperation. "Look, Capett, you got to know Miss McMarion pretty well, didn't you? And here she's only been on my boat for three days, and already I know better than to say something like that to her. She's not the type to get scared off by implied threats. We need to make our case like reasonable men, and she'll respond because she's a reasonable woman. Try to shorten that process with threats and all you'll get is what I just got."

Capett looked Prudence over. She could just about see what he was thinking. He had not seen her at her best during those few days in Carraçao — she'd started out with girly problems with candles and matches and moved on to weepy hysteria in the wake of Eleanor's disappearance, and finished out her time there as a broken-down shell of a woman who had been easily suckered into thinking herself crazy, getting swindled into voluntarily entering a madhouse. Surely she hadn't given him much reason to respect her.

Yet something in her eyes must have given him reason for that respect now. "I believe you're right," he grunted to Bancroft, and lowered and decocked his pistol, and reached to put it away in his holster.

"Hey! Don't do that!" Rick yelled, with a panic-stricken glance at Prudence. "Keep that gun out!"

Prudence's hand, with the tiny silver .32 in it, came up out of her pocket and level with Rick's face just as Capett's big revolver whipped around to cover her.

"This is for your own good, Miss McMarion," Rick said firmly, looking at her over the barrel of the little silver heater. Prudence's finger was wrapped so tightly around the trigger that the hammer was halfway back, but her eyes were locked on Capett's Colt. "After you've had a little time to think this over, you'll understand that. But for right now, um, I just need you to put the gun down on the floor and walk away from it… Prudence? Look at me, Prudence."

Prudence tore her eyes off Capett for a second and caught Rick's eye. And in that instant, on the side of his face that was away from Capett, he flashed her the tiniest, quickest and sneakiest of winks.

In a flash it dawned on Prudence what he was trying to do. For a fraction of a second she wondered if he was sincere; then Eleanor's words flashed through her mind: "You can trust Rick Bancroft. Him alone."

And in the next instant, Prudence the Vaudeville Girl had her stage directions and was ready to go. She just hoped that her face, which Capett had been looking directly at the whole time over the barrel of his pistol, hadn't betrayed too much of the epiphany she'd just had.

"Prudence, put the gun down," Capett was telling her. "I do not want to have to shoot you."

It was time. She went straight into character, hoping Rick would recognize it as such but knowing it didn't really matter if he did not. She arched an eyebrow at him, turned for a leisurely glance at Capett, and looked back at Rick once more.

"I see how matters stand," she said, icily and a bit dramatically. "You filthy turncoat bastard. Oh, don't worry, I'm not going to kill you. You're not worth getting shot over."

Her gun muzzle moved steadily downward until it covered his feet. "But I *am* going to teach you to dance," she purred.

Smoke and noise filled the room. Chips of stone flew at Rick's feet as he leaped into the air, trying to avoid the little storm of bullets that were zipping around his feet and ankles.

Five shots. Then all was silent and Prudence was scornfully throwing away the empty pistol. It clattered to the stone floor, sounding, in the stunned silence, almost as loud as the gunshots had been.

Rick looked down at his feet, now covered with a light coating of rock dust. He looked as if he were taking inventory of his toes.

The silence hung in the room for a moment more as the echoes of the tumbling gun died away. Then it was broken by Capett. He'd been staring at Prudence in obvious shock; then the corners of his mouth had started to twitch, and a tentative, dawning chortle emerged from his lips. A moment later he was doubled over, his gun drooping from his fingers, nearly helpless with mirth.

"Guess I shoulda saved a round," Prudence growled to Rick. Capett was laughing too hard to hear her.

When he finally was done, he looked up at Prudence, who met his frankly admiring gaze with a look of icy hostility.

"Oh, Prudence, Prudence, I so hope we can be friends again someday," he said. "You really are magnificent. Magnifique, as I used to say."

"And you," she growled back, "are really lucky you got the drop on me with that giant heater, or I wouldn't have bothered making YOU dance. I owe you big for those two days in your loony locker doped up on whatever the hell you spiked that wine with to make me think I was crazy."

"I do feel bad about that," said Capett. "But business is business, Prudence. You know now why I couldn't let you stay on the loose exploring after your missing friend. My associate, Marco the Bull, he really wanted to take you out back and shoot you. Said it was the only safe way to handle it. He near mutinied on the night we loaded you up to go to the asylum, you know. That business with the straitjacket, that was for his benefit, not yours."

"I think we'd better put her in the cooler now," said Rick, his voice shaking a little. "And Capett — don't put your gun away again. Some of those came pretty close to my ankles."

Prudence knew this was not true, and she knew he knew it too. Her eyes met his again, and she found in them the ghost of an approving smile. She broke away.

"Very well," Capett was saying. "I know just the room."

And he led the way to a small doorway just behind the gold smelter, a heavy wooden door with a bar across it.

"Miss McMarion, I hope you'll change your mind," Rick told her as she moved toward the open doorway. "I understand why you're upset. But so help me, if you ever make me dance again, I'll… I'll…"

She snorted and looked down her nose at him, a scornful and haughty look accompanied by a slight disgusted wrinkle of her nose. He looked back at her sternly, but the corner of his mouth was twitching again, as if he were trying to hold back a smile.

Then the door was closed and barred and she was alone in the almost-blackness; the only source of light in the room was the light that streamed through the crack beneath the door.

rudence felt her way to the wall, next to the door, and sank down against it. Had she done this right? Was shooting at Rick's feet overdoing it? Had he really meant what he'd said about her making him dance? She thought she'd seen something in his eyes that made her think otherwise, but he'd sure sounded sincere about it.

The wink had told her what she'd really needed to know, and she was a little disappointed in herself for having been so quick to assume the worst. But there were still so many other questions.

Sitting there in the dark, Prudence rested her head against the door. The strenuous activities of the day had finally caught up with her, all in a rush. All the running through the brush, and sprinting up the stairs, the emotional whiplash of not finding Eleanor, of getting caught, of thinking Rick was a traitor, of learning who Raoul really was…

Suddenly she was alert again. She realized that she could hear everything the two men said in the other room through the door. She pressed herself closer to it.

"That's a big goddamn relief," Rick was saying. "What a bearcat. I mean, that woman is a tiger."

"No kiddin'," said Capett. "And she seemed like such a pushover back when I had a French accent. Are you sure she's worth the risk? We could just leave her in that room. Ten percent is ten percent."

"Five minutes ago I would never have considered that," said Rick. "Now I'm dusting rock chips off my socks and being more broad-minded about things. But let's see what happens."

"Fair enough. Let's talk about what I'm getting for your ten percent, if I agree to your terms."

"OK. My proposal is, my boat and piloting services are at your disposal. I don't want to be exploring around the city looking for more stuff to melt down, but I'm well known and trusted on this river. I make runs up and down it all the time; I have regular smuggling routes in place for when greater discretion is needed; and I have contacts and relationships with all the nearby Indian tribes. I can get your stuff out of here and onto the international gold market — all of it, faster than you think — without anybody ever figuring out something funny's going on."

There was silence while Capett thought about this. Then he said, "I dunno. I got a boat, you know that, right?"

Rick laughed. "Fat lot of good that thing's going to do you," he said, "even if it were already floating."

"No, no," said Capett. "Not the old steamboat in the piranha pond. We gotta new steam launch, and it's on the way right now. It's the one the broads thought they'd hired for their movie. The pilot is one of my men. He was delayed a bit, because he had to get rid of the actor who was coming up the river with him so that I could offer my services as a replacement."

Behind the door, Prudence sat motionless, her jaw hanging open. So that's why Charles Conners had suddenly gotten arrested and deported. Leonard Stevens was a traitor, and had set him up to put him out of the way. More and more things were making sense.

Capett was still talking: "Then just when he was supposed to be leaving, Lenny was delayed some more when I tasked him with collecting the skirt from your boat and delivering —"

"Lenny?" Rick said, in a dangerously rising voice. "You're talking about Lenny DeKock? Lenny DeKock is your man in Porto Escuro?"

"Easy, big fella," Capett said. "I know he stepped on your toes last time you were in port. It's actually my fault."

Rick made a spitting noise that she could hear even through the door. Then, "It's gonna be a little while before I can work with Lenny," Rick said. "Or even see his face, unless you're OK with me rearranging it a little bit with my fist."

"You and me both, Ricky," Prudence whispered silently. She remembered those feet that she'd briefly glimpsed when the oily-voiced man had almost discovered her hiding in the captain's cabin. And that oily-voiced man had been *working* for her!

"Wait a sec," Rick was saying. "How did you know me and Lenny got into it? I came straight from there to here. What, are you using the local telegraph line or something?"

"No, we've got a portable wireless kit," said Capett. "We communicate in cipher. It works great. I used it when you dropped me off after we went looking up the river for that Martins bitch. Jonesy, the big dumb drunken bastard, had forgotten to pull the fake foliage over the path to hide it. I saw it from the other side of the river when we were on our way up. That's why I suddenly remembered a pressing engagement at four o'clock on our way back, because then you'd be forced to race down the middle of the river. I figured you'd probably take the dame and come back up, but by that time I would'a had a chance to wireless Jonesy to get his ass down there and cover the path up."

"Oh, I see," said Rick. "And it would have worked great if it hadn't been for that caiman trick."

"Yep. When that happened, that's when I realized I was going to have to rub you out. I almost decided not to, after I had Prudence filled up with scopolamine and she claimed she didn't trust you and hadn't told you about it. But she also told me she learned about it from a dream, which made me think the scopolamine wasn't working like it should, because obviously that's not how she learned about the place."

"Ah. How do you think she found out?" said Rick.

"Obviously that Martins whore snuck back and told her all about it," said Capett. "There's no other way."

"So Eleanor Martins is alive? And why do you keep calling her the Martins Whore?"

"She's alive, or she was this morning, but it's not for lack of trying on our part. The dirty bitch has top-notch commando skills. She's like a ghost in this place. She comes out at night and breaks our equipment and steals our stuff. Just a few minutes ago she snuck in here while we were melting our first batch, cut the lines and let out all the gas while I was out of the room for a minute. Once she dropped a rock on Jonesy, made him drop a really nice gold headpiece shaped like a snake. That's it over — Jesus goddamn Christ!"

This last phrase came out in an enraged bellow. In the darkness behind the door, Prudence smirked. She was pretty sure she knew what he was angry about.

"What are you yelling about, Capett?" Rick was saying.

"That Martins bitch has been in here again. The head-dress was right over there, by the furnace."

"You probably mislaid it. And anyway, who cares? There's enough loot here without it. Looks like a cool three million to me, and that's just what's in this room."

"It's just the audacity of the thing," said Capett. "That whore just runs around here like she owns the place, screwing with our stuff and scaring the boys. Marco's shot at her twice now, can never seem to connect. Hell, we'll get her eventually, but it's really frustrating."

She heard Rick give a sympathetic grunt.

"Anyway, you can imagine how annoying that was, back when she first left the village and showed up here," Capett continued. "But then, back in town, the bearcat starts asking questions and claiming she's had dreams that she couldn't possibly really have had, and we realize she's still in contact with the Martins bitch somehow. So me and the boys talk it over, and we decide we really need to get her the hell out, and figure something else out for why we're running around in the boat. Sending her to the loony bin was perfect. They'd figure out she wasn't crazy in a couple months, but by then we'd have all the loot out of this joint and be long gone. Marco wanted to handle her in a more simple fashion, but Marco's kinda dumb. We were gonna have a helluva time explaining how my patient got disappeared while in my care. My assistant, Beatriz, she's discreet and not too smart, but ...."

There was a brief pause.

"And then it occurred to you that maybe something bad could happen to her on the way down the river to the asylum, and me too," Rick said, and even through the door Prudence could hear the edge on his voice. "Indians could attack us."

"Yeah." Capett actually sounded a little sheepish. "Not my brightest idea, I gotta admit."

Another pause.

"And if it had worked, you probably would have had to run your launch at night," Rick went on. "It's not big enough to take all this loot in one trip, right?"

"Not even close. It would have been a pain in the ass without 'movie business' to use as a cover story."

"Man, that would've been a neat scam," Rick said. "You could've had Lenny running all over the place in his little boat, and everybody would think he was doing errands for the movie. Too bad you had to run your cover story out of town with a one-way ticket to the bin."

"That's all because of that goddamn Martins bitch," Capett shouted. "Jesus Christ would I like to get my fingers around that perfect little throat of hers."

"You don't think that Eleanor Martins thing is a little weird and creepy?" Rick said. "This is a giant empty city full of nothing. Where could she be staying? What could she be eating? Why on Earth would she *want* to stay here, all by herself like that?"

"Goddamned if I know," Capett growled. "Or care. I just want her gone. Period. In fact, if you can catch her or put a bullet in her, I'll cut you in at a full twenty percent."

"Thanks," said Rick. "I don't have those skills, though. Like I said, I just want to be your boat guy."

"Fine. We'll get her sooner or later, anyway."

"All right. But now you've really got a problem on your hands," said Rick. "You show up with your new boat, do a bunch of running around, somebody will notice even if you do it all at night. Then one day you up and vanish. A few months later, somebody else stumbles on this jungle Ritzburg and figures out what you were up to, and you've got people on your tail asking questions. Wouldn't you rather deal me in, and let me help you get your pretty things out of here quietly over the next couple months — and then all of a sudden there's a family emergency calling you back to La Patrie, and away you go back to France? Nobody asks you any questions, nobody thinks anything's funny, and I'm still running my boat up and down this river same as ever, telling everybody who asks that we didn't get along at first but you turned out to be a pretty good guy and the village misses you, but duty called, et cetera. Clean, neat. No loose ends."

"What about you? You'll be stuck here."

A moment of silence. Then, "I'm stuck here anyway, for reasons I'm not going to go into. But I don't mind. I found, to my surprise, I like it here. It's my home now."

Capett was silent for a moment, obviously thinking. "I don't see that as being worth ten percent," he said at last. "Make it five and we got a deal."

"I think you should take it and be glad to have it," said Rick. "You're in a pretty big pickle right now. I'm the only boat on this river. You bring in a new boat, people will notice and wonder why. You can kill me off, but that will be real suspicious, and somebody will replace me in a month or two because Carraçao needs the service. But listen, I hate to just throw your good-faith offer back in your face. I'm willing to do it for nine percent. I won't go lower than that."

"Done," said Capett. "But I'll bump you back to ten if you can get the bearcat to join us. She's worth ten ordinary henchmen. My God, what a woman. I think I'm in love."

Rick's laugh sounded harsh and strained and — maybe a little jealous? In spite of the circumstances, Prudence couldn't help smiling mischievously to herself.

"So," Rick was saying. "Tell me about your operation. What am I buying into here?"

"Well, it all started with my search for a good place to set up my printing operation," said Capett. "I got outta the joint, see, three Januaries ago, after a ten-year stretch for makin' five-dollar bills. I realized it's just too damn easy to get caught if you make U.S. currency inside the U.S. So I set out looking for an out-of-the-way place close to the international markets where I can make money and pass it on to people who don't know real well what it looks like, see? I figured out pretty quick that in the international market, when people pass around dollars, they're usually using big bills. So I settled on hundreds. So far it's worked out pretty good. Been printing these things for over two years now, and not even one close call."

"You've been in this city for two years, and you're just now getting around to looting the place?"

"Oh no," said Capett. "My press was set up in that padded room I put the bearcat in. Didn't you ever wonder why I needed a padded cell in my office? It's for sound-proofing. Of course, I told everybody it was for professional reasons, in case I had a patient who needed it. My fake French medical degree was in psychiatry, you know."

"So you're actually not even a doctor?"

"I'm a doctor," said Capett bitterly. "But, thanks to the goddamn American So-Called Medical Association, I can't legally go into practice, in the U.S. at least. I'm a genuine homeopathic physician. Got my degree from the Hahneman Medical School in Philadelphia in 1908. Life was grand for a few years, but by the time the war broke out my degree and years of training were not worth a hot-pink damn. That's why I bought the fake degree."

"Right. So then you stumbled across this city, and moved all your stuff up here," said Rick. "I can see how it works well for that. But how did you find it?"

"I went to explore that little creek entrance as a possible place to hide a boat," Capett said. "And I found that sunken steamboat there. Then I noticed there was a rowboat on the shore. I went and looked it over, and found human bones wearing 1890s clothes. I mean, they weren't full skeletons or anything like that, the skulls were gone, but there were a few bones left. So, you know, I checked the pockets and found some really interesting pieces of gold jewelry that was obviously from some kind of archaeological find."

"Ah, and you followed the trail to here," Rick said. "Very good."

"Bancroft, this place is loaded," Capett said. "You cannot believe how much treasure there is here. I've got my boys out getting more now. We're going to be rich men. There is literally so much treasure here it's not worth fighting over how much we get. When we leave, the last thing we're going to do is dump the printing press in the river and burn all these hundred-dollar bills. Why take chances pushing funny money for a few thousand smackers when we've got a hundred million in gold in our back pockets?

"Anyway, remember that big crate you brought up to Carraçao last month? That was this smelting kiln right here. I just got it set up and started melting down jewelry and gold cups and stuff like that, making it into ingots. You picked a helluva great time to stick your nose into the business, Bancroft, you really did."

"Why are you bothering to melt the stuff down?" Rick said. "Seems to me the stuff's probably more valuable as it is. Old and historical and all that, right?"

"Yeah, but also easy to trace. Think about it, Bancroft. Say we get rich sellin' this amazing Indian art, nobody knows where it came from. Then all of a sudden some idiot like that British bastard Fawcett shows up and claims this place for the Crown or whatever, and next thing you know everybody in the world knows where we got the stuff, and that we didn't really have a legal claim on it. They'd freeze our assets and we'd have to go on the lam. No, trust me, this is better. To hell with history and culture, they're not worth the risk."

"Hello, Trudie," said a soft feminine voice at Prudence's elbow.

XX.

THE IMAGINARY FRIEND.

"Eleanor!" Prudence gasped.

Eleanor, barely visible in the darkness, held a finger to her lips, smiling. Behind the door, Prudence heard a sudden silence, and realized the men outside had heard her cry out.

"Goddamn," Capett grunted. "That woman really is like a ghost in this place. I can't seem to get rid of her."

"Yeah, I still don't get that, and it makes me nervous," said Rick. "How can she just be here? How does she live? There's no food in this place, is there?"

"She must have a stash, I don't know. She just showed up, and she's scaring the hell out of my boys. Follows them around, steals the things they're collecting. Only some of them—like, she seems to have some special favorites. That snaky headdress I was telling you about, for instance.

Anyway, I can't explain it but it's really maddening. Listen, do you suppose if we got the bearcat to join us she could do something about the Eleanor Martins problem? I wanna kill her right now, but if what it takes to get her off my back is to deal her in, I'm ready to do it."

"I guess so. They're best friends."

Capett grunted and was silent for a moment, apparently mulling this possibility over.

"So," said Rick then. "You're not the one who marked up that boat like a giant caiman had eaten it, right? I wonder who did that."

"Maybe she did it herself," growled Capett. "If I was going to put tooth marks on a boat, make it look like a caiman did it, I'd at least make 'em look like caiman tooth marks. The marks on that boat, the only way they could be the real thing would be if the caiman's head was six feet wide."

"Humph," Rick was saying. "Well, if you guys didn't do that, I'd like to know who did. Maybe two caimans worked it over, who knows."

"I think the little whore did it herself," Capett said. "I think she staged the whole thing as publicity for her rotten movie. When she found out what happened to her aunt and uncle, she marked up that boat and hid out here, planning to stumble out of the woods with a story about a giant caiman, but then she found all this gold and loot and decided to stick around."

"Maybe," said Rick. "Listen, you got anything to drink around here? I'm ready to get started, but I think we should start off with a little toast to the new partnership."

"I got nothing here," said Capett. "The only way I can get any work out of Jonesy is to not have the stuff around. He doesn't know when to stop."

"Well, I've been saving some actual Scotch for a special occasion and I'm thinking this is it," Rick said. "Let's go down to the boat and get the bottle. It's my way of saying thanks for dealing me in on what looks to be a very lucrative operation. I won't bring enough to get Jonesy looped."

"Now you're talkin' my language!" Capett bellowed. "Why don't you go get the booze while I get the kiln fixed? I got another bottle of gas, thank God. By the time you're back, I'll have it warmed up and ready for action, and the boys should be back with their day's haul. Remember there's four of us."

"Of course!" Rick said. "Five, counting Miss McMarion. All I got to drink out of is a couple of tin cups, though. We might have to pass the bottle around."

"Cups will not be a problem," said Capett. "You'll see what I mean when Marco and Jonesy get back."

Eleanor now reached out in the darkness and took Prudence by the hand. "Come with me," she said, and led the way to the back of the room.

Wonderingly, Prudence followed her friend to the darkest corner of the room, where Eleanor stood facing away from the wall. Prudence could just barely see her in the darkness.

"Come here and stand close to me, on my left," Eleanor said. "Keep your arms straight down at your sides; that's right, just like that. A little farther over — good."

Eleanor reached one arm around Prudence and with the other reached somewhere behind her in the dark. Then Prudence felt the floor beneath her feet start to move. It slowly and silently pivoted, and she found herself dazzled and blinking in the bright light of day.

She and Eleanor were now standing in the corner of a well-lit room furnished with comfortable if archaic-looking teakwood furniture. Seated together on a sort of love-seat-shaped chair was a particularly noble-looking Indian couple, dressed in the clothing of mainstream Brazilians.

"Prudence," Eleanor said, "meet my aunt Kayifu and my uncle Essimat, also known as Aunt Marcita and Uncle Carlo. We were staying in their home in Carraçao, while they were away."

"Yes, and I am so sorry we left it so empty for you," Kayifu said, smiling at Prudence with that same indefinable sweetness that was so characteristic of Eleanor. "We were called back very suddenly. We had no time to make preparations."

"I — that's — the tooth marks," Prudence stammered. "We all thought you were dead. How is it that —"

"I'll explain soon," Eleanor interrupted. "We need to focus right now on the invaders."

"Should we —" Kayifu started.

"No," said Eleanor. "It's too risky. The Guardian is still far away."

"But Mr. Bancroft is out of the city," said Essimat. "Is not now the best time?"

"If we allow the strike now, one of them may escape," said Eleanor. "We must wait just a little longer."

"But even now they may be melting down one of the Mystical Pieces," said Kayifu, looking a little frightened. "Do you not think we must take the chance? If we lose the Headdress —"

"Prudence saved the Headdress," said Eleanor. "She sensed its importance without knowing what it meant, and cast it out the window when no one was looking. I have retrieved it, and it is safe. And I have temporarily disabled their kiln."

"Eleanor?" Prudence interrupted. "You are kind of

frightening me right now."

Eleanor's face brightened as she turned to look at Prudence. "Don't be frightened, Trudie," she said softly. "Trust me. There is not time to fully explain. Just know that I will not let anything happen to you or to Rick."

Prudence looked quizzically at her for a moment. "That has to be the least reassuring reassurance I've ever heard," she said at last.

"You are sure, Eleanor, that Mr. Bancroft is clean?" Kayifu asked.

Eleanor turned to face her aunt. "He is clean," she said. "But it would not matter if he were not. My spir — my best friend is in love with him. Were he unclean, we would have to redeem him. He cannot be endangered."

A silence of perhaps one and a half seconds elapsed, during which Prudence reeled a little. The implications of that quiet, matter-of-fact line, ringing out in Eleanor's lyrical and lovely voice, hit her like a hammer. Eleanor, it seemed, could read her deepest thoughts — thoughts so deep she hadn't even admitted them to herself. She was, she realized, in love with Rick Bancroft. It was true. She had been fighting, with varying degrees of success, against an inexplicable attraction to him since they'd first met.

Prudence realized suddenly that she was making a wholly unladylike face: jaw hanging open, eyes bugging out. She quickly composed herself.

"How — how do you know these things?" she whispered.

Eleanor smiled at her. "I have known you ever since I can remember," she whispered. "We have been spending time together in our dreams for our entire lives, you and I. I am — I am Eleanor, your imaginary friend from childhood. But of course, you almost never remember your dreams, so you did not recognize me when we finally met in person. And I didn't remember my dreams either, so I didn't recognize you, not until I came home here, to the city of Azæsia — my city. When we met, in that rustic hotel, I instantly knew you would be my best friend, but what I didn't realize was that you already were. When I arrived here, back home, in my city, those forgotten dreams were unlocked and I cried tears of joy. You have no idea how I've looked forward to this moment, here, with you."

She paused for a moment, looking into Prudence's eyes. "No," she said. "Actually, I think you do know."

Prudence stared back at her. Her emotions were so turbulent and joyful and terrible that she couldn't move her face. She felt a tear run down her cheek.

Eleanor was speaking again. "Do you remember, Trudie, that dark day when you came home to find that letter from poor dear Jonah, and that very afternoon your father died on stage?" she said. "You fell asleep crying and wanting to kill yourself. And you woke up knowing you were not alone. I was there for you that night. It was a hard night. Do you remember it now, too?"

The tears were now coursing freely and unhindered down Prudence's cheeks. Memories were pouring into her mind as if released from a great cistern, or as if they'd been locked in a secret room that had just been opened: memories of forgotten dreams from the previous twenty years — a lifetime of them. Memories of what she'd thought was her imaginary friend, and whole conversations about their lives. Her imaginary friend, who was a princess — a princess of a faraway kingdom that had once ruled a mighty realm and today was a secret kingdom, tucked away where no one knew about it but her, a kingdom that was —

Prudence tottered toward a chair and collapsed into it.

"I've been trying to find you for decades," said Eleanor. "You remember now; we've talked about this, us two, in our dreams. We'd make our plans, and then when I awoke, my dreams forgotten, I just knew I had to find something. I know it was the same with you. Wasn't it?"

"Eleanor," Prudence whispered. "My God. My Eleanor."

Then suddenly a horrible realization blazed across her mind, and she gave a little gasp.

"What is it, Prudence?" Eleanor asked, concern furrowing her lovely face.

"You were in North America looking for me," Prudence said, in a horrified whisper that slowly rose to a wail. "You were looking for me, and you were away, and now your home is full of vandals and thieves and the treasures of your kingdom are being melted into slag, and it's all my fault!"

"It is not your fault," Essimat broke in, with what she somehow knew was uncharacteristic sharpness. "We called her back the moment we knew."

"And it wouldn't have mattered if they hadn't called me back," Eleanor said quickly. "The City of Azæsia has its own defenses. It does not need me, or Auntie and Uncle either, to repel unwelcome intruders."

"And Prudence," Kayifu added, "this is more complicated than you know. You are the most important thing in our niece's world and have been since she was four years old, when she made the dream-connection to you. She is our hereditary princess-priestess, the first and most important citizen of Azæsia. So we have done our best to watch over you, even though we didn't know who you were or where you lived. We could not pierce the veil and learn who you were, but we were able to glimpse a few bits of Eleanor's dreams that told us that you lived in Los Angeles. Later, Essimat was able to tune you in, and he learned that you were on a path that would lead to your death. We knew your death would destroy our niece, our princess-priestess. That, in turn, would destroy all of us."

"Yes," said Essimat. "Until Eleanor has a girl-child, she is the last of our line of hereditary princess-priestesses, and if anything happens to her, Azæsia would —"

"This is too complicated to fully explain just now," Eleanor interrupted firmly.

"Yes," said Kayifu. "It is. But suffice it to say that because we are vulnerable, Eleanor had to be protected. The City, as Eleanor says, can protect itself. So we moved her out of the city when she was three years old, because it is not good for a little girl to be brought up in a city full of nothing but echoes and because awareness of her... unusual origins would cause trouble for her in the outer world during those childhood years before one has learned to dissemble. Our Princess-Priestess grew up first in our house in Carraçao, and later in a happy, loving family in Los Angeles, a family that thought she was an orphan."

"Kayifu and I are what are called outriders," said Essimat. "What that fully means, we haven't time to get into just now; but the important part is, we live out in the outside world, like secret agents, under cover. And when our City needs us, we are summoned back, and we must go. This happened to us last month, when the thieves and vandals again discovered the portal. But this time, we faced a new quandary. The thieves and vandals were making plans not only to steal our treasures, but to melt them down before leaving the city. This was new. Always before when thieves and vandals came, they merely tried to steal the treasures, and once they were stopped, no harm was done. This is the first time thieves have actually undertaken to destroy them on the spot. It was new, and it forced upon us a new quandary. On the one hand, we faced the loss of our ancient treasures; on the other, the loss of our very connection to our home world."

"Essimat," said Kayifu sharply. Essimat flinched, almost imperceptibly, and exchanged glances with Kayifu. Then Kayifu continued.

"We had to save you so that you could save Eleanor," she said. "So we found you, stalked you, learned of your vacation plans in Oregon, and arranged for Eleanor to meet you there. You know what happened then. But just as you got to Carraçao, we were called back to the City.

"You should know, Prudence," she added, "that there are two kinds of treasure in this city. There are Mystical and non-mystical pieces. The non-mystical pieces are mere baubles, although they are fine and treasured works of art, and we were very sad to see the vandals melting them down. The other ones, the Mystical Pieces, they are what we were called in to protect."

"Like that headdress that I dropped in the bushes?" said Prudence.

"Yes," said Essimat. "That piece is the most important one of them all. If it is ever destroyed, Eleanor's father will be forever lost in the outer —"

"That is all Essimat and I can tell you," Kayifu broke in, sharply and firmly. "Eleanor, with her deep connection to you, must be the one to explain all that must be explained about Azæsia and its people. She alone will know what she can tell you, and what you might be unable to understand at this time."

Eleanor stood up. "Prudence, you will soon know all," she said. "All my secrets, as you have let me know all of yours. Right now, though, time is short, and we must act quickly. The most important thing to understand is that the city is not truly abandoned. Rather, its residents are away from home. But when mystical pieces are destroyed, they lose their ability to find their way back."

Prudence looked at her blankly.

"Oh, Trudie, this is such a lot to take in, isn't it?" Eleanor said then. "Come sit by me."

Prudence tottered over to the couch next to Eleanor and put her arms around her and gave full vent to the sobs and tears of confused contentment and frightened joy.

XXI.

THE UNSEEN GUARDIAN.

Eleanor gave Prudence a little time to recover and accustom herself to the realization that her imaginary friend had been real. But it wasn't long before Prudence felt herself being gently shaken.

"Trudie, dear, we have to move now," Eleanor said. "Everything is coming together, but the timing is going to be very important. Come with me. Can you come with me?"

Prudence nodded, and, getting to her feet, followed Eleanor out of the room. Eleanor led the way across the courtyard to a spiral staircase set into the wall, and up and up and up. Soon they emerged on the top of a tall watchtower, from which she could look out over the landscape below and see, in the distance, the river snaking lazily by. She wondered how she had failed to see the tower from the path when she and Rick had been approaching. Then, looking around her, she realized that the entire city should be plainly visible from the river. How had she not noticed it?

Eleanor pointed to a distant figure, approaching the city's tower. The figure was just near enough for Prudence to see that it held a bottle in one hand. It was Rick, she knew, on his way back from the boat with the Scotch.

"He's brought a gun with him," said Eleanor. "That makes things much easier."

"What?" said Prudence. "How do you know?"

Eleanor paused for a moment. "It is best that you not know yet," she said. "I cannot tell you until after — after the men leave.

"Prudence, listen to me," she said then, and she took her friend's face between her hands and looked very earnestly into her eyes. "I am princess-priestess of this city. To me falls the duty to defend it from the men who are in it. In defending it, I am not permitted the luxury of mercy. They are evildoers, but they are men, and all men have a core of goodness, the destruction of which is an evil deed. It is I who am required, fated, destined to shoulder the burden of that evil deed. And I would not share that burden with anyone, least of all my dream-sister, but Prudence, if I do not, Rick will die."

"What? Why? How?"

Eleanor looked long and earnestly into Prudence's face. "Trudie," she said softly, "this city is — alive. It is a living thing. It knows and resents the step of the intruders and even now it is preparing itself to crush them. Uncle is holding it back, but like a horseman riding a great stallion, he only has so much control over it. And when it strikes, it will not discriminate."

Prudence was silent for a moment. "Is there no way we can stop this, this bloodshed?" she asked at last.

Eleanor was silent. Prudence glanced up and caught her eye. Tears were sliding down Eleanor's cheek and she looked ashamed of herself.

"Please, Eleanor," Prudence pressed on. "Do you — do your people really want to be the kind that slaughters without even giving a chance at redemption? Do you want to turn yourself into a — a murderess, or rather an accessory to murder? Is there no other way?"

Eleanor raised her head and looked straight at her. "I am not permitted to take such a chance," she said, in a flat, almost mechanical voice. "But you, my dream-sister, you can be the angel of mercy for both of us."

She paused for a moment before continuing. "It is risky," she said then. "It is especially risky because the Guardian is not here. The Guardian is the heart of the City's defenses. They will work when he is not here, but in dangerous and unpredictable ways. And he will not be back for another quarter-hour at least."

"Who is the Guardian? Why is he not here?"

"He is coming back from Porto Escuro, where he … eliminated a threat to the city," said Eleanor.

"A threat to — you mean Leonard DeKock, don't you?"

"Yes."

Prudence shivered a little. "Who — what — is this Guardian?"

"It is better that you should not know just yet."

Prudence shook her head, trying to clear it.

"What must I do?" she asked.

Eleanor did not pretend to misunderstand. "You must warn them," she said. "But you must not warn them in such specific terms that they are able to escape the city. If they are to be spared, they must remain here, in this city and in the world of which it is an outpost, forever; they can never be permitted to return to the outside world. And above all, you must not permit yourself to fall into their power. If they try to use you as a hostage, in the absence of the Guardian, the City will — will call their bluff. And I do not know if I could —"

She broke off, looking overcome. Prudence thought she'd never seen Eleanor looking so much like a lost little girl.

"This is so hard on you, darling," she murmured. "On one hand, your duty calls on you to become a murderess. On the other, you risk seeing me destroyed by your own city while trying to save the lives of three men, three — evil men."

Eleanor nodded. She actually looked frightened now. "Be careful, Trudie," she whispered. "Oh, do be careful."

Eleanor's eyes were liquid pools shining in the semi-darkness. Looking into them, Prudence felt something harden inside her. She knew what she had to do. Without her, Eleanor would be forced by her duty to her city to do a deed that would oppress and haunt her sensitive spirit for the rest of her life. Yet if she failed, Eleanor would be unable to save her and would have to watch her die. There was only one path she could take, and she knew it would require everything she had.

She didn't have to nod or speak. Eleanor instantly knew. She gave a grateful smile.

"I will guide you, my dream-sister," she said. "Listen for my voice."

"I take care of my friends," Prudence said evenly. "You were there for me once. It is my turn to be there for you."

"Are — are those Rick's words?" Eleanor said. "They

are, are they not?"

"Yes. Eleanor, thank — thank you for telling me to trust him. I wouldn't have, you know, not so far as I could kick him."

"I know. Now: come."

The two of them hurried back across the open expanse of the courtyard — Prudence looking furtively about, but Eleanor calm and confident, apparently knowing where the men were. They soon arrived in the room where Kayifu and Essimat still reclined, both looking very worried.

"Oh good, you're back," said Essimat, rising to his feet. "It is time."

"Yes," said Eleanor. "Uncle, please go to the north tower. Auntie, the temple top."

The two relatives hurried from the room. Eleanor stepped, with Prudence beside her, to the pivoting corner, and a moment later they were back in the dark room with the light streaming out from beneath the door.

They arrived just in time. Prudence heard footsteps outside, and she realized that Rick was just coming in. She glanced at Eleanor, and saw that she was seated close to the wall in the corner, legs folded beneath herself, spine perfectly straight. She looked at Prudence.

"Listen for me," she said.

Prudence was about to ask what she meant when she heard voices break out in the outside room.

"Twenty-year-old Glenfarclas, boys," Rick was yelling. "Come on, you mugs, this is the best hooch in my cabinet. Let's have a nip and then start making money!"

A general shout of approval greeted this, and Prudence realized that Capett's colleagues had returned to the room, no doubt loaded down with more gold artifacts to melt. She wondered if any of the new finds were mystical pieces.

Then Capett's voice rang out: "Don't forget the bearcat, Bancroft. I want her to drink with us. Get her out here!"

Eleanor looked up at her again. "Listen carefully, Trudie," she said. "I do not believe those men will respond or believe when you tell them about the city. If that is correct, at least one of those men, possibly all of them, will soon be chasing you and Rick. You must first lead them away from the room they are in now — and then back to it. This is necessary to give the Guardian time to return. Uncle is holding the city's defenses back, but without the Guardian, he will not be fully able to control the city once he releases it, and it will lash out blindly, and probably destroy Rick and possibly you as well. Listen for my voice; I will guide you. When you return, you must lead Rick into this room, this very room. This storeroom, which he thinks leads to only starvation and death, will be the only safe place in the entire city for him. It will be difficult to do this, but you can and you must. Rick's life depends on it."

"And mine too?"

"Yes, at first. But once the Guardian returns, your life will not be in danger from the city; only from the intruders. Be strong, Trudie. I love you."

"I love you too, Eleanor," Prudence whispered. "I will not let you down."

Prudence gave her hand a little squeeze, then walked back to where she had been standing, in front of the door. Right on cue, it opened, and there before her stood Rick Bancroft, holding her tin cup in his hand.

"Miss McMarion," he said, "will you come and drink with us?"

"Oh, Prudence!" Capett sang out from behind. "We want you to drink this toast with us, and then we want you to join our gang and share our treasure. Come on, sweetheart, don't be like that. Marco says he's very sorry. Don't you, Marco?"

A resentful grunt sounded behind him.

It was showtime. Prudence, once again drawing on all her Vaudeville training, first winked at Bancroft and then strolled out of the storeroom like a queen, head held high and eyes flinty and disdainful, and moved to stand over the table at which the men sat. They gaped up at her, wondering at the transformation in her attitude.

She directed her eyes around the little table, training them on each man in turn. While she'd been in the cooler, Capett had been joined by the burly, taciturn Marco Morais and by another fellow, a slender and wiry man with gray hair and a distinctly seedy air, whom she recognized as the bartender from Katakuona who had served her the drugged wine. Rick, who had been moving toward the chair next to Morais with obvious intent to sit down in it, paused with his hand on its back, gazing at her with a puzzled expression.

Capett tried to break the spell. "Prudence, you already know Marco, of course," he said. "And this is Hiram K. Jones, who you've also met but probably you don't remember that. The other member of our merry band, Lenny DeKock, is on his way from Porto Escuro right now — you've spoken with him a great deal, I know, but I don't believe you've met him."

She did not respond, only eyed him coldly for a moment. Then she spoke.

"Leonard DeKock is already dead," she said, slowly and coldly, like an oracle; "and his nemesis is on its way here, even now. Listen to me. All of you are given this one chance for life. The city you have invaded is hostile to you. The very floors ache to be bathed in your blood and the very walls yearn to be dappled with fragments of your flesh and splinters of your bones. You will never leave the city, and the world to which it is a portal, again. You now have a choice to make: will you remain here, in this other world, in peace? Or will you try to escape it, and be crushed and destroyed, as was Leonard DeKock?"

Capett gaped at her, momentarily speechless. Then he found his voice.

"What the hell kind of game are you playing, Prudence?" he rasped. "You think you can talk your way out of this, do you?"

"Out of what?" Prudence replied, with icy tranquility. "Your doom does not threaten me. Only, I give you a chance for life. You must accept it in the next sixty seconds, or it will pass from you, forever."

"She's a pretty good bluffer," remarked Jones, trying to shake off the spell of her words.

"I am," agreed Prudence tranquilly. "But I am not bluffing now. What would be the point? I am merely offering you a choice between life, here, in this other world; and death, swift and terrifying, exactly nine minutes from now."

"What a head job," Capett sneered; he seemed to have recovered from the initial surprise. "Honey, I don't know what kind of game you're playing, but whatever it is, you better stop before one of us decides to call your bluff."

"This is all too rich for my blood," growled Marco Morais. "Sorry, Emil, I know you're a little sweet on the dame, but I think she's too hot to handle."

"Well," said Capett coldly, "be my guest, then."

Morais raised his pistol. Prudence, looking directly into his eyes, saw a weird light in them, mocking, anticipating. Then his pistol was pointing directly at her face, and she saw the muscles in his forearm start to tighten.

Then Bancroft sprang forward and knocked the big thug sprawling to the stone floor with a colossal left cross. Morais' pistol, dropped from his hand, fell to the tabletop and slid across toward Capett, who reached to catch it with his one good arm. At that moment, taking advantage of the distraction, Bancroft picked up the table and threw it straight into Capett's face, knocking Hiram K. Jones over backward into the letterpress with a crash of breaking machinery.

"Run, Tru!" Rick shouted, and, pulling a small silver revolver from his pocket — it looked like a twin to the one she had used to make him "dance" — he ran for the door, with Prudence close behind. A pistol bellowed behind them, and then another; a bullet knocked chips off the stony doorframe as the two of them plunged through it and raced around into the blinding sun of the street.

And as they left the building, Prudence suddenly heard a tiny voice in her mind — tiny and faint, but perfectly clear and distinctive.

"Run to the right," it said. "Around the side of the building."

Eleanor! Eleanor was guiding her!

"This way!" she shouted to Rick, and they ducked down by the building as roars of rage continued to ring out behind them. Another gunshot, and another piece of brickwork flew off the wall behind Rick as they fled.

"Down this alley!" she gasped, snatching Rick's hand. "To the end. Then turn and shoot twice. Just to slow them down. We need a little time."

"That looks like a dead end!" Rick said. "Don't go —"

"Don't argue with me, Bancroft," she hissed back. "I know what I'm doing."

Rick, taken aback, followed her into the narrow corridor.

When they got to the end, they saw that indeed there was an entryway, a narrow arch, not even wide enough for the two of them to walk through abreast. Rick turned around and got his pistol ready.

"Don't hit them," Prudence said. "Shoot to miss and delay them. Whatever you do, don't leave them wounded, especially in the legs."

Rick was too busy to do more than nod, but she knew that questions were swimming furiously in his mind. She hoped they'd live long enough for her to answer them all.

Then Capett rounded the alley end, gun first. His big revolver bellowed once — unaimed cover fire, no doubt, intended to prevent Rick from plugging him from cover. Rick's little handgun answered it with two quick blasts, sending their three pursuers scrambling back to take cover behind the wall.

"Come on!" Prudence whispered, and led Rick at a run through the tunnel. It was a long, narrow tunnel, and she could see why Eleanor had "told" her to have Rick do as he did. By the time Capett figured out that it was safe, she and Rick would be on the other side.

"Stop here," she said, when they'd reached it. "Do you have more bullets?"

Rick broke the pistol open, pulled out the three fired shells, and replaced them with fresh bullets. Then he closed the gun again.

Prudence stooped and picked up the three shell casings he'd dropped. She placed them carefully in the dirt outside so that it would be obvious that they'd turned to the right at the tunnel exit. "Now let's go," she said. "This way."

The two of them hustled to the end of the wall and ducked around it.

"Wait here with me for a moment," she said.

"How do you know all these things?" Rick said wonderingly.

"I'll explain later," she said. "Right now, let's just get out of this alive."

"I'm for that," he said. "But what I don't understand is, why are we just waiting here? Are you deliberately leading him someplace? What do you have in mind?"

"Yes, I am," she said. "Eleanor says the Guardian will be here in just a few minutes. We have to keep them busy until the Guardian returns. But I don't actually — just, please, please, Rick just trust me. In about five minutes I'm going to ask you to go into a room that — hold on a minute. Stick your gun around that wall and fire one shot. Don't look when you do, he's waiting for you to stick your head out."

Wonderingly, Rick did as she asked, and was rewarded with a yelp of surprise from not far behind.

"Now — when I say go, make a break across this open space, firing as you run. Remember, you've got four bullets left. Shoot no more than three times, but be sure you don't hit them … go!"

The two of them launched themselves across the road. Capett, Jones and Morais, taken by surprise, each popped off a round; all three shots flew well behind Prudence, and then Rick opened up on them with the .32. Three shots, well spaced out, and then they were across the path and behind the wall again.

"Down to the end and turn the corner," she panted to him as they ran.

When they got there, she pointed back the way they'd come. "Aim at the dirt right at the end of the wall and shoot when I tell you to shoot," she said.

And about three seconds later: "Now!"

BLAM. The dirt scuffled at the end of the wall, and a yelp of surprise could be heard from behind it. Prudence broke into a run back along the wall, and then suddenly Rick stopped in his tracks, obviously just realizing where they were.

They were standing outside the door they had left a few minutes before — the door that led into the room with the printing press and the gold-smelting kit — and the prison room.

"What the —" Rick said.

"Rick," Prudence said then. "Listen to me. I am about to ask you to do something that you will be 99 percent sure will lead to death for both of us. Every fiber of your body will be screaming at you to not do it, and that I'm just nuts, and that we're both going to die. I need you to trust me instead of your instincts, just this one time, because your instincts are wrong and the trap that you think I'm leading you into is the only place in this city that will be safe for you. Promise me, Rick? Promise me you'll do as I ask?"

Rick, by way of an answer, grabbed a handful of the front of her blouse and pulled her into a kiss. It was a short, hot, passionate kiss that tasted of sweat and desire. It was over quickly, of course; there were, after all, three men with guns racing up behind them. But after he released her, Prudence felt as if her entire world had shifted beneath her feet.

"Trudie McMarion, you can lead me anywhere. I don't care," he told her. "You can —"

"Stop!" said Prudence, her voice thick with passion. "You'll spoil my concentration. There will be time for that sort of thing tonight and" — she looked meaningfully at him — "and tomorrow morning. Let's go!"

"Should I reload?"

"No need. This is almost over. Follow me."

The two of them ran through the doorway and into the smelting room.

Then Prudence ran to the heavy wooden doorway behind which she had been imprisoned — the one that had led to the room with Eleanor and her aunt and uncle — the one that Eleanor, as far as she knew, still sat in, meditating in the dark, guiding her like a living wireless beacon.

"Drop your pistol here, in the middle of the floor," she said. Then she sat down on the floor just inside the doorway that led into the prison room, her feet just visible from the door of the room.

"Stand behind me and be ready to drag me into this room and close the door behind us," she whispered. "We want them to see my feet being dragged into the room, as if I'm hurt. And when you close the door, do it softly, as if you're trying to be sneaky. Wait for my signal."

"Are you sure about this?" Rick whispered nervously. "There's no way out of this room, and he knows it. He'll bar the door and leave us to starve!"

"There's a way out, trust me. Remember what I told you... now! Pull me, Rick!"

With a heave, Rick dragged Prudence's body into the dark, windowless room and then hurried to close the heavy wooden door — softly, as if trying to hide.

Prudence looked up at his face, softly lit by the tiny stream of light coming under the now-closed door. She felt tears starting to come. It was all done now. All except —

Footsteps rang out in the other room: three sets of them, walking briskly across the floor. Then the door rattled and they heard the heavy pounding of the wooden bar being slammed into place.

"I've got you now, you sneaky bastards," Capett shouted.

"I think I'll just leave you in there to die. I'm going to bring you water, because I want you to die of starvation. That way, when you get hungry enough, maybe —"

"Yeah!" shouted Morais. "Me an' Emil will be out here the whole time, listening to your pitiful cries for mercy and laughing. You pathetic sons of bitches."

Capett said something else after that, or maybe it was Jones; but Prudence barely heard. She was listening to the tiny soundless voice of her imaginary friend, telling her it was almost over.

"Raoul!" she screamed then. "Open this door and come in here with us. It's your only hope. Do it now before it's too late!"

"Nice try, you crafty little bitch," rasped a voice — she thought it was Morais, but it might have been Jones. "You're just gonna —"

The voice broke off suddenly, and Prudence knew the die was cast. She dropped to her knees facing the closed and barred door. "G — goodbye, Raoul," she wailed. "I am so sorry."

"What the hell?" Capett shouted back, his voice full of alarm.

Then came the sound of rock sliding on rock, and the light that shone beneath the heavy wooden door went dim and then black.

"Jesus Christ!" shouted a voice. She thought it was Capett. And then there were gunshots — more of them than she could count — and a scream.

She collapsed prone onto the floor. A flood of emotion poured over her: vicarious fear, and horror, and terror, and shame, and under it all a deep, inconsolable sadness and grief. As Rick rushed to her side in the inky blackness and gathered her in his arms, her sobs came thick and unhindered, almost masking the increasingly horrifying sounds coming from the other side of that heavy wooden door. The screams had stopped now — the last one cut short in the middle and followed by a series of sloppy crunching sounds. Prudence's body was wracked with sobs. Rick held her tight and stroked her dark-brown hair as she buried her face, wet with tears, in his chest.

Then all was still and silent, and the only sound was that of Prudence weeping for the souls of the dead.

XXII.

A NEWSPAPER CLIPPING.

I melda Ribeiro stood by the counter at Old Man Paulo's store and watched the proprietor as he pored over the ancient printing telegraph machine in the corner. It was always interesting when that machine clattered to life. When it did, Old Man Paulo would instantly stop whatever he was doing and hurry over to the machine — once she'd even seen him stop in the middle of giving a customer change for a purchase when the teletype clattered, and by the time he got back to her, both of them had forgotten how much he owed her, so he'd just pulled her money back out of the drawer and told her the groceries were on the house. Old Man Paulo was like that. Everybody loved him.

The teletype was clattering now, so she waited patiently for the message to come through while Old Man Paulo eagerly watched the machine.

Finally it was finished, and he came to the counter.

"Any news?" she asked.

She wasn't talking about the telegram, as Old Man Paulo well knew. Imelda had been asking the same question, every time she came into the store, since the woman she'd taken to calling "Aunt Prudence" had left town. She'd left all her things in the Martins house, and she'd asked Imelda especially to watch over it for her, promising that she would come back — but adding that it would be some time before she did. Six whole months, she'd said, maybe more. And that had been nine months ago.

Imelda had known Aunt Prudence when she had first come to Carraçao with Miss Martins, before Captain Bancroft had rescued her from Dr. LeCourt and his gang of criminals. But she hadn't really gotten to know her, and to call her Aunt Prudence, until after Captain Bancroft had brought her back from that rescue.

She still remembered that day vividly. Imelda had been standing on the dock waiting for the *Amazon Princess* to come in, as she always did — although just thirteen years old, Imelda thought of herself as nearly a grown woman, but she still ran with the village children to see the boat arrive the instant they heard its distinctive, low-pitched flute-like steam whistle moaning from far away down the river — and she still remembered how shocked she had been that day to see Captain Bancroft steering the boat, standing in the wheelhouse with one hand on the wheel and the other arm around the waist of Aunt Prudence. Aunt Prudence, who had seemed to positively hate him just a week before.

Then the boat had reached the dock and Aunt Prudence had hustled around the deck tying off the *Amazon Princess*, like a seasoned deck hand, and as she'd done so, Imelda had noticed the look on Captain Bancroft's face as he watched her.

I hope someday I can find a boy who looks at me like that, she'd thought.

There had been a big, festive supper that night at Ana and Paulo Silva's big house, with all of Aunt Prudence's other friends from the village. And she had told them all about what had happened to her — how Dr. LeCourt had tried to get her shipped off to the insane asylum after she stumbled across his counterfeiting operation on board a partly-sunken riverboat in a backwater pond full of piranhas; how Captain Bancroft, hired to transport her, had figured everything out when they were halfway there, and turned around to bring her back; how *Signior* Morais had shot at them with his pistol when they approached, and Captain Bancroft, shooting back, had made him fall into the water with the piranhas; and how he fought on the deck of the old derelict with Dr. LeCourt until Dr. LeCourt picked up a stick and clobbered Captain Bancroft with it, knocking him out; and how, when Dr. LeCourt had picked up Captain Bancroft to throw him to the piranhas, Aunt Prudence had shoved him from behind so that he dropped Captain Bancroft and tripped over him and tumbled into the water with the piranhas.

Aunt Prudence had said the federal policemen were skeptical at first, when she and Captain Bancroft told them about this; but when they returned to the derelict with two police boats, they had found everything there: the printing press and stacks of phony American hundred-dollar bills, all set up to operate in the wheelhouse of the old half-sunken riverboat; cots and blankets for the two counterfeiters; and a supply of food and rum. They could find no trace of the bodies, but then, they hadn't expected to. The pond was still brimming with famished piranhas, two of which actually had leaped into the dinghy as they'd rowed toward the old steamboat. Imelda thought that must have been very exciting. She wished she could have gone along.

Aunt Prudence had said her friend, Miss Martins, had gone suddenly back to Los Angeles. Something very important had happened, and she had not been able to tell anyone, but she had found her aunt and uncle and the three of them had paddled down the river in a canoe to Porto Escuro, which had taken them almost a week, and shipped out from there. They had sent Aunt Prudence a letter from Porto Escuro, but the mail had taken a long time to come to Carraçao, so Aunt Prudence hadn't received it until after her return.

Imelda had not been surprised at *Senhorita* Martins' strange departure. The whole Martins family was weird. Since she had been a baby, she had known about the Martins family's reputation for strangeness, and its connections to certain old stories about "elder things" that had been whispered around hearth fires on cold winter nights for decades, maybe even centuries, in the town. Imelda did not believe any of it, of course, those old myths of eldritch creatures from the stars and their mysterious vanishing city that sometimes was there but usually was not; but she was pretty sure the Martins family did. And happy though everyone in Carraçao had been to see *Senhorita* Eleanor when she'd come, no one Imelda knew of was surprised to see her go, and it actually came as something of a relief.

Well. After her return, for about two months, Aunt Prudence had lived there in the old Martins home, emerging every morning an hour before dawn to sit on the front porch and write in her little journal and sometimes, very rarely, smoke one of her long dark-brown cigarettes. It was at that time that Imelda had begun to call her Aunt Prudence. Seeing how much pleasure Aunt Prudence took in the pre-dawn quiet time, she had come over one morning with her own sketchbook, planning to join her; but then, realizing it would be rude to just walk right up, she'd paused in confusion there before the house. Seeing her there lingering in the street, Aunt Prudence had called out to her: "Come sit on the porch with me, Imelda; let's watch the sunrise together."

After that morning, Imelda had gotten out of bed extra early every morning so that she could be at Aunt Prudence's house the minute she stepped outside, and the two of them would sit there in companionable silence, writing and sketching and just drinking in the cool tranquility of the morning.

That's when Aunt Prudence had started teaching Imelda English. She already knew some English, although not nearly as much as her bratty little brother Alberto. Now, with Aunt Prudence's help and guidance, she had made great strides, and the two of them would often converse in English after their morning journal times.

Aunt Prudence had also established a village library. Captain Bancroft had helped her enclose the front porch of the Martins home, and they had gone down the river all the way to Belem to get books for it. Aunt Prudence had insisted on having books in Spanish and English as well as Portuguese for their library. It was free and open to everyone in the village. Aunt Prudence was the primary librarian, but Imelda always acted as her assistant. Since Aunt Prudence had gone away to north America, Imelda had been the only librarian, and it was a responsibility she took very seriously.

Aunt Prudence and Captain Bancroft had made plans to be married, but it was not to be done until the following summer. In the meantime, Aunt Prudence had told her, she and Captain Bancroft were going to have to go back to the United States one last time. Both of them, she said, had some affairs that they needed to wrap up there.

And then that day had come, and Aunt Prudence and Captain Bancroft had said goodbye to all the villagers; Captain Bancroft had even given almost everyone in the village a hug, which was something Captain Bancroft never, ever did.

"Goodbye, Mellie," Aunt Prudence had said tearfully as she stood on the pier. "I will write you letters in English. And I am going to do something else for you, too. I am going to sign you up for a Sunday subscription to the Los Angeles Times. It's a newspaper in my home town. They will come on the mail boat, every two weeks you'll get two of them. They will help you keep up with your English, and when you're done with them you can share them with the other villagers through the library."

Then, promising that they would be back as soon as they could, Aunt Prudence and Captain Bancroft had chugged away down the river, disappearing from sight with a double blast of the *Amazon Princess's* distinctive low-pitched steam whistle.

That had been nine months ago. Aunt Prudence had written to her several times, but she hadn't gotten a letter in three months. And for the last month at least, Imelda had come down to Old Man Paulo's shop every chance she got, hoping to hear news from Aunt Prudence.

Old Man Paulo gave her a big smile as he turned away from the teletype machine and saw Imelda standing there patiently waiting at the counter.

"No, that telegram wasn't from Miss McMarion," he said. "She hasn't sent any telegrams at all. I'm sorry."

Disappointed, Imelda started to turn away.

"But the mail boat came late last night, and brought you your newspapers," he continued.

Thanking Old Man Paulo effusively, Imelda happily gathered the two fat gray newspapers in her arms and hurried down to the dock, where she liked to sit on the edge and dangle her toes in the water while she read.

She took the latest one first. It was old; it always took a long time for Aunt Prudence's newspapers to get to Carraçao. This one was dated Sunday, November 27, 1928, so it was more than a month old. But she was especially interested in it, because of the date.

Imelda always looked at the society pages first. It was there that she had read, four months before, an article announcing that Aunt Prudence and Captain Bancroft were to be married. It was supposed to have happened on November 24, so she was particularly eager to see the society page this time, hoping there would be a wedding announcement and maybe a story and picture. She was just sure Aunt Prudence would be the most gorgeous thing anyone had ever seen in a wedding dress. She wished she could have traveled to Los Angeles to see them married, but she would have to settle for reading about it.

As she opened the Society page, her eyes fell to the biggest headline on the page, and then she gave a start and fell to reading it, carefully and thoroughly and with a growing horror:

LADY FILMMAKERS' PLANS FALL APART.

Scheme to Make Grand Adventure-Romance Picture in Amazon Jungle Founders on Extreme Run of Bad Luck.

SURVIVOR TELLS HER STORY.

LOS ANGELES — A badly frightened would-be lady moving-picture director has given up on a plan to make a moving picture on location in the wilds of the savage Amazon after three members of her cast and crew vanished into the red-toothed maw of the hungry jungle.

Miss Prudence McMarions is the charming little filmmaker's name, and she entered the Amazon jungle in December of last year as part of an independent film company chartered by the late Miss Ellen R. Martin, who was to have been the film's producer. Both ladies hailed from this city, and had hoped to represent the intrepidity of the fair sex in that faraway land of crocodiles, tigers and other frightful monsters.

The project seemed at first to be going well, but bad luck seemed to follow the little ladies around like a lovesick suitor.

The first sign of trouble was when the actor who was to play the lead part in the little ladies' motion picture, Charles Conners, was caught with $50,000 in counterfeit $100 bills in his valise. Mr. Conners claimed not to recognize the valise, and said the cash had been planted there, and

U.S. authorities are inclined to believe him, but the Brazilian authorities, declaring him persona non grata, deported him forthwith.

MYSTERIOUS DISAPPEARANCE.

The very next day, the lovely Miss Martin sallied forth on a midnight paddle on the river and failed to return. She is feared dead, no doubt a hapless victim to the great Amazon crocodiles that the native savages call "caimen."

Miss McMarions was fortunate enough to secure an actor to replace Mr. Conners, but this new gentleman, who gave his name as Raul LeCourte', vanished soon afterward when it was learned that he was really Emil Cappet, the notorious murderer, counterfeiter and international racketeer.

HER BOAT IS DESTROYED.

The final blow to Miss McMarions' dream came when a mysterious fate befell the steam launch that was to be used in the film, and its captain. The launch was found upside down in the river and covered with deep scars as if it had been struck many mighty blows with a pick-axe, looking almost as if a giant dog had picked it up and bitten and shaken it and dashed it to the ground. The launch's captain, Leonard D. Cock, has not been found and is also presumed dead.

THE BOOTLEGGER'S DEMISE.

As if all this tragedy were not enough, Miss McMarions has also had her heart tragically broken, although it is probably for the best. Her engagement to "Captain George Bancroft," whom she also met on location in the Amazon, ended in tragedy after it was learned that Mr. Bancroft was in reality Richard Thrasher, the notorious bootlegger and gun-runner whose Manhattan Island operations were discovered and dismantled by Prohibition Agents in 1925. Apparently eager to take up his old pursuits now that he was back on American soil, Mr. Thrasher purchased a gasoline-powered motor yacht shortly after his return, clearly for use in rum-running — the 39-foot *Piranha*.

Readers will doubtless recall the fate of the *Piranha*, which was caught by the Coast Guard Cutter *CG-811* off Catalina Island with a cargo of illegal tequila. The *Piranha's* captain refused to stop or even acknowledge the cutter's hail, even ignoring a warning shot over the bows; and so, in an attempt to disable the vessel, the cutter fired a shell into the *Piranha's* stern, aiming for the rudder. The shell caused a great explosion aboard the *Piranha*, the concussion of which blew the little ship into fragments, leaving nothing behind but scraps of debris and tequila bottles floating upon the sea. No sign of captain or crew was ever found.

Miss McMarions is now back in Los Angeles, a sadder and wiser damsel, having learned the folly of aspiring to a man's job. She now is once again employed as a film editor in the cartoon studio of Mr. Walter Disney, and most recently assisted Mr. Disney's studio in the release of its popular and acclaimed cartoon, "Steamboat Willy," earlier this month.

We wish Miss McMarions the best of luck in her work at Disney, as well as in finding once again the love she found and lost in the Amazon jungle, and we hope she has learned her lesson.

But when this reporter spoke with her on Monday of this week, she expressed a desire to return at her very next opportunity to the jungle village that was so recently the scene of her misfortunes, so it seems to him quite likely that she has not.

Imelda laid the newspaper down. A tear ran down her face. She felt hollowed-out and raw inside, as if someone had opened her chest and scooped out her heart. A tear ran down her cheek. Captain Bancroft, dead? And poor Aunt Prudence was left all alone and heartbroken in Los Angeles, far away from everyone who loved her — far away from Imelda. She thought about Captain Bancroft — or was that Captain Thrasher? Was that really his name? — torn to pieces in the explosion, or maybe drowning alone and shivering in the cold northern sea.

Laying the newspaper aside, she covered her face with her hands and sobbed.

But then, between sobs, she heard something that made her pick her head up and turn her tear-streaked face toward the river. Had she really heard it?

Yes — yes! there it was again!

It was the familiar moan of a low-pitched, flute-like steamboat whistle, coming from far away down the river.